By Wit of Woman

Arthur W. Marchmont

By Wit of Woman

The present edition is a reproduction of previous publication of this classic work. Minor typographical errors may have been corrected without note; however, for an authentic reading experience the spelling, punctuation, and capitalization have been retained from the original text.

ISBN: 978-1-63637-640-0

CONTENTS

CONTENTS

CHAPTER I

FROM BEYOND THE PALE

"To John P. Gilmore, Jefferson City, Missouri, U.S.A.

"MY DEAR BROTHER-IN-LAW,—For years you have believed me dead, and I have made no effort to disturb that belief.

"I am dying now, alone in Paris, far from my beloved country; unjustly degraded, dishonoured and defamed. This letter and its enclosure will not be despatched until the grave has closed over me.

"To you I owe a debt of deep gratitude. You have taken and cared for my darling child, Christabel; you have stood between her and the world, and have spared her from the knowledge and burden of her father's unmerited shame. You can yet do something more— give her your name, so that mine with its disgrace may be forgotten; unless—it is a wild thought that has come to me in my last hours, the offspring of my hopeless melancholy—unless she should ever prove to have the strength, the courage, the wit and the will to essay that which I have endeavoured fruitlessly—the clearance of my name and honour.

"When ruin first fell upon me, I made a vow never to reveal myself to her until I had cleared my name and hers from the stain of this disgrace. I have kept the vow—God knows at what sorrow to myself and against what temptation in these last lonely years—and shall keep it now to the end.

"The issue I leave to you. If you deem it best, let her continue to believe that I died years ago. If otherwise, give her the enclosed paper—the story of my cruel wrong—and tell her that during the last years of my life my thoughts were all of her, that my heart yearned for her, and that my last conscious breath will be spent in uttering her name and blessing her.

"Such relics of my once great fortune as I have, I am sending to you for my Christabel.

"Adieu.

"ERNST VON DRESCHLER, COUNT MELNIK."

"To my Daughter, Christabel von Dreschler.

"MY DEAREST CHILD,—If you are ever to read these lines it will be because your uncle believes you are fitted to take up the task of clearing our name, from the stain of crime which the villainy of others has put upon it. But whether you will make the effort must be

1

decided finally by yourself alone. For two years I have tried, with such strength as was left to me by those who did me this foul wrong, and I have failed. Were you a son, I should lay this task upon you as a solemn charge; but you are only a girl, and left in your hands, it would be all but hopeless, because of both its difficulty and probable danger. I leave you free to decide: for the reason that if you have not the personal capacity to make the decision, you will not have in you the power to succeed. One thing only I enjoin upon you. If you cannot clear my name, do not bear it.

"I have not strength to write out in full all the details of the matter, but I give you the main outline here and send in this packet many memoranda which I have made from time to time. These will give you much that you need.

"At the time of your mother's death and your leaving Hungary for the United States I was, as you may remember, a colonel in the Austro-Hungarian army, in possession of my title and estates, and in favour with one of the two most powerful of all the great Slav nobles, Ladislas, Duke of Kremnitz. I continued, as I believed, to enjoy his confidence for two years longer, up to the last, indeed. He was one of the leaders of the Patriots—the great patriotic movement which you will find described in the papers I send you—the other being the Hungarian magnate, Duke Alexinatz of Waitzen. Two of my friends, whose names you must remember, were Major Katona, my intimate associate, and Colonel von Erlanger, whom I knew less well.

"If the Patriots were successful, the Hungarian Throne was to be filled by Duke Alexinatz with reversion to his only son, Count Stephen; and it is necessary for you to understand that this arrangement was expressly made by Duke Ladislas himself.

"So matters stood when, one day, some hot words passed between young Count Stephen and myself, and he insulted me grossly. Two days later, Major Katona came to my house at night in great agitation. He declared that the Count had sworn to shoot me, and that his father had espoused his side in the quarrel and threatened to have me imprisoned; and that Duke Ladislas, unwilling to quarrel with Duke Alexinatz, although taking my part in the affair, desired me to absent myself from Buda-Pesth until the storm had blown over. He pressed me to leave instantly; and, suspecting nothing, I yielded. I had scarcely left my house when the carriage was stopped, I was seized, gagged, and blindfolded, and driven for many hours in this condition, and then imprisoned. I believed that I was in the hands of the agents of Duke Alexinatz; and continued in this belief for six years, during the whole of which time I was kept a close prisoner.

"Then at length I escaped: my strength sapped, my mind impaired and my spirit broken by my captivity; and learned that I had been branded as a murderer with a price set on my head.

"On the night when I had left, the young Count Stephen had been found shot in my house; my flight was accepted as proof of my guilt, and, most infamous of all, a confession of having murdered him had been made public with my signature attached to it.

"That is the mystery, as it stands to-day. The God I am soon to meet face to face knows my heart and that I am innocent; but prove it I cannot. May He give you the strength and means denied to me to solve the mystery.

"With this awful shadow upon me, I could not seek you out, let my heart ache and stab as it would with longing for a sight of your face and a touch of your hand. I thank God I have still been man enough—feeble as my mind is after my imprisonment—to keep away from you.

"This sad story you will never know, unless your uncle deems it for the best.

"That God may keep you happy and bless you is the last prayer of your unhappy father,
"ERNST VON DRESCHLER."

*****

My Uncle Gilmore had been dead three months, having left me his fortune and his name, when, in sorting his old papers to destroy them, I came upon these letters.

They were two years old; and it was evident that while my uncle had intentionally kept them from me, he had at the same time been unwilling to destroy them.

My poor, poor father!

CHAPTER II

A CHESS OPENING

"If your Excellency makes that move I must mate in three moves."

His Excellency's long white fingers were fluttering indecisively above the bishop and were about to close upon it, when I was guilty of so presumptuous a breach of etiquette as to warn him.

He was appropriately shocked. He fidgeted, frowned at me, and then smiled. It was one of those indulgent smiles with which a great man is wont to favour a young woman in his employment.

"Really, I don't think so," he replied; and having been warned by one whose counsel he could not condescend to rank very high, he did what most men would do under the circumstances. He made the move out of doggedness.

I smiled, taking care that he should see it.

The mate was perfectly apparent, but I was in no hurry to move. I had much more in view just then than the mere winning of the game. The time had arrived when I thought the Minister and I ought to come to an understanding.

"Your Excellency does not set enough store by my advice," I said slowly. "But there are reasons this evening. Your thoughts are not on the game."

"Really, Miss Gilmore! I am sorry if I have appeared preoccupied." He accompanied the apology with a graceful, deprecatory wave of his white hand. He was very proud of the whiteness of his hands and the grace of many of his gestures. He studied such things.

"I am not surprised," I said. "The solution of the mystery of those lost ducal jewels must naturally be disturbing."

His involuntary start was sufficiently energetic to shake the table on which the board was placed, and to disturb one or two of the pieces. He looked intently at me, and during the stare I put the pieces upon their squares with unnecessary deliberation. Then I lifted my eyes and returned his look with one equally intent.

Some of the family jewels of the Duke Ladislas of Kremnitz had been stolen a few days before, and the theft had completely baffled the officials of the Government from His Excellency, General von Erlanger, downwards. It had been kept absolutely secret, but—well, I had made it my business to know things.

"It has been a very awkward affair," I added, when he did not speak.

"Shall we resume our game, Miss Gilmore?" The tone was stiff. He intended me to understand that such matters were not for me to discuss.

I made the first move toward the mate and then said—

"Chess is a very tell-tale game, your Excellency. The theft occurred seven days ago, and for six of them you have been so preoccupied that I have won every game. To-night you have been alternately smiling and depressed; it is an easy inference, therefore,

4

that the solution of the mystery is even more troublesome than the mystery itself. In point of fact, I was sure it would be."

Instead of studying his move, he began to fidget again; and presently looked across the board at me with another of his condescending, patronizing smiles.

"The loss you may have heard spoken of, but you cannot know anything more. What, pray, do you think the solution is?" It never entered his clever head that I could possibly know anything about it.

"I think you have been an unconscionable time in discovering what was palpably obvious from the outset."

He frowned. He liked this reply no better than I intended. Then the frown changed to a sneer, masked with a bantering smile, but all the same unmistakable.

"It is a serious matter for our Government to fall under your censure, Miss Gilmore."

"I don't think it is more stupid than other Governments," I retorted with intentional flippancy. I was not in the least awed by his eminent position, while he himself was, and found it difficult therefore to understand me. This was as I wished.

"Americans are very shrewd, I know, especially American ladies, who are also beautiful. But such matters as this——" and he waved his white hand again loftily; as though the problem would have baffled the wisdom of the world—any wisdom, indeed, but his.

Now this was just the opening I was seeking. I had only become governess to his two girls in order to make an opportunity for myself. I used the opening promptly.

"Will your Excellency send for your daughter, Charlotte?"

He started as if I had stuck a pin in him. If you wish to interest a man, you must of course mystify him.

"For what purpose?"

"That you may see there is no collusion."

"I don't understand you," he replied. I knew that as clearly as I saw he was now interested enough to wish me to do so. I let my fingers dawdle among the chessmen during a pause intended to whet his curiosity, and then replied:

"I wish you to ask her to bring you a sealed envelope which I gave her six days ago, the day after the jewels disappeared."

"It is very unusual," he murmured, wrinkling his brows and pursing his lips.

"I am perhaps, not quite a usual person," I admitted, with a shrug.

He sat thinking, and presently I saw he would humour me. His brows straightened out, and his pursed lips relaxed into the indulgent smile once more.

5

"You are a charming woman, Miss Gilmore, if a little unusual, as you say;" and he rang the bell.

"You have not moved, I think," I reminded him; but he sat back, not looking at the board and not speaking until his daughter came. I understood this to signify that I was on my trial.

"Miss Gilmore gave you a sealed envelope some days ago, Charlotte," he said to her. "She wishes you to bring it to me. Has it really any connexion with this case?" he asked, as soon as she had left to fetch it.

I laughed.

"How could it, your Excellency? What could a girl in my position, here only a few weeks, possibly know about such a thing?"

As this was the thought obviously running in his own mind, he had no difficulty in assenting to it politely.

"Then what does this mean?" he asked, with a little fretful frown of inquisitiveness.

"I am only proving my self-diagnosis as a somewhat unusual person. Will you move now?"

He bent forward and scanned the pieces; but his thoughts were not following his eyes, and with an impatient gesture he leaned back again. I continued to study the board as though the game were all in all to me.

"You are pleased to be mysterious, Miss Gilmore;" he said, his tone a mingling of severity, sarcasm and irritation. I was to understand that a man of his exalted importance was not to be trifled with. "I appreciate greatly your valuable services, but I do not like mysteries."

I raised my eyes from the board as if reluctantly.

"I am unlike your Excellency in that. They have a distinct attraction for me. This has." I indicated the mate problem with my hand, but my eyes contradicted the gesture. He believed the eyes, and again moved uneasily in his chair. "It is naturally an attractive problem. I have moved, you know."

He was a very legible man for all his diplomatic experience; and the little struggle between his sense of dignity and piqued curiosity was quite amusing. But I was careful not to show my amusement. Nothing more was said until the envelope had been brought and Charlotte sent away again.

He toyed with it, trying to appear as if it were part of some silly childish game to which he had been induced to condescend in order to please me.

"What shall I do with this?"

"Suppose you open it?" I said, blandly.

He shrugged his shoulders, waved his white hand, lifted his

6

eyebrows and smiled, obviously excusing himself to himself for his participation in anything so puerile; and then opened it slowly.

But the moment he read the contents his manner changed completely. His clear-cut features set, his expression grew suddenly tense with astonishment, his lips were pressed close together to check the exclamation of surprise that rose to them; even his colour changed slightly, and his eyes were like two steel flints for hardness as he looked up from the paper and across the chessmen at me.

I enjoyed my moment of triumph.

"It is your Excellency's move," I said again, lightly. "It is a most interesting position. This knight——"

He waved the game out of consideration impatiently.

"What does this mean?" he asked, almost sternly.

"Oh, that!" I said, with a note of disappointment, which I changed to one of somewhat simpering stupidity. "I was trying my hand at adapting the French proverb. I think I put it 'Cherchez le Comte Karl el la Comtesse d'Artelle,' didn't I?"

"Miss Gilmore!" he exclaimed, very sharply.

I made a carefully calculated pause and then replied, choosing my words with deliberation: "It is the answer to your Excellency's question as to my opinion of the solution. If you have followed my formula, you have of course found the jewels. The Count was the thief."

"In God's name!" he cried, glancing round as though the very furniture must not hear such a word so applied.

"It was so obvious," I observed, with a carelessness more affected than real.

He sat in silence for some moments as he fingered the paper, and then striking a match burnt it with great deliberation, watching it jealously until every stroke of my writing was consumed.

"You say Charlotte has had this nearly a week?"

"The date was on it. I am always methodical," I replied, slowly. "I meant to prove to you that I can read things."

His eyes were even harder than before and his face very stern as he paused before replying with well-weighed significance:

"I fear you are too clever a young woman to have further charge of my two daughters, Miss Gilmore. I will consider and speak to you later."

"I agree with you, of course. But why later? Why not now? My object in coming here was not to be governess to your children, but to enter the service of the Government. This is the evidence of my capacity; and it is all part of my purpose. I am not a good teacher, I know; but I can do better than teach."

He listened to me attentively, his white finger-tips pressed together, and his lips pursed; and when I finished he frowned—not in anger but in thought. Presently a slight smile, very slight and rather grim, drew down the corners of his mouth. And then I knew that I had matriculated as an agent of the Government.

"Shall we finish the game, your Excellency?"

"Which?" he asked laconically, a twinkle in the hard eyes.

"It is of course for your Excellency to decide."

"You are a good player, Miss Gilmore. Where did you learn?"

"I have always been fond of problems."

"And good at guessing?"

"It is not all guessing—at chess," I replied, meaningly. "One has to see two or three moves ahead and to anticipate your opponent's moves."

A short laugh slipped out. "Let us play this out. You may have made a miscalculation," he said, and bent over the board.

"Not in this game, your Excellency."

"You are very confident."

"Because I am sure of winning."

He grunted another laugh and after studying the position, made a move.

"I foresaw your Excellency's move. It is my chance. Check now, of course, and mate, next move."

"I know when I am outplayed," he said, with a glance. "I resign. And now we will talk. You play a good game and a bold one, Miss Gilmore, but chess is not politics."

"True. Politics require less brains, the stakes are worth winning, and men bar women from competing."

"It is rare to find girls of your age wishing to compete."

"I am twenty-three," I interjected.

"Still, only a girl: and a girl at your age is generally looking for a lover instead of nursing ambitions."

"I have known men of your Excellency's age busy at the same sport," said I. "Besides, I may have been a girl," I added, demurely; taking care to infuse the suggestion with sufficient sentiment.

"And now?" he asked, bluntly.

"I am still a girl, I hope—but with a difference."

"You are not thinking of making a confidant of an old widower like me, are you?"

"No, I am merely laying before you my qualifications."

"You know there is no room for heart in political intrigue? Tell me, then, plainly, what do you wish to do?"

"To lend my woman's wit to your Excellency's Government for a fair recompense."

"What could you do?"

8

There was a return to his former indulgent superiority in the question which nettled me.

"I could use opportunities as your agents cannot."

"How? By other clever guesses?"

"It was no guess. I have seen the jewels in Madame d'Artelle's possession."

He tried not to appear surprised, but the effort was a failure.

"I have been entertaining a somewhat dangerous young woman in my house, it seems," he said.

"It was ridiculously easy, of course."

"Perhaps you will explain it to me."

"A conjuror does not usually give away his methods, your Excellency. But I will tell this one. Feeling confident that Count Karl had stolen the jewels, and that his object would only be to give them to the Countess, I had only to gain access to her house to find them. I found a pretext therefore, and went to her, and—but you can probably guess the rest."

"Indeed, I cannot."

It was my turn now to indulge in a smile of superiority.

"I am surprised; but I will make it plainer. I succeeded in interesting her so that she kept me in the house some hours. I was able to amuse her; and when I had discovered where she kept her chief treasures, the rest was easy."

"You looked for yourself?"

"You do me less than justice. I am not so crude and inartistic in my methods. She showed them to me herself."

"Miss Gilmore!" Disbelief of the statement cried aloud in his exclamation.

"Why not say outright that you find that impossible of credence? Yet it is true. I mean that I led her to speak of matters which necessitated her going to that hiding-place, and interested her until she forgot that I had eyes in my head, so that, in searching for something else, she let me see the jewels themselves."

"Could you get them back?" he asked, eagerly.

I drew myself up and answered very coldly.

"I have failed to make your Excellency understand me or my motives, I fear. I could do so, of course, if I were also—a thief!"

"I beg your pardon, Miss Gilmore," he exclaimed quickly, adding with a touch of malice. "But you so interested me that I forgot who you were."

"It was only an experiment on my part; and so far successful that I won the Countess' confidence and she has pressed me to go to her."

9

"You didn't refer her to me for your credentials, I suppose?" he said, his eyes lighting with sly enjoyment.

"She asked for no credentials."

"Do you mean that you talked her into wanting you so badly as to take you into her house without knowing anything about you?"

"May I remind your Excellency that I was honoured by even your confidence in giving me my present position without any credentials."

He threw up his hands.

"You have made me forget that in the excellent discretion with which you have since justified my confidence. I have indeed done you less than justice."

"The Countess thinks that, together, we should make a strong combination."

"You must not go to her, Miss Gilmore—unless at least——"

He paused, but I had no difficulty in completing his sentence.

"That is my view, also—unless at least I come to an understanding with you beforehand. It will help that understanding if I tell you that I am in no way dependent upon my work for my living. I am an American, as I have told you, but not a poor one; and my motive in all this has no sort of connexion with money. As money is reckoned here, I am already a sufficiently rich woman."

"You continue to surprise me. Yet you spoke of—of a recompense for your services?"

"I am a volunteer—for the present. I shall no doubt seek a return some time; but as yet, it will be enough for me to work for your Government; to go my own way, to use my own methods, and to rely only upon you where I may need the machinery at your disposal. My success shall be my own. If I succeed, the benefits will be yours; if I fail, you will be at liberty to disavow all connexion between us."

He sat thinking over these unusual terms so long that I had to dig in the spur.

"The Countess d'Artelle is a more dangerous woman than you seem at present to appreciate. She is the secret agent of her Government. She has not told me that, or I should not tell it to you; but I know it. Should I serve your Government or hers? The choice is open to me."

He drew a deep breath.

"I have half suspected it," he murmured; then bluntly: "You must not serve hers."

"That is the decision I was sure you would make, General. We will take it as final."

"You are a very remarkable young woman, Miss Gilmore."

10

"And now, a somewhat fatigued one. I will bid you good-night. I am no longer your daughter's governess, but will remain until you have found my successor."

"You will always be a welcome guest in my house," and he bade me good-night with such new consideration as showed me I had impressed him quite as deeply as I could have wished. Perhaps rather too deeply, I thought afterwards, when I recalled his glances as we parted.

CHAPTER III

MY PLAN OF CAMPAIGN

When my talk with General von Erlanger over the chess board took place, I had but recently decided to plunge into the maelstrom whose gloomy undercurrent depths concealed the proofs of my father's innocence and the dark secret of his cruel wrongs.

My motive in coming to Pesth was rather a desire to gauge for myself at first hand the possibility of success, should I undertake the task, than the definitely formed intention to attempt it.

I had studied all my father's papers closely, and in the light of them had pushed such inquiries as I could. I had at first taken a small house, and as a reason for my residence in the city had entered as a student of the university.

I was soon familiar with the surface position of matters. Duke Alexinatz was dead: his son's death was said to have broken his heart; and Duke Ladislas of Kremnitz was the acknowledged head of the Slavs. Major Katona was now Colonel Katona, and lived a life of seclusion in a house in a suburb of the city. Colonel von Erlanger had risen to be General, and was one of the chief Executive Ministers of the local Hungarian Government—a very great personage indeed.

The Duke had two sons, Karl the elder, his heir, and Gustav. Karl was a disappointment; and gossip was very free with his name as that of a morose, dissipated libertine, whose notorious excesses had culminated in an attachment for Madame d'Artelle, a very beautiful Frenchwoman who had come recently to the city.

Of Gustav, the younger, no one could speak too highly. He was all that his brother was not. As clever as he was handsome and as good as he was clever, "Gustav of the laughing eyes," as he was called, was a favourite with every one, men and women alike, from his father downwards. He was such a paragon, indeed, that the very praises of him started a prejudice in my mind against him.

I did not believe in paragons—men paragons, that is. Cynicism this, if you like, unworthy of a girl of three and twenty; but the result of a bitter experience which I had better relate here, as it will account for many things, and had close bearing upon what was to follow.

As I told General von Erlanger, I am not a "usual person;" and the cause is to be looked for, partly in my natural disposition and partly in my upbringing.

My uncle Gilmore was a man who had made his own "pile," and had "raised" me, as they say in the South, pretty much as he would have "raised" a boy had I been of that sex. His wife died almost directly after I was taken to Jefferson City; but not before my sharp young eyes had seen that the two were on the worst of terms. His nature was that rare combination of dogged will and kind heart; and his wife perpetually crossed him in small matters and was a veritable shrew of shrews. He was "taking no more risks with females," he told me often enough, with special reference to matrimony; and at first was almost disposed to send me back to Pesth because of my sex. That inclination soon changed, however; and all the love that was in his big heart was devoted to my small self.

But he treated me much more like a boy than a girl. I had my own way in everything; nothing was too good for me. In a word, I was spoiled to a degree which only American parents understand.

"Old Gilmore's heiress" was somebody in Jefferson City, I can assure you; and if I gave myself ridiculous airs in consequence, the fault was not wholly my own. I am afraid I had a very high opinion of myself. I did what I liked, had what I wished, went where I pleased, and thought myself a great deal prettier than I was. I was in short "riding for a fall;" and I got it—and fell far; being badly hurt in the process.

The trouble came in New York where I went when I was eighteen; setting out with the elated conviction that I was going to make a sort of triumphal social progress over the bodies of many discomfited and outclassed rivals.

But I found that in New York I was just one among many girls, most of them richer and much prettier than I: a nobody with provincial mannerisms among heaps of somebodies with an air and manner which I at first despised, then envied, and soon set to work at ninety miles an hour speed to imitate.

I had all but completed this self-education when my trouble came—a love trouble, of course. I became conscious of a great change in myself. Up to that point I had held a pretty cheap opinion of men in general, and especially of those with whom I had flirted. But I realized, all suddenly, the wrongfulness of flirting. That was, I think the first coherent symptom. The next was the painful doubt whether a very handsome Austrian, the Count von Ostelen, was merely flirting with me.

I knew German thoroughly, having spoken it in my childhood; and I had ample opportunities of speaking it now with the Count. We both made the most of them, indeed; until I found—I was only eighteen, remember—that the world was all brightness and sunshine; the people all good and true; and the Count the embodiment of all that a girl's hero should be.

I was warned against the Count, of course: one's intimate friends always see to that; but the warnings acted as intelligent persons will readily understand—they made me his champion, and plunged me deeper than ever into love's wild, entrancing, ecstatic maze. To me he became not only the personification of manly beauty and strength, but the very type of human nobility, honour, and virtue.

To think such rubbish about any man, one must of course have the fever very badly; and I had it so intensely that, when he paid me attentions which made other girls tremble with anger and envy, I was so happy that I even forgot to exult over them. I must have been very love sick for that.

I came to laugh at it afterwards—or almost laugh—and to realize that it was an excellent discipline for my silly child's pride: but to learn the lesson I had to pass through the ordeal of fire and passion and hot scalding tears that go to the hardening of a young heart.

He had been merely amusing himself at the expense of a "raw miss from the West;" and the knowledge came to me as suddenly as the squall will strike a yacht, all sails standing, and strew the proud white canvas a wreck on the waves.

At a ball one night we had danced together as often as usual, and when, as we sat out a waltz, he had asked me for a ribbon or a flower, I had been child enough to let him see all my heart as I gave them to him. Love was in my eyes; and was answered by words and looks from him which set me in a very seventh heaven of ecstatic delight.

Then, the next day, crash came the dream-skies all about me.

I was riding in the Central Park and he joined me. I saw at once he was changed; and my glad smile died away at his constrained formal greeting. He struck the blow at once, with scarcely a word of preamble.

"I am leaving for Europe to-morrow, Miss von Dreschler," he said. "I have enjoyed New York immensely."

The chill of dismay was too deadly to be concealed. I gripped the pommel of the saddle with twitching, strenuous fingers.

"You have been called away suddenly?" I asked; my instinct being thus to defend him even against himself.

He paused, as if hesitating to use the excuse I offered.

"No," he answered. "It has been arranged for weeks. These things have to be with us, you know."

In a flash his baseness was laid bare to me; and the first sensation of numbing pain dumbed me. I had not then acquired the art of masking my feelings. But anger came to my relief, as I realized how he had intentionally played with me. I knew what a silly trusting fool I had been; and knew too that had I been a man, I would have struck him first and killed him afterwards for his dastardly treachery. I was like a little wild beast in my sudden fury.

He saw something of this; for his eyes changed. "I am so sorry," he said. As if a lip apology were sufficient anæsthetic for the stabbing pain in my heart.

"For what, Count von Ostelen?" I asked, lifting my head and looking him squarely in the eyes. The question disconcerted him.

"I did not know——" he stammered, and stopped in confusion.

"Did not know what?" I asked; and he was again so embarrassed by the direct challenge that he kept silent. His embarrassment helped me; and I added: "I think your going is the best thing for all concerned, Count, except perhaps for the unfortunate country to which you go. Bon voyage!" And with that I wheeled my horse round and rode away.

It was months before the wound healed; months of sorrow, self-discipline and rigidly suppressed suffering. I took it fighting, as our Missouri men say. No one saw any difference in me. My moods were as changeable, my manner as frivolous, my words as light and my smiles as frequent as before; and I was as careful not to over-act the frivolous part as I was to hide the truth. It was a period of as hard labour as ever a convict endured in Sing-Sing prison.

But I won. Not a soul even suspected the canker in my heart which had changed the point of view of all things in life for me. I came in the end to be glad of the stern self-discipline which had made me a woman before my girlhood had fully opened. I learnt the lesson thoroughly, and never again would I be tempted to trust myself to any man's untender mercies.

I grew very tired of a girl's humdrum routine life. I longed for activity and adventure. I wanted to be doing something earnest and real, to pit myself against men on equal terms; and for this I sought to qualify myself both physically and mentally. I travelled through the States alone; meeting more than once with adventures that tested my nerve and courage.

I made a trip to Europe; and when my uncle insisted upon sending a good placid dame to chaperone me, I found occasion to quarrel with her on the voyage out so that I might even sample Europe by myself.

Unconsciously, I was fitting myself for the work which my father's letters were to lay upon me; and when in Paris on that trip I had an adventure destined to prove of vital import to that task.

The big hotel in which I was staying caught fire one night, and the visitors, most of them women and elderly men, were half mad with panic. I was escaping when I found crouching in one of the corridors, fear-stricken, helpless, and hysterical, a very beautiful woman whom I had seen at the dinner table, the laughing centre of a noisy and admiring crowd of men. I first shook some particles of sense into her and then got her out.

It was a perfectly easy thing to do without any risk to me; but she said I had saved her life. Probably I had: for she might have lain there till she was suffocated by the smoke; and she insisted upon showering much hysterical gratitude upon me; and then wished to make me her close friend. She was a Madame Constans; and, as I can be cautious enough upon occasion, I had some inquiries made about her from our Embassy. The caution was justified. She was a secret Government agent; a police spy with a past.

I parted from her therefore amid vivid evidences of affection from her and vehement protestations that, if ever she could return the obligation, her life would willingly be at my disposal. I accepted her declarations at their verbal worth and expected never to see her again.

But the Fates had arranged otherwise; and it was with genuine astonishment that when Madame d'Artelle was pointed out to me one day driving in the Stadwalchen of Pesth, I recognized her as Madame Constans.

This fact set me thinking. What could she be doing in Buda Pesth? Why was she coiling the net of intrigue round the young Count—the future Duke? Was she still a secret Government agent promoted to an international position? Who was behind her in it all? These and other questions of the kind were started.

15

Then came the mysterious theft of the ducal jewels; and through my instinct, or intuition, call it by what term you may, that which was a mystery to so many became my key to the whole problem. Count Karl was in the toils of the lovely French-woman; he was one of the very few persons who had access to the jewels; he was admittedly a man of dissipated habits; and it was an easy deduction that she had instigated the robbery; more to test the extent of her power over him, perhaps, than because she coveted the jewels. There was much more than mere vulgar theft in it; that was but one of the coils she threw round him. She was in the Hungarian capital because others had sent her to find out secrets; and she was drawing the net about his feet to ruin him for other and greater purposes.

Here then was my course ready shaped for me. I had entered the Minister's household to win his confidence as a possible means to the end I had in view; but the study of my father's papers had shown me that the General might have had a hand in the grim drama, and in such an event I might find my way blocked.

But if I took the field against Madame d'Artelle and cut the meshes of the net of ruin being woven round Count Karl, I should have on my side the future Duke, the man with the power in his hands, and himself quite innocent of all connexion with my father's fate. Success might easily lie that way.

I acted promptly. I went to Madame d'Artelle's; and the interview was one which would have greatly interested his Excellency. I posed as the student and governess with my own way to make in the world; and the Frenchwoman, eager to buy my silence and wishing to separate me from the Minister, urged me to trust to her to advance my interests, and to live with her in the meantime.

I consented, of course; and it was then I spoke out to General von Erlanger. Thus with one stroke I established close relations with two sides in the intrigue.

It was with a feeling of some inward satisfaction at the progress I was making that I went to stay in Madame d'Artelle's house; and, as I had not yet seen the man whom I planned to deliver from her hands, I looked forward with much curiosity and interest to meeting him. I should need to study him very closely; for I was fully alive to the infinite difficulties of what I had undertaken to do.

But those difficulties were to prove a hundred-fold greater than I had even anticipated; and my embarrassment and perplexity were at first so great, that I was all but tempted to abandon the whole scheme.

I was sitting with Madame d'Artelle one afternoon reading—I

16

kept up the pretence of studying—when Count Karl was announced. I rose at once to leave the room.

"Don't go," she said. "I wish to present you to the Count."

"Just as you please," I agreed, glad of the chance, and resumed my seat.

He was shown in, and as I saw him I caught my breath, my heart gave a great leap, and I felt a momentary chill of dismay.

Count Karl was no other than the Count von Ostelen—the man whose treatment of me five years before in New York had all but broken my heart and spoilt my life.

Here was a development indeed.

CHAPTER IV

MADAME D'ARTELLE

For a moment the situation oppressed me, but the next I had mastered it and regained my self-possession. I was not recognized. Karl threw a formal glance at me as Madame d'Artelle mentioned my name, and his eyes came toward me again when she explained that I was an American. I was careful to keep my face from the light and to let him see as little of my features as possible. But I need not have taken even that trouble. He did not give me another thought; and I sat for some minutes turning over the pages of my book, observing him, trying to analyze my own feelings, and speculating how this unexpected development was likely to affect my course.

My first sensation was one which filled me with mortification. I was angry that he had not recognized me. I told myself over and over again that this was all for the best; that it made everything easier for me; that I had no right to care five cents whether he knew me or not; and that it was altogether unworthy of me. Yet my pride was touched: I suppose it was my pride; anyway, it embittered my resentment against him.

It was an insult which aggravated and magnified his former injury; and I sat, outwardly calm, but fuming inwardly, as I piled epithet upon epithet in indignant condemnation of him until my old contempt quickened into hot and fierce hatred. I felt that, come

17

what might, I would not stir a finger to save him from any fate to which others were luring him.

But I began to cool after a while. I was engaged in too serious a conflict to allow myself to be swayed by any emotions. I could obey only one guide—my judgment. Here was the man who of all others would be able by and by to help me most effectively: and if I was not to fail in my purpose I must have his help, let the cost be what it might.

It was surely the quaintest of the turns of Fate's wheel that had brought me to Pesth to save him of all men from ruin; but I never break my head against Fate's decrees, and I would not now. So I accepted the position and began to watch the two closely.

Karl was changed indeed. He looked not five, but fifteen, years older than when we had parted that morning in the Central Park. His face was lined; his features heavy, his eyes dull and spiritless, and his air listless and almost preoccupied. He smiled very rarely indeed, and seemed scarcely even to listen to Madame d'Artelle as she chattered and laughed and gestured gaily.

The reason for some of the change was soon made plain. Wine was brought; and when her back was toward him I saw him look round swiftly and stealthily and pour into his glass something from a small bottle which he took from his pocket.

I perceived something else, too. Madame d'Artelle had turned her back intentionally so as to give him the opportunity to do this; for I saw that she watched him in a mirror, and was scrupulous not to turn to him again until the little phial was safely back in his pocket.

So this was one of the secrets—opium. His dulness and semi-stupor were due to the fact that the previous dose was wearing off; and she knew it, and gave him an opportunity for the fresh dose.

I waited long enough to notice the first effects. His eyes began to brighten, his manner changed, he commenced to talk briskly, and his spirits rose fast. I feared that under the spur of the drug his memory might recall me, and I deemed it prudent to leave the room.

I had purposely held my tongue lest he should recognize my voice—the most tell-tale of all things in a woman—but now I rose and made some trivial excuse to Madame d'Artelle.

As I spoke I noticed him start, glance quickly at me, and pass his hand across his forehead; but before he could say anything, I was out of the room. I had accomplished two things. I had let him familiarize himself with the sight of me without associating me with our former relations; and I had found out one of the secrets of

18

Madame's influence over him—her encouragement of his drug-taking.

But why should she encourage it? It seemed both reasonless and unaccountable. Did she care for him? I had my reasons for believing she did. Yet if so, why seek to weaken his mind as well as destroy his reputation? I thought this over carefully and could see but one answer—she must be acting in obedience to some powerful compelling influence from outside. Who had that influence, and what was its nature?

When I knew that Karl had gone I went down stairs and had another surprise. I found Madame d'Artelle plunged apparently in the deepest grief. She was a creature of almost hysterical changes of mood.

"What is the matter?" I asked, with sparse sympathy. "Don't cry. Tears spell ruin to the complexion."

"I am the most miserable woman in the world," she wailed.

"Then you are at the bottom of a very large class. Tears don't suit you, either. They make your eyes red and puffy. A luxury even you cannot afford, beautiful as you are."

"You are hateful," she cried, angrily; and immediately dried her eyes and sat up to glare at me.

I smiled. "I have stopped your crying at any rate."

"I wish to be alone."

"I think you ought to be very grateful to me. Look at yourself;" and I held a hand mirror in front of her face.

She snatched it from me and flung it down on the sofa pillow with a little French oath.

"Be careful. To break a mirror means a year's ill luck. A serious misfortune for even a pretty woman."

"I don't believe you have a grain of sympathy in your whole heart. It must be as hard as a stone."

"My dear Henriette, the heart has nothing to do with sympathy or any other emotion. It is just the blood pump. I have not read much physiology but...."

"Nom de Dieu, spare me your science," she cried, excitedly.

I laughed again without restraint. "We'll drop physiology, then. But I know other things, and now that I have brought you out of the tear stage, we'll talk about them if you like. I agree with you that it is most exasperating and bitterly disappointing."

Her face was a mask of bewilderment as she turned to me swiftly. "What do you mean?" The question came after a pause.

"It is so ridiculously easy. I mean what you were thinking about when the passion of tears came along. What are you going to do about it?"

19

I had seated myself and taken up a book, and was turning over the leaves as I put the question. She jumped up excitedly and came and stood over me, her features almost fiercely set as she stared down.

"What do you mean? You shall say what you mean. You shall."

"Not while you stand there threatening me with a sort of wild glare in your eyes. I don't think it's fair to be angry with me just because you can't do what you wish."

She stretched out her hands as if she would shake me in her exasperation. Then she laughed, a little wildly, and went back to her seat on the couch.

"What was in my thoughts then?"

"At the foundation—the inconvenience of your religious convictions as a member of the Roman Catholic Church."

"You are mad," she cried, with a toss of her shapely head and a ringing laugh. But as the laugh died away her eyes filled with sobering perplexity. "At the foundation," she said slowly, repeating my words. "You are a poor thought-reader. What else was I thinking of?"

I paused to give due significance to my next words, and looked at her fixedly as I spoke. "Of your marriage with M. Constans; and that in your church, marriage is a sacrament."

"You are a devil," she exclaimed, with fresh excitement, almost with fury indeed. "Say what you mean and don't torment me."

"The Count has been urging you to marry him of course, and—"

"You have been listening. You spy." The last vestige of her self-control was lost as she flung the words at me.

I paused. I never act impetuously with hysterical people. With studied deliberation I closed my book, having carefully laid a marker between the pages, and looked round as if for anything that might belong to me. Then I rose. Her eyes watched me with growing doubt and anxiety.

"I shall be ready to leave the house in about an hour, Madame," I said icily, and walked toward the door.

She let me get close to it. "What are you going to do?"

My answer was a cold smile, in which I contrived to convey a threat. I knew how to frighten her.

She jumped up and rushed to the door and stood with her back against it—as an angry, over-teased child will do. "You shall not go. You mean to try and ruin me." I had known before that she was afraid of me; but she had never shown it so openly.

"Yes, I shall do my best." I spoke so calmly and looked her so firmly in the face that she was convinced of my earnestness.

"I didn't mean what I said," she declared.

20

"It is too late for that," I replied, with a sneer of obvious distrust and disbelief. She had very little courage and was a poor fighter. Her only weapon was her beauty; and it was useless of course against me.

Her eyes began to show a scared, hunted expression. "Don't go. Forgive me, Christabel. I didn't mean it. I swear I didn't. You angered me, and you know how impetuous I am."

"I am surprised you should plead thus to—a spy, Madame."

"But I tell you I didn't mean it. Christabel, dear Christabel, I know you are not a spy. Don't make so much of an angry word. Come, let us talk it over. Do, do"; and she put her arm in mine to lead me back to my chair.

I let her prevail with me, but with obvious reluctance. "Why are you so afraid of me?" I asked.

"I am not afraid of you; but I want you to stay and help me."

I sat down then as a concession and a sign that I was willing to talk things over; and she sat near me, taking care to place her chair between me and the door.

"If that is so, it is time that we understood one another. Perhaps I had better begin. You cannot marry Count Karl."

"I love him, Christabel."

"And Monsieur Constans—your husband?"

"Don't, don't. He deserted me. He is a villain, a false scoundrel. Don't speak of him in the same breath with—with the man I love."

"He is your husband, Madame." She moaned and waved her arms despairingly.

"I am the most wretched woman on earth. I love him so."

"And therefore encourage him to take opium. I do not understand that kind of love. Had you not better tell me the truth?"

"I shall save him. You don't understand. My God, you don't understand at all. The only way I can save him is to do what he asks."

"Who is it that is forcing your hand?"

She winced at the question, as if it were a lancet thrust. "You frighten me, Christabel, and mystify me."

"No, no. It is only that you are trying to mystify me, and are frightened lest I should guess your secret. Let us be fair to one another. I have an object here which you cannot guess and I shall not tell you. You have an object which I can see plainly. You have been brought here to involve Count Karl in a way which threatens him with ruin, and you have fallen in love with him—or think you have. You are now anxious to please your employer and also secure the man you love from the ruin which threatens him. He has asked you to marry him; and a crisis has arisen which you have neither the nerve to face nor the wit to solve."

"Nom de Dieu, how you read things!" she exclaimed under her breath, her eyes dilated with wonder and fear.

"But for my presence you would marry him; and trust to Fate to avoid the discovery being made that M. Constans is still alive. To yourself you would justify this by the pretence that if you were once the Count's wife you could check instead of encourage his opium habit and so save him. Who then is it with the power to drive you into this reckless crime?"

She was too astounded to reply at once, but sat staring at me open mouthed. Suddenly she changed, and her look grew fierce and tense. "Who are you, and what is your motive in forcing yourself upon me here?"

"I depend on my wits to make a way for me in the world, Madame; and I take care to keep them in good condition. But I am not forcing myself upon you. I am ready to go at this moment—if you prefer that—and if you think it safer to have me against you."

"Mon Dieu, I believe I am really afraid of you."

"Of me, no. Of the knowledge I have, yes. And you will do well to give that fear due weight. You have been already induced to make one very foolish move. To receive stolen jewels is a crime, even when the thief is——"

"How dare you say that!"

"You forget. The day I came first to you you had occasion to go to the secret drawer in the old bureau in your boudoir, and I saw them there. You are a very poor player, Madame, in such a game as this."

The colour left her cheeks, and hate as well as fear was in her eyes as she stared helplessly at me.

"It is all your imagination," she said, weakly.

I smiled.

"It can remain that—if you wish. It is for you to decide."

"What do you mean?"

"You had better trust me. You can begin by telling me what and whose is this evil influence behind you?"

A servant interrupted us at that moment.

"His Excellency Count Gustav is asking for you, Madame."

She gave a quick start, and flashed a look at me.

"I will go to him," she answered.

I had another intuition then. I smiled and rose.

"So that is the answer to my question. You may wish to consult him, Madame. I will see you afterwards; and will use the interval to have my trunks packed in readiness to leave the house should he deem it best."

"I am right. You are a devil," she cried, with another burst of impetuous, uncontrollable temper.

I turned as I reached the door.

"Should he decide that I stay, Madame, and wish to see me, I shall be quite prepared."

I went out then without waiting for any reply.

CHAPTER V

A NIGHT ADVENTURE

I felt completely satisfied with the result of my conversation with Madame d'Artelle. I had had some qualms about the manner in which I had entered her house; feeling, it must be confessed, something like a spy. But our relations would now be changed. It would be at most an alliance of hostility. I should only remain because she would deem it more dangerous for me to leave; she would trust me no further than she dared; and as I had openly acknowledged that I had an object of my own in view, I need no longer have any scruples about staying.

I had made excellent use of my opportunities, moreover; and if my last shaft had really hit the bull's-eye—that the influence behind her was that of Karl's brother—the discovery would be of the utmost value.

Could it be Count Gustav? Instead of packing my trunks I sat trying to answer that question and the others which flowed from it. I had always heard him spoken of not only as a man of high capacity and integrity but as a staunch friend to his brother Karl. Yet he was a man; and he might be as false as any other. I would take no man's good faith for granted.

There was the crucial fact, too, that Karl's ruin meant Gustav's advantage. Every one expressed regret that Karl and not Gustav was to be the future Duke; and if others felt this, was Gustav himself likely to hold a different opinion? From such an opinion it was no doubt a far cry to form a deliberate plot to secure the dukedom; but

Gustav was no more than a man; and men had done such things before.

I hoped they would send for me, that I might judge for myself. I could understand how my interference with such a scheme, if he had formed it, would rouse his resentment; and the difficulty it would present. To send me out of the house would in his view be tantamount to giving away the whole scheme at once to General von Erlanger; and I settled it with myself therefore that, if he was really at the back of the plot, he would be as eager to see me as I was to see him.

An hour passed and I was beginning to think I was wrong, when Madame's French maid came to my room, saying that her mistress would very much like to speak to me.

"Where is she, Ernestine?"

"In the salon, mademoiselle."

"Alone?"

"M. le Comte Gustav is with her."

"I will go to her," I said; and as she closed the door I laughed. I was not wrong, it seemed, but very much right; and I went down to meet them with the confidence borne of the feeling that I knew their object while they were in ignorance of mine.

People did the Count no less than justice in describing him as a handsome man. He had one of the handsomest faces I had ever looked upon; eyes of the frankest blue, a most engaging air, and a smile that was almost irresistibly winning.

He held out his hand when Madame presented him, and spoke in that ingratiating tone which is sometimes termed caressing.

"I have desired so much to know Madame d'Artelle's new friend, Miss Gilmore. I trust you will count me also among your friends."

"You are very kind, Count. You know we Americans have a weakness for titles. You flatter me." I was intensely American for the moment, and almost put a touch of the Western twang in my accent.

"You are really American, then?"

"You bet. From Missouri, Jefferson City: as fine a town in as fine a State as anywhere in the world. Not that I run down these old-world places in Europe. Have you been in the States?"

"To my regret, no."

"Ah, then you haven't seen what a city should be. Fine broad straight streets, plenty of air space, and handsome buildings."

"I know that American women are handsome," he replied, with a look intended to put the compliment on me. But I was not taking any.

24

"I guess we reckon looks by the dollar measure, Count. You should see our girls at home."

"You must regret living away from your country."

"Every man must whittle his own stick, you know, and every woman too. Which means, I have to make my own way."

"You are more than capable, I am sure."

"I can try to plough my own furrow, sure."

"You have come to Pesth for that purpose?"

"Yes—out of the crowd."

"What furrow do you think of ploughing here?"

"Well, just at present I'm in Madame's hands, you see. And I think we're getting to understand one another, some. Though whether we're going to continue to pull in the same team much longer seems considerably doubtful."

"I am very anxious to help you, Christabel, dear," put in Madame d'Artelle; and I knew from that "dear," pretty much what was coming.

"It would give me much pleasure to place what influence I have at your disposal, Miss Gilmore."

"I must say I find everybody's real kind," I answered, demurely. "There is General von Erlanger saying very much the same thing."

"You speak German with an excellent idiom," said the Count, with a pretty sharp look. "One is tempted to think you have been in Europe often before."

I laughed. "I was putting a little American into the accent, Count, as a matter of fact. I have a knack for languages. I know Magyar just as well. And French, and Italian, and a bit of Russian. I'm a student of comparative folk lore, you know; and I'm getting up Turkish and Servian and Greek."

"But surely you have been much in Europe?"

"I was in Paris three years ago;" and at that Madame d'Artelle looked away.

"So Madame told me," he said, suggestively. "It was there you met, of course. It was there you made your mistake about her, I think."

"What mistake was that?"

"That Madame's husband was still alive."

So he was a scoundrel after all, and this was to be the line of tactics.

"Oh, that is to be taken as a mistake, is it?" I said this just as though I were ready to fall in with the suggestion.

"Not taken as a mistake, Miss Gilmore. It is a mistake. We have the proofs of his death."

"'We'?" I rapped back so sharply that he winced.

"Madame has confided in me," he replied.

"Well, from all accounts she has not lost much; and must be glad to be free to marry again."

His eyes smiled. "You are very quick, Miss Gilmore."

"I am not so quick as Madame," I retorted; "because she has got these proofs within the last hour. It is nothing to me, of course; but I don't think we are getting on so quickly to an understanding as we might."

"You know that I am my brother's friend as well as Madame's in this?"

"What does that mean?"

"In regard to the marriage on which my brother's heart is so deeply set. You are willing to help it also?"

"How can it concern me? What for instance would happen to me if I were not?" I paused and then added, significantly: "And what also if I were?"

"I think we shall arrive at a satisfactory understanding," he answered, with obvious relief. "Those who help my family—a very powerful and influential one, I may remind you—are sure to secure a great measure of our favour."

"I desire nothing more than that," said I, with the earnestness of truth—although the favour which I needed was not perhaps in his thoughts.

"Madame would of course like to know a good deal about all who co-operate with her," he declared, very smoothly and suggestively.

"What do you wish to know about me; and what do you wish me to do?"

"Americans are very direct," he replied, bowing. "She would leave you to tell us what you please, of course, and afford such means as you think best for her to make inquiries."

"Every one in Jefferson City knew my uncle, John P. Gilmore, knows that he educated me, and that what little money he left came to me. My father was a failure in life, and my mother died when I was a little child. I'm afraid I haven't made much history so far. And that's about all there is to it. What matters to me is not the past but the present and, perhaps, the future."

"You have no friends in Pesth?"

"None, unless you count General von Erlanger; I was his children's governess and used to play chess with him."

"And your motive in coming here?" There was a glint in his eyes I did not understand.

"I thought I had told you. I am a student in the University."

"That is all?"

I laughed. "Oh no, indeed it isn't. I am just looking around to shake hands with any opportunity that chances to come my way. I am a soldieress of fortune. That's why I came to Madame d'Artelle. Not to study folk lore."

"In Paris you were not a student?"

"Oh, you mean I was better off then? My uncle Gilmore was alive; and we all thought he was rich."

"Pardon my inquisitiveness yet further. You know New York well?" This was the scent, then.

"I know Fifth Avenue, have walked about Broadway, and once stood in a whirl of amazement on Brooklyn Bridge. But I haven't a friend in the whole city."

"Were you there five years ago?"

I affected to search my memory. "That would be in ninety-five. I was eighteen. I have been about so much in the States that my flying visits to New York are difficult to fix. Was that the year I went to California? If so, I did not go East as well, and yet I fancy I did. No, that was to Chicago and down home through St. Louis."

"I mean for a considerable stay in New York?"

"Oh, I shouldn't forget that. That was three years ago before I started for Paris," I said, laughing lightly. "I had the time of my life then."

"Did you ever meet a Miss Christabel von Dreschler?"

Where was he leading me now? What did he know? I shook my head meditatively. "I have met hundreds of girls but I don't remember her among them."

"She must resemble you closely, Miss Gilmore, just as she has the same Christian name. My brother knew her and declares that you remind him of her."

I laughed lightly and naturally. "I should scarcely have believed he had eyes or thoughts for any woman except Madame d'Artelle."

"Pardon me if I put a very plain question. You have acknowledged to be seeking your fortune here. You are doing so in your own name? You are not Miss von Dreschler?"

I took umbrage at once and showed it. I rose and answered with all the offended dignity I could assume. "When I have cause to hide myself under an alias, Count, it will be time to insult me with the suggestion that I am ashamed of my own name of Gilmore."

He was profuse in his apologies. "Please do not think I intended the slightest insult. Nothing was farther from my thoughts. I was merely speaking out of my hope that that might be the case. I am exceedingly sorry. Pray resume your seat."

I had scored that game, so I consented to be pacified and sat down again. I was curious to see what card he would play next.

He pulled at his fair moustache in some perplexity.

"You expressed a desire just now to have the advantage of my family's influence, Miss Gilmore."

"Am I to remain with Madame, then?" I asked, blandly.

"Of course you are, dear," she answered for herself.

"You are willing to help her and my brother in this important matter?" said the Count.

"How can I help? I am only a stranger. And I should not call it helping any one to connive at a marriage when one of the parties is already married. I would not do that."

The handsome face darkened; and in his impatience of a check he made a bad slip.

"Our influence is powerful to help our friends, Miss Gilmore, and not less powerful to harm our antagonists."

I laughed, disagreeably. "I see. A bribe if I agree, a threat if I do not. And how do you think you could harm an insignificant person like me? I am not in the least afraid of you, Count."

"I did not mean to threaten," he said, rather sullenly, as he saw his mistake. "You can do us neither harm nor good for that matter. You are labouring under a mistake as to Madame d'Artelle's husband—her late husband; and by speaking of the matter might cause some temporary inconvenience and slander. We do not wish you to do so. That is all."

"I have not yet been shown that it is a mistake."

"The proofs shall be given to you." He spoke quite angrily. "In the meantime if you speak of the matter, you will offend and alienate us all."

"It seems a very lame conclusion for all this preamble," I answered, lightly, as I got up. "Produce the proofs and I of course have no more to say. But until they are produced I give no pledge to hold my tongue;" and without troubling myself to wait for a reply, I left the room.

I had obtained the information I needed as to the power behind Madame d'Artelle, and I had something to do. They intended to produce proofs of M. Constan's death, and I resolved to get the proof that he was still living.

Leaving a message for Madame that I had to go to the university for an evening lecture, I drove to the house which I had taken on coming to Pesth.

In passing through Paris I had seen the friend who had formerly given me the information about Madame, and I now telegraphed to him that I must know the whereabouts of M.

Constans at once, and that no expense was to be spared in getting the information.

I had brought three servants with me from home, John Perry and his wife and their son, James. The last was a sharp, clever young fellow, and he was now in Paris where I had sent him to get information about Madame d'Artelle. I wired to him also, telling him what further information I needed; and I instructed him to help in the matter and wire me the instant M. Constans had been traced.

That done I set out to return to Madame's. I was not nervous at being out alone at such a time, night prowling having long been a habit with me. I was perfectly able to take care of myself, too; for at home I had been accustomed to carry a revolver, and was an excellent shot. If any one interfered with me, it was not I who was likely to come worse off.

I think it is just nonsense that girls must always be "seen home" in the dark. It is a good excuse for flirtation, possibly; but an extremely undignified admission of inferiority. A humiliation I have never countenanced and never will.

The night was fine and clear, and a bright moon was nearly at the full; so I turned out of my way a little to a very favourite spot of mine—the great Suspension Bridge which constitutes the hyphen between Buda and Pesth. My house was close to the bridge in that part of Pesth known as the "Inner Town;" and I strolled across to a point on the Buda side from which a glorious view can be had of the stately Danube.

I stood there in the deep shadow of the high Suspension Arches, gazing at the dotted lights along the quays, across the flat country on the Pesth side, up the river toward the witching Margaret Island, and away to the old hilly Buda on my left, with the Blocksberg and its citadel keeping its frowning watch and ward over all.

There is not much poetry in my nature; but the most prosaic and commonplace soul must feel a quickening of thought and sentiment at the appeal of that majestic waterway and its romance-filled setting.

I did that night; and stood there, thinking dreamily, until I was roused abruptly by the sound of laughter. I recognized the voice of Count Gustav; and glancing round saw him on the other side of the bridge with a companion. He stooped a second and pointed down the river; and as they walked on, I heard her laugh sweetly in response.

I was considering what to do, when I caught the sound of footsteps, and shrank into the shadow of the deep buttress as two men came slouching past me stealthily; and I heard enough to tell

29

me they were following Count Gustav. I let them pass and then followed in my turn.

The Count and his companion left the bridge, turned to the right, and presently entered the old garden of Buda—a deserted spot enough at such an hour. Presently, as the two reached an open place, I saw the Count hesitate, glance about him, stand a moment, and take off his hat. Then they continued their walk.

I was struck by the action. It looked as though it might have been a signal; for the next moment the two men quickened their pace and closed up to the pair. A momentary scuffle followed; the girl gave a half-smothered cry for help; and then the Count came running past me, making for the bridge at the top of his speed. He had left his companion in the hands of the two men.

Convinced now that mischief was on foot, I resolved to see the matter through. I hid myself as the men came hurrying back with the girl, half-leading, half-carrying her; and I noticed that her face was closely muffled.

Near the entrance to the place they halted, and drew back under the shadow of the trees. They stood there some moments, when one of them went out into the road and stood listening. I heard in the distance the sound of wheels, and guessed it was a carriage for which the two were waiting.

Clearly, if I was to make an attempt to save the girl, I must act at once; and to save her and learn her story, I was now determined.

I took a deep breath, as one will when about to plunge into a cold stream, and keeping my hand on my revolver I darted across to where the girl and her one captor stood. It was a point in my favour that the two men were just then separated.

He did not hear my footsteps until I was close to him, and gave a great start of surprise when I spoke.

"Let my friend go at once," I said, in a loud, firm tone.

The man's start was the girl's opportunity. Snatching her arm out of his grasp, she rushed to me, tearing at the wrapper which covered her face.

The man swore and called his companion, who ran swiftly back. A couple of words were exchanged hurriedly between them, and then they came at me, one of them brandishing a heavy stick and threatening me.

The girl uttered a sharp cry of fear.

I whipped out my revolver, and the two scoundrels pulled up at the sight of it.

"If you make me fire I shall not only shoot you," I called, "but bring the police up, and you'll have to explain this to them."

And as we stood thus, the carriage drove up.

30

CHAPTER VI

GARETH

I was quite as anxious to avoid police interference as the men themselves could be; but I knew the threat was more likely to drive them off than any other.

To recover the girl, they would have bludgeoned me readily enough, if they could have done it without being discovered; but my weapon made that impossible. Moreover, they liked the look of the business end of the revolver as little as many braver men.

The stick was lowered; they whispered together, and then tried to fool me. They began to edge away from one another, so as to be able to rush in from opposite directions.

"You stand just where you are, or I fire, right now," I called.

They stopped and swore.

"Can't a man take his own daughter home?" growled one of them.

"I am not his daughter," protested the girl.

"I know that. Don't be afraid, I shan't give you up."

"Who are you to interfere with us?" asked the other.

"I'm a man in woman's clothes," I answered, intending this tale to be carried to their employer. "And I'll give you five seconds to clear. You get into that carriage and drive off, the lot of you together, or I'll bring the police about your ears. Now, one, two, if you let me count to five, you'll eat nothing but prison fare for a year or two. Off with you;" and emboldened by my success I made a step toward them.

It was good bluff. They shrank back; then turned tail and scurried to the carriage, swearing copiously, and drove off in the direction of Old Buda.

I watched the vehicle until the darkness swallowed it, and then hurried with my companion in the opposite direction. We recrossed the bridge and made for my house.

When we were near it I stopped, and she began to thank me volubly and with many tears.

"Don't thank me yet. Tell me where you wish to go."

"I have nowhere to go in Pesth, sir," she answered.

I smiled at her mistake. "Let me explain. I said that about my being a man to frighten those ruffians. I am a girl, like yourself, and have a home close by. If you like to come to it, you will be quite safe there."

"I trust you implicitly," she said, simply; and with that I took her to my house.

As we entered I managed to draw out a couple of hairpins, so that when I took off my hat, my hair came tumbling about my shoulders in sufficient length to satisfy her of my sex. She was quick enough to understand my reason; and with a very sweet smile she put her arm round my waist and kissed me on the cheek.

"I did not need any proof, dear," she said. "But you are wonderful. How I wish I were you. So brave and daring."

"You are very pretty, my dear," I answered, as I kissed her. She was; but very pale and so fragile that I felt as if I were petting a child.

"I am so wretched," she murmured, and the tears welled up in her great blue eyes. "If I were only strong like you!"

"You shall tell me your story presently; but first I have something to do. Sit here a moment."

I went out and told Mrs. Perry to get us something to eat and to prepare a bed for my friend; and I wrote a hurried line to Madame d'Artelle that I was staying for the night with a student friend, and sent it by Mr. Perry.

When I went back the girl was sitting in a very despondent attitude, weeping silently; but she started up and tried to smile to me through her tears. Then I made a discovery. She had taken off her gloves, and on her left hand was a wedding ring.

"How can I ever thank you?" she cried.

"First by drying your tears—things might have been much worse with you, you know; think of that; then by having some supper; I am positively famished; and after that, if you like, you can tell me your story, and we will see whether, by putting our heads together, we cannot find a way to help you further."

"I am afraid——" and she broke down again.

With much persuasion I induced her to eat something and take a little wine; and this seemed to cheer her. She dried her eyes and as we sat side by side on a couch, she put her hand in mine and gradually nestled into my arms like a weary wee child.

"I'll begin," I said. "My name is Christabel Gilmore. I'm an American, and a student at the University here;" and I added some details about the States and so on; just talking so as to give her time to gather confidence.

"You haven't told me your name yet," I said, presently.

"I am the Countess von Ostelen. You have heard the name?" she said, quickly, at my start of surprise.

"I was surprised, that is all. Yes. I knew the name years ago in America. I knew the Count von Ostelen."

"He is my husband," she said, very simply. "My Christian name is Gareth. You will call me by that, of course." With a sweet little nervous gesture she slipped her arm away and began to finger her wedding ring.

"I had seen that, my dear."

"Your eyes see everything, Christabel;" and her arm came about me again and her head rested on my shoulder.

I sat silent for a few moments in perplexity. If she were Karl's wife, how came his brother to have been——what a fool I was! Of course the thing was plain. Gustav was the husband, and he had used his brother's name. My heart was stirred, and my intense pity for her found vent in a sigh.

"Why that sigh, Christabel?" Her sweet eyes fastened upon my face nervously, and I kissed her.

"The sigh was for you, child, not for myself. Had you not better tell me everything? Have you your husband's likeness?"

"I had it here in a locket," she said, wistfully, as she drew a chain from her bosom. "But to-day he said the locket was not good enough for me. I wish I had kept it now. You would have said he was the handsomest man you had ever seen. Oh, how selfish I am," she broke off, with a quick cry of distress and sat up.

"What is the matter?"

"I never thought of it. He was with me when those men attacked us. Oh, if he should have been hurt!"

"You can make your mind easy about that," I said, a little drily. "I saw the attack and that he escaped."

"He is so brave. He would have risked his life for me."

"I saw him—get away, dear," I replied. I nearly said run away; but could not yet undeceive her.

"If anything had happened to him, it would have killed me. I would rather have died than that." Then with a change of manner she asked: "Did you see his face, Christabel?"

"Yes, in the moonlight, but he passed me quickly."

"But you saw he was handsome?"

"One of the handsomest men I have ever seen," I assented, to please her.

"Yes, yes. That is just it, and as good as he is handsome."

"I could not see that, of course," I answered; and then was silent. I was growing very anxious as I saw the problem widening and deepening. Poor trustful little soul! How should I ever break the truth to her and not break her heart at the same time?

There was a long pause, which she broke. "Oh, how I hope he has really escaped, as you say."

33

"How came you to be where I saw you?" I asked. This reminded her, as I intended, that she had told me nothing yet.

"I said I was selfish, Christabel, didn't I? I had quite forgotten I had told you nothing. I will tell you: but you must first give me a promise not to repeat it. Our marriage is only a secret so far, you know."

"On my honour, I will do nothing to harm you. Why is your marriage a secret?"

"My husband is afraid of his father's anger. You see, Karl—"

"Karl?" I exclaimed, involuntarily.

"That is my husband's name," she replied, with a touch of rebuke and pride. He had taken his brother's Christian name, it seemed.

"Of course," I agreed.

"My husband is a Count, but as yet only a poor one, dependent upon the good will of his father who wishes him to marry some one else. So we dare not let it be known yet that we are married."

"But your own friends know?" I said.

She seemed to resent this in some way as a reflection upon her husband. "I have no friends in Pesth except my dear father. He is alive and I know he loves me; but I don't know why, I have never lived at home for more than a week or so at a time. I did wish to tell him; but Karl would not let me—I mean, we decided it was better not until the truth could be told to all." Then she showed me her innocent heart again. "It is when I think of my father that I am so wretched. He will believe I have deserted him so cruelly;" and her eyes were full of tears again.

"Who is your father, dear?"

"Colonel Katona. My dear, dear father!" and her grief so overcame her that my fresh start of surprise passed unnoticed. He had been that friend of my father's who was believed to hold the secret of the great wrong in his keeping. And it was his daughter whom I had thus saved.

Her tears passed soon, like a summer storm. She was a creature of strangely variable moods.

"I know, of course, that Karl was right. My father is a stern, gloomy and sometimes hard man. He would have forced us to announce the marriage; and then Karl would have been ruined."

"But did not your father know that he wished to marry you?"

"Oh, no," she cried, smiling now. "That was the lovely part of it. He never saw Karl. I meant it to be a surprise. I was at Tyrnau, staying with friends, when we met, and it was all settled in a few weeks. You see Karl loved me and I loved him, and—that was all."

"You were married at Tyrnau?"

34

She shook her head gaily. "No. It was such fun. We ran away together, and were married by a friend of Karl's in his house at Sillien, in the mountains. A heaven of a place. My home is there. Oh, the loveliest of homes, Christabel. You will say so when you see it."

"I may never see it, my dear."

"Oh, but of course you will. You will come and stay with me. You will be my dear friend always; and Karl's too, when he knows how you saved me to-night. And it will never be lonely there any more."

"How came you to be in Pesth to-night then?" I asked, smothering the sigh which her last words impelled.

"I suppose I did wrong to come. A wife should obey her husband, of course, but I couldn't help it. You see, lately his father has kept Karl so much here that I have scarcely seen him; and something is going to happen; I shan't be alone then; and—you understand, I wanted to let my father know I was married before my child was born. I wrote this to Karl, and—it was naughty and wicked of me, I know—but when he would not consent, I came to Pesth to-day and surprised him."

"Yes, I think I understand," said I. It was easy to read now, indeed. Her visit meant discovery for him, and he had improvised the means of getting rid of her which I had prevented. "He was very angry, I suppose?"

"At first, yes. He tried to make me go back to Sillien; but I could not. I could not, could I, Christabel? And when he saw I was in earnest—I can be firm when I will"—and she made a great effort to look resolute and determined—"and said I would go to my father to-morrow, he gave in and kissed me, and agreed to take me to his father and admit everything. We were on our way there when we were attacked. I knew his love for me would conquer in the end. How delighted he will be when he knows that after all I am safe."

"You will see him to-morrow and tell him. You know where to find him in the city here?"

Her face clouded. "That is a strange thing. He was so afraid of his father's anger that he dared not let me write to his home. He gave me an address in the Altgasse, but it is only a place where letters are received. But I shall find him, of course, easily."

"Would you take my advice, if I gave it?"

"In that, oh yes, of course. I know you are clever."

"It is to go straight to your father, Colonel Katona, and tell him all."

"Oh, no, no, no, I dare not now," she cried, shrinking timidly. "Karl made me take an oath to-day on the holy crucifix that,

35

whatever happened, I would never tell my father without his permission."

"Why?"

"Because no one but Karl must break the news of our marriage to his father. No, no. I dare not. I dare not. I cannot break my oath. I should be false to the Holy Church." And at the mere thought of it she began to tremble.

It was clever; a stroke of almost diabolical cleverness; knowing the simple, trusting child, to close her lips by such an oath.

"You will not betray us?" she cried, taking alarm at my silence and serious expression. "You are my friend?"

"Yes, I am your friend, my dear, and will always be, if you want one." She was a very tender little thing, and as I kissed her she threw her arms round my neck and clung to me. "And now, I'll give you some other advice—to go to bed; and after a night's rest, I daresay we shall see our way."

After I had seen her into bed and shown her that her room opened into mine, I went downstairs to think over all she had told me, all the tangle of trouble ahead for her, and its possible effects upon my course.

It was quite late when at length I went to bed; and I was lying unable to sleep in my perplexed anxiety when I heard her call out as if in fear. I started up and then she came running into my room.

"Are you awake, Christabel?"

"What is it, dear?"

"I have had a dream and am frightened. Let me come to you."

And just like a child she crept into my bed and into my arms.

"I dreamt that Karl was dead and that my father had killed him," she moaned. "And he was going to kill me and my child when I screamed out and woke."

Was it an omen? The thought stayed with me long after I had calmed her fright and soothed her to sleep.

God help the helpless, trustful, clinging child! It might well be an omen, indeed. My heart was heavy for her and her trouble.

CHAPTER VII

GARETH'S FATHER

The next day was a busy one for me, for I had to find a place in which Gareth could remain safely hidden.

This I felt to be impracticable in my present house. I had rented it on first coming to Pesth, and it was recorded as my address in the register of the University. It was, of course, certain that Count Gustav would have every possible inquiry made about me; and if he or his agents came to the house, Gareth's presence would at once become known.

Fortunately, I had already commenced some negotiations to take a villa in a secluded part of the hilly district of Buda; and my first step that morning was to go out and complete the matter, so that I could remove that day. I wrote to Madame d'Artelle that I was called out of Pesth, and should return to her on the following day.

I knew quite enough of Count Gustav already to be fully aware that my discovery of his secret in regard to Gareth might prove a source of danger to me. Discreetly used, it might be of the most vital importance for my purposes. But he was a very formidable antagonist; and unless I acted with the utmost wariness and caution, I knew he would beat me.

If I had read his actions aright, he would go to any length to prevent the secret of his marriage getting known; and until I was quite prepared for emergencies, I must guard my knowledge of it jealously.

I was to score the first point. The next morning brought me news from Paris—a telegram from James Perry telling me the whereabouts of M. Constans. I should therefore have that knowledge to take with me to Madame d'Artelle's.

With Gareth, however, I had some difficulty. The view she took of Count Gustav was of course diametrically opposed to mine. This was natural enough. To her he was just the loving husband who would be in an agony of suspense until he knew of her safety. The belief that he was suffering such suspense added to her own grief and worry; and during the day we were removing to the villa she was very impatient of the delay involved.

She was ill both in body and mind; and how to deal with her caused me much thought and anxiety. To tell her what I was convinced was the truth in regard to the Count was impossible, even had I wished to do so. She would not have accepted me as a witness against her faith in him. Moreover, I had no wish to break down that faith yet. What I desired, rather, was to find means to compel him to do her justice; and unwittingly she made that task, hard as it was, more difficult by her attitude.

I repeated my urgent advice—that she should go to her father and tell him everything; but she would not listen to me. On the contrary, she declared that no earthly consideration would induce her to break the solemn vow she had taken; and nothing I could say made the slightest impression upon that resolve.

I could not tell her what I knew well enough was the case—that unless she took that course she would be in danger. I was convinced that Count Gustav would have a very sharp search made for her and that, if he discovered her, he would contrive to get her to a place where she would be prevented from causing him any trouble.

But her faith in him was unshakable. "I shall show myself in the streets," she said, smiling, "and go everywhere until I meet him. He will be desperate until he knows I am safe."

I had to frighten this intention away. "What will happen if you do is this," I told her. "Either your father will meet you; or the men who attacked you will see you, and in order to prevent your accusing them will make away with you. If you will trust me to make this search for you, I will do it; but only on condition that you promise me not to stir from the house unless I am with you."

Scared in this way, she at length was induced to give the promise.

It was at best but an unsatisfactory compromise; and more than once I debated with myself whether, in her interests, I should not be justified in breaking the pledge of secrecy and going to Colonel Katona myself.

But I put that course aside for the moment and set out for Madame d'Artelle's house.

I had not been two minutes with her before I saw that a considerable change had come over the position in my absence. She was so affectionate that I knew she was deceiving me. She over-acted her new role outrageously. She overwhelmed me with kisses and caresses, called Heaven to witness how much she had missed me, and declared she had been inconsolably miserable in my absence. Considering the terms on which we had parted, I should have been a mole not to have seen that this was false.

She was so afraid of offending me indeed, that she scarcely dared to show a legitimate curiosity as to the cause of my absence. She had obviously been coached by Count Gustav; and when a man coaches a woman, he generally makes her blunder. I could see that she was quivering to know what I had been doing, and on tenterhooks lest I had been working against her.

I thought it judicious, therefore, to frighten her a little; and when the due moment came I asked, significantly: "Have you the proofs yet of M. Constan's death?"

"You are not going to talk of disagreeable things directly you get back, are you?"

"His death would not be disagreeable to you, Henriette?"

"You cannot guess what I have endured from that man. I tell you, Christabel, he is a man to raise the devil in a woman."

"A good many men can do that," I said, sententiously. "But if he is dead he can raise no more devils in either man or woman. Where did he die and when?"

"It does not matter to me now whether he is dead or living. You have had your way. I shall not marry Count Karl."

"And your gratitude to me for this is the reason of your kisses and caresses on my return?"

She was very easy to stab; and her eyes flashed with sudden anger. She was too angry indeed to reply at once.

"You are a very singular girl, Christabel—very difficult to love," she said, as if to reproach me.

"Easier to hate, perhaps; but you should not pretend to love me. We need not make believe to love each other, Henriette. I do not love you. I saved your life in Paris, and when I found you here you wished me to come into your house because you thought you could more easily prevent my saying what I knew about you. That has more to do with fear than love—much more. And it does not seem to have occurred to you that I too might have a selfish motive in coming."

"What was it?" She rapped the question out very sharply.

"For one thing I thought it would be interesting to know what the information was which your employers in France wished you to obtain."

"Then you are a spy, after all?" she cried, angrily.

"No. A spy, in the sense you mean, is a person paid by employers to obtain information—as the police used to pay Madame Constans in Paris. I have no employers. I am seeking my own way, and acting for myself. You will see the difference. Now will you tell me what you were sent here to do?"

"You are right in one thing, Christabel—you are easier to hate than to love."

"That does not answer my question."

"I am no spy."

"Henriette! I have been in communication with Paris since I

39

saw you, and a special messenger is now on his way here to me with full tidings. Let us be frank with one another. You promised to advance my fortunes: Count Gustav has made the same promise—why then should you try to deceive me? It is not playing the game fairly."

"I have not tried to deceive you."

"Henriette!" I cried again, this time with a laugh. "What! when you have changed your plans entirely within the last few hours?"

She could not suppress a start at this, and tried to cover it with a laughing suggestion of its absurdity. "You are ridiculous—always finding mysteries," she said.

"Finding them out, you mean," I retorted, slowly and significantly. "Will you leave me to do this now, or will you tell me frankly?"

"There is no new plan."

"You will find it not only useless but unsafe to attempt to deceive me. I know already much of the new plan and within a few hours shall know all." She had been already so impressed by the discoveries I had made that she was quite prepared to believe this bluff; and she was so nervous and agitated that she would not trust herself to speak.

I paused some moments and then said with impressive deliberation:

"Henriette, our relative positions here are changing fast. I came here that you might help me to push my fortunes. I know so much and am so much better and stronger a player than you, that either I shall leave you altogether to carry my knowledge to those who need it badly, or I shall stay to protect you and your fortunes from the man who is threatening both. Think of that while I go upstairs to my room; and think closely, for your future—ruin or success—is the stake at issue; and one false step may cost you everything."

"You mean to threaten me?" she cried, half nervously, half in bravado.

"It is more an offer of help than a threat; but you can regard it as you please;" and I went out of the room.

I ran up hastily to my room full of a new idea which had just occurred to me; but fortunately not so preoccupied as to keep my eyes shut. As I passed Madame d'Artelle's room the door was not quite closed, and through the narrow slit I caught a glimpse of Ernestine. She was vigorously dusting some object that was out of my line of sight.

I am accustomed to study trifles; they often act as finger posts at the forked roads of difficulty and point the proper way. Ernestine was a very particular lady's maid indeed, and never dreamt of dusting out rooms. Why then was she so busy?

I paused and managed to get a peep at the object of her unusual industry. It was a travelling trunk; large enough to hold a big suggestion for me. I pushed the door open.

"Good-morning, Ernestine. I've come back, you see," I said, smiling.

"Ah, good-morning, Mademoiselle Gilmore. I am glad to see you." Ernestine was very friendly to me. I had bought her goodwill.

"Madame and I have been talking over our arrangements," I said, lightly. "It is all rather sudden. Do you think you will have time to alter that black silk bodice for me before we start?"

"I'm afraid not, mademoiselle. You see every thing has to be packed."

"Of course it has. If I had thought of it, I would have left it out for you before I went, the day before yesterday."

"If I had known I would have asked you for it, mademoiselle. But I had not a hint until this morning."

"Come up and see if we cannot contrive something. A bertha of old lace might do for the time."

I did not wish Madame to catch me in her room, so Ernestine and I went on to mine. We talked dress for a couple of minutes and, as I wished her not to speak of the conversation, I said that as the alteration could not be made, I might as well give her the dress. It was nearly new, and delighted her.

"I suppose you'll be ready in time? You are such a clever packer. But the time is short."

She repudiated the suggestion of being behind. "I have all to-day and part of to-morrow. I could pack for you as well," she cried, with a sweep of her hand round the room.

"Never mind about that. I may not go yet."

"Oh no, of course not;" and she laughed archly. "They will not want Mademoiselle la Troisième."

"Mèchante," I cried, dismissing her with a laugh, as though I fully understood the joke. And in truth she had given me a clue which was very cheap at the price of a silk dress.

Instinct had warned me of the change in the position, and now I began to understand what the new plan was. Madame had made her avowal about not marrying Karl much too clumsily; and the dusting of that travelling trunk, coupled with Ernestine's sly reference to "Mademoiselle la Troisième," was too clear to be misunderstood. They meant to hoodwink me by an apparent abandonment of the marriage; and then make it clandestinely.

I laughed to myself as I left the house to hurry up my own plan.

41

Having made sure that I was not being followed, I hailed a carriage and drove to the neighbourhood where Colonel Katona lived.

I finished the distance on foot, and scanned the house closely as I walked up the drive. It was a square, fair-sized house of two floors, and very secluded. Most of the blinds were down, and all the windows were heavily barred and most of them very dirty. It might well have been the badly-kept home of a recluse who lived in constant fear of burglars. Yet Colonel Katona was reputed a very brave man. Barred windows are as useful however, for keeping those who are inside from getting out, as for preventing those who are out from getting in; and I remembered Gareth's statement that she had scarcely ever lived at home. Why?

When I rang, a grizzled man, with the bearing of an old soldier, came to the door and, in answer to my question for Colonel Katona, told me bluntly I could not see him.

"I am a friend of his daughter and I must see the Colonel," I insisted.

He shut me outside and said he would ask his master.

Why all these precautions, I thought, as I waited; and they strengthened my resolve not to go away without seeing him. But my use of Gareth's name proved a passport; and presently the old soldier returned and admitted me.

He left me in a room which I am sure had never known a woman's hand for years; and the Colonel came to me.

He had as stern and hard a face as I had ever looked at; and it was difficult to believe that the little shrinking timorsome child who had nestled herself to sleep in my arms the night before could be his daughter. The colouring pigment of the eyes was identical; but the expression of Gareth's suggested the liquid softness of a summer sky, while those which looked down at me were as hard as the lapis lazuli of the Alps.

"Accept my excuses for your reception, Miss Gilmore. I am a recluse and do not receive visitors as a rule; but you mentioned my daughter's name. What do you want of me?"

I assumed the manner of a gauche, stupid school-girl, and began to simper with empty inanity.

"I should never have taken you for Gareth's father," I said. "I think you frighten me. I—I—What a lovely old house you have, and how beautifully gloomy. I love gloomy houses. I—I——"

He frowned at my silliness; and I pretended to be silenced by the frown.

"What do you know of my—of Gareth?"

"Please don't look at me like that," I cried, getting up as if in dismay and glancing about me. "I didn't mean to disturb you, sir—

Colonel, I mean. I—I think I had better go. But Gareth loved you so, and loved me, and—oh——" and I stuttered and stammered in frightened confusion.

If she has a really stern man to deal with, a girl's strongest weapon is generally her weakness. His look softened a little at the mention of Gareth's love for us both, as I hoped it would.

"Don't let me frighten you, please. I am a gruff old soldier and a stern man of many sorrows; but a friend of Gareth's is a friend of mine—still;" and he held out his hand to me.

The sorrow in that one syllable, "still," went right to my heart.

"I am very silly and—weak, I know," I said, as I put my hand timidly into his and met his eyes with a feeble smile.

I could have sighed rather than smiled; for at that moment everything seemed eloquent to me of pathos. The dingy, unswept room, the dust accumulating everywhere, his unkempt hair and beard, his shabby clothes, the dirt on the hand which closed firmly on mine—everywhere in everything the evidences of neglect; the silent tribute to a sorrow too absorbing to let him heed aught else.

"What can I do for you?" he asked much more gently, after a pause.

"Oh please," I cried, nervously. "Let me try and collect my poor scattered wits. I ought not to have come, I am afraid."

"Don't say that. I am glad you have come. What could I be but glad to see one who was a friend of Gareth's?"

"Was a friend. Is a friend, I hope, Colonel, and always will be. She always wanted me to come and see her home—but she was hardly ever here, was she? So she couldn't ask me."

Sharp, quick, keen suspicion flashed out of his eyes, but I was giggling so fatuously that it died away.

"Part of my sorrow and part of my punishment," he murmured.

I misunderstood him purposely. "Yes, she always looked on it as a kind of punishment. You see, she loved you so—and then of course we girls, you know what girls are, we used to tease her about it."

He winced and passed his hand across his fretted brows as if in pain.

"You don't know how it hurts me to hear that," he said, simply. "God help me. When did you see her last?"

I knew the anguish at the back of the eager look which came with the question. But I laughed as if I knew nothing. "Oh, ages ago now. Months and months—six months quite."

"Where? My God, where?"

The question leaped from him with such fierceness, that I

43

jumped up again as if in alarm. "Oh, Colonel Katona, how you frighten me!"

"No, no, I don't wish to frighten you. But this is everything to me. Twelve months ago she disappeared from Tyrnau, Miss Gilmore, lured away as I believe by some scoundrel; and I have never seen or heard of her from that time. You have seen her since, you say—and you must tell me everything."

It was easy to heap fuel on fire that burned like this; and I did it carefully. I affected to be overcome and, clapping hands before my face, threw myself back into my chair.

"You must tell me, Miss Gilmore. You must," he said, sternly.

"No, no, I cannot. I cannot. I forgot. I—I dare not."

"Do you know the scoundrel who has done this?"

"Don't ask me. Don't ask me. I dare not say a word."

"You must," he cried, literally with terrifying earnestness.

"No, no. I dare not. I see it all now. Oh, poor Gareth. Poor, dear Gareth."

"You must tell me. You shall. I am her father, and as God is in heaven, I will have his life if he have wronged her."

I did not answer but sat on with my face still covered, thinking. I had stirred a veritable whirlwind of wrath in his heart and had to contrive to calm it now so as to use it afterwards for my own ends.

CHAPTER VIII

COUNT KARL

Colonel Katona's impatience mounted fast; and when he again insisted in an even more violent tone that I should tell him all I knew, I had to fall back upon a woman's second line of defence. I became hysterical.

I gurgled and sobbed, choked and gasped, laughed and wept in regulation style; and then, to his infinite confusion and undoing, I fainted. At least I fell back in my chair seemingly unconscious, and should have fallen on the floor, I believe in thoroughness, had he not caught me in his rough, powerful arms and laid me on a sofa.

I can recall to this day the fusty, mouldy smell of that couch as I lay there, while he made such clumsy, crude efforts as suggested themselves to him as the proper remedies to apply. He chafed and slapped my hands, without thinking to take off my gloves; he called for cold water which the soldier servant brought in, and bathed my face; lastly he told the man to bring some brandy, and in trying to force it between my teeth, which I clenched firmly, he spilt it and swore at his own clumsiness.

Then, fearing he would try again and send me out reeking like a saloon bar, I opened my eyes, rolled them about wildly, began to sob again, sat up, rambled incoherently and asked in the most approved fashion where I was.

I took a sufficiently long time to come round, and was almost ashamed of my deceit when I saw how really anxious and self-reproachful he was. But I had forged an effective weapon; and had only to show the slightest disposition to "go off" again, to make him abjectly apologetic.

I always maintain that a woman has many more weapons than a man. He can at best cheat or bribe; while a woman can do all three, and in addition can wheedle and weep and, at need, even faint.

It was a long time before I consented to talk coherently; and during the incoherent interval I managed to introduce my father's name.

"I am getting better. Oh, how silly you must think me," I murmured.

"It was my fault. I was too violent," he said. "I am not used to young ladies."

"Oh dear, oh dear, I am so ashamed. But she told me you were a very violent man. I wish I hadn't come."

"Who told you? Gareth?"

"No, no. In America. Miss von Dreschler. Oh, what have I said?" I cried, as he started in amazement. "Oh, don't look so cross. I didn't know you'd be so angry;" and I began to gasp, spasmodically.

"I am not angry," he said, quickly. "What name did you say?"

"That horrible girl with the red hair. I don't suppose you've ever seen her, in America. She said you were a villain and had been her father's friend; Colonel von Dreschler, he was. She said you'd kill me. But I'm sure you're kind and good, or dear Gareth would never be your daughter. She said horrible things of you. That you'd ruined her father and imprisoned him; and much more. But of course she would say anything. She was jealous of my friendship with Gareth, and red haired. And I don't know what I'm saying, but she was really a wicked girl. And, oh dear, if it's true, I wish I hadn't come. Give me some water please, or I know I shall go off again."

45

I gabbled all this out in a jerky, breathless way, pausing only to punctuate it with inane giggles and glances of alarm; and at the end made as if I were going to faint.

Had I been in reality the giggling idiot I pretended, I might well have fainted at the expression which crossed his stern, sombre face. At the mention of my father and his imprisonment, he caught his breath and started back so violently that he stumbled against a chair behind him and upset it; and only with the greatest effort could he restrain himself from interrupting me.

He was trembling with anger as he handed me the water I asked for; and when he had put down the glass, he placed a chair and sat close to me.

"Do you mean that Colonel von Dreschler's daughter knows Gareth?"

"Oh, yes, of course."

"Mother of Heaven, I see it now," he murmured into his tangled beard. "It is he who has taken her away. What do you know of this?"

"Oh, Colonel Katona, what on earth could he want to do that for? Besides, how could he?" I cried, with an empty simper.

"You don't understand, Miss Gilmore. Can you tell me where to find this girl—Miss von Dreschler."

"Oh yes. In Jefferson City, Missouri. I come from there. It's a long way off, of course; but it's just the loveliest town and well worth a visit;" and I was babbling on when he put up his hand and stopped me.

"Peace, please. And do you know Colonel von Dreschler?"

"Lor', how could I? He's been dead ever so long. Two years and more, that horrid little red-haired thing said. But of course she may have been fibbing."

He stared down at me as if to read the thoughts in my brain; his look full charged with renewed suspicion. But I was giggling and trying to put my hat straight; and with a sigh he tossed up his hand and rose.

"I can't understand you," he said. "Can you tell me anything about Gareth, when you saw her last?"

"Not much, I'm afraid. I have such a silly memory. It must be quite six months ago—yes, because, I had this hat new; and I've had it quite six months."

"Where was it?" he asked, growing keener again.

"Karlsbad; no, Marienbad; no, Tyrnau; no, Vienna; I can't remember where it was, but I have it down in my diary. I could let you know."

"Did she—she speak of me?"

"Oh yes. She said she was happy and would have been quite happy if only she could have let you know where she was."

"Why couldn't she?"

"I suppose he wouldn't let her; but I'm sure——"

"What he? For heaven's sake, try to speak plainly, Miss Gilmore. Do you mean she was with any one?"

"I don't know. I only know what we thought. Oh, don't look like that or I can't say any more."

His eyes flashed fire again. "Tell me, please," he murmured restraining himself.

"We thought she had run away with him." I said that seriously enough.

He paused, nerving himself for the next question. It came in a low, tense, husky voice. "Do you mean she was—married?"

I hung my head and was silent.

"'Fore God, if any one, man or woman dares to hint shame of my child——" he burst out, and stopped abruptly.

It was time to be serious again, I felt, as I answered, "I love Gareth dearly, and would say no shame of her. If I can help you to find her and learn the truth, will you have my help?"

"Help me, and all I have in the world shall be yours. And if any one has wronged her, may I burn in hell if I do not make his life the penalty." The vehement, concentrated earnestness of the oath filled me with genuine awe.

A tense pause followed, and then, recovering myself, I began to display anew my symptoms of hysterics. This time I was not going to get well enough to be able to speak of the matter farther; and I declared I must go away.

I was going to play a dangerous card; and when he asked me when he should see me again, I told him that if he would come that afternoon to me—I gave him Madame d'Artelle's address—I would tell him all I could.

I went away well satisfied with the result of my visit; and then planned my next step. It was to be a bold one; but the crisis called for daring; and if I was to win, I must force the moves from my side.

I walked back, glad of the exercise and the fresh air, and as I was passing through the Stadtwalchen, busily occupied with my thoughts, I met Count Karl. He was riding with an attendant and his look chanced to be in my direction. He stared as if trying to recollect me, then he bowed. I responded, but he passed on; and I concluded he had not placed my features in his muddled memory. But a minute later I heard a horse cantering after me; and he pulled up, dismounted, and held out his hand.

"You are Madame d'Artelle's friend, Miss Gilmore?"

"Yes," I said, scarce knowing whether to be glad or sorry he had come after me.

"May I walk a few steps with you?"

"Certainly, if you wish."

"Take the horses home," he said as he gave the reins to the servant. "I have been wishing to speak to you alone, Miss Gilmore. Shall we walk here?" and we turned into a side path at the end of which some nursemaids and children were gathered about the fountains.

He did not speak again for some moments, but kept staring at me with a directness which, considering all things, I found embarrassing.

"Would you mind sitting down here?" he asked, as we reached a seat nearly hidden by the shrubbery.

"Not in the least," I agreed; and down we sat.

"You will think this very singular of me," he declared after a pause.

"One person could not very well be plural," I said inanely; and he frowned at the irrelevant flippancy. "I am a student you know, and therefore appreciate grammatical accuracy."

"I wish to ask you some questions, if I may."

"They appear to be very difficult to frame. You may ask what you please."

"I wish you would smile," he said, so unexpectedly that I did smile. "It is perfectly marvellous," he exclaimed with a start.

I knew what that meant. In the old days he had talked a lot of nonsense about my smile.

"If I smile it is not at the waste of your life and its opportunities, Count Karl," I ventured.

"Opportunities!" he repeated with a laugh. "I have seized this one at any rate. I have been thinking about you ever since I saw you two days ago at Madame d'Artelle's."

"Why?" I asked pointedly.

"That is a challenge. I'll take it up. Because your name is Christabel. Is it really Christabel?"

"My name seems to cause considerable umbrage," I said, with a touch of offence. "Two days ago your brother not only doubted the Christabel, but wished to give me a fresh surname as well, von Decker or Discher, or Dreschler, or something."

He frowned again. "Gustav is a good fellow, but he should hold his tongue. You're so like her, you see, and yet so unlike, that——" he finished the sentence with a cut of his riding whip on his gaiters.

"I am quite content to be myself, thank you," I declared with a touch of coldness.

48

"Your voice, too. It's perfectly marvellous."

"May I ask what all this means?" I put the question very stiffly.

"Chiefly that I'm an idiot, I think. But I don't care. I'm long past caring. Life's only rot, is it?"

"Not for those who use it properly. It might be a glorious thing for a man in your position and with your future."

"Ah, you're young, you see, Miss Gilmore," he exclaimed, with the self-satisfaction of a cynic. "I suppose I thought so once, but there's nothing in it."

"There's opium," I rapped out so sharply that he gave a start and glanced at me. Then he smiled, heavily.

"Oh, you've found that out, eh; or somebody has told you? Yes, I can't live without it now, and I don't want to try. What does it matter?" and he jerked his shoulders with a don't-care gesture.

"I should be ashamed to say that."

"I suppose you would. I suppose you would. I should have been, at one time, when I first began; but not now. Besides, it suits everybody all right. You see, you don't understand."

"I have no intention of trying it."

"No, don't. It's only hell a bit before one's time. But I didn't stop you to talk about this. I don't quite know why I did stop you now;" and he ran his hand across his forehead as if striving to remember.

A painful gesture, almost pathetic and intensely suggestive.

"I suppose it was just a wish to speak to you, that's all," he said at length, wearily. "Oh, I know. You reminded me so much of—of another Christabel of the name you mentioned, Christabel von Dreschler, that I wondered if you could be any relation. You are an American, are you not?"

"Yes. But that is not an American name."

"But she was American. I knew her in New York years ago. Lord, what long years ago. You are not a relation of hers?"

"I have no relative of that name, Count Karl."

"I wish you had been one."

"Why?"

"That's just what I've been asking myself these two days. It wouldn't have been any good, would it? And yet—" he sighed—"yet I think I should have been drawn to speak pretty freely to you."

"About what?"

He turned at the pointed question and looked quizzically at me. "I wonder. You're so like her, you see."

"Were you in love with her, then?"

He started resentfully at the thrust. Coming from me it must have sounded very much like impertinence.

"Miss Gilmore, I——" then he smiled in his feeble, nothing-matters manner. "Of course that's a question I can't answer, and you oughtn't to ask. But life's much too stupid for one to take offence when it isn't meant. And I don't suppose you meant any, did you?"

"No, on the contrary. I should very much like to be your friend," I said, very earnestly.

"Would you? I daresay you would. Lots of people would like to be the friend of the Duke Ladislas' eldest son. If they only knew! What humbug it all is."

"I am not a humbug," I protested.

"I daresay you have a motive in that clever little brain of yours. No clever people do anything without one, and they both agree you're clever and sharp. I wonder what it is. Tell me."

"'They both?'" I repeated, catching at his words.

His face clouded with passing doubt and then cleared as he understood. "I'm getting stupid again; but you don't get stupid. You know what Henriette and Gustav are in my life. You've spotted it, of course. It saves a heap of trouble to have some one to think for you. You mayn't believe it—you like to think for yourself; but it does, a regular heap of bother. And after all, the chief thing in life is to dodge trouble, isn't it?"

"No." I said it with so much energy that he laughed.

"That's only your point of view. You're American, you see. But I'm right. I hate taking trouble. Of course I know things. They think I don't, but I do. And I don't care."

"What things do you know?"

He stopped hitting his boots with his whip and looked round at me, paused, and then shook his head slowly. "You don't understand, and it wouldn't do you any good if you did."

But I did understand and drove the spur in. "I don't understand one thing—why the elder son should think his chief object in life is to make way for the younger brother."

He leant back on the seat and laughed. "They're right. You have a cute little head and no mistake. That's just it. I'm not surprised Gustav warned me against you. But he needn't. I shouldn't let you worry me into things. I'm glad I spoke to you, though. You've got old fox Erlanger round that little finger of yours, too, haven't you?"

"I was governess to General von Erlanger's daughter."

"And played chess with the old boy. I know;" and he laughed again. "And he sent you to look after Henriette, eh?"

"No. I knew Madame d'Artelle in Paris, years ago; and I went to her thinking her influence would help me."

"Did you? I'm not asking. But if you did, you can't be so clever as they think. She hasn't any influence with any one but me—and I don't count. I never shall either."

"Whose fault is that but your own?"

"I don't want to. I don't care. If I did care, of course——" The momentary gleam of energy died out in another weary look and wave of the hand. He waited and then asked. "But won't you tell me that motive of yours, for wanting to be my friend, you know?"

"I did not say I had one."

"I hoped you might want me to do something for you."

"Why?"

"Because you might do something for me in return."

"I'll promise to do that in any case."

"Ah, they all say that. The world's full of unselfish people willing to do things for a Duke's son," he said, lazily.

"What is it you wish me to do?"

"You have friends in America, of course?"

"Yes."

"Do you think they could find that other girl—the one you're like, Christabel von Dreschler?"

"Yes, I've no doubt they could."

"Well, I'd like to hear of her again."

"Would you like her to know what your life is and what you have become?"

That made him wince.

"By God, that hurts!" he muttered, and he leant back, put his hand to his eyes, and sat hunched up in silence. Presently he sighed. "You're right. I'm only a fool, am I?"

"If she cared for you, it might have hurt her to know," I said.

"Don't, please. You make me think; and I don't want to think."

"If she loved you then, she would scarcely love you now."

"Don't, I say, don't," he cried, with sudden vehemence. "You are so like her that to hear this from you is almost as if——I beg your pardon. But for a moment I believe I was almost fool enough to feel something. No, no; don't write or do any other silly thing of the sort. It doesn't matter;" and he tossed up his hands helplessly.

We sat for a few moments without speaking, and presently he began to fumble in his pocket. He glanced at me rather shamefacedly, and then with an air of bravado took out a phial of morphia pills.

"Since you know, it doesn't matter," he said, half-apologetically.

"It does matter very much," I declared, earnestly.

He held the little bottle making ready to open it, and met my eyes. "Why?"

"Would you take it if she were here?"

"I don't know;" and he heaved a deep sigh.

"Think that she is here, and then you daren't take it."

51

He laughed. "Daren't I?" and he partly unscrewed the cap.

I put my hand on his arm. "For her sake," I said.

"It means hours of hell to me if I don't."

"It means a life of hell if you do."

"I must."

"For her sake," I pleaded again, and held out my hand for the phial.

"You would torture me?"

"Yes, for your good."

The struggle in him was acute and searching. "It's no good; I can't," he murmured, his gaze on the phial.

I summoned all the will power at my command and forced him to meet my eyes. "For her sake; as if she were here; give it me," I said.

"I shall hate you if you make me."

"For her sake," I repeated. We looked each into the other's eyes, until I had conquered.

"I suppose I must," he murmured with a sigh; and let the little bottle fall into my hand. I threw it down and ground it and the pellets to powder with my heel. He watched me with a curious smile. "How savage you are. As if you thought that could finish it."

"No. It is only the beginning—but a good beginning."

He got up. "We'd better go now, before I begin to hate you."

"You will think of this and of her when the next temptation comes."

"Oh, it will come right enough; and I shan't resist it. I can't. Good-bye. I like you yet. I—I wish I'd known you before."

And with that and a sigh and a smile, he lifted his hat and left me.

CHAPTER IX

I COME TO TERMS WITH MADAME

My interview with Karl led to a very disquieting discovery. I sat for some time thinking about it—and my thoughts increased rather than diminished my uneasiness.

To use a very expressive vulgarism one often hears at home, I began to fear that I "had run up against a snag." In other words, I had misunderstood the real nature of my feelings for Karl; and that miscalculation might cost me dear.

It was true that when I had seen him at Madame d'Artelle's I had hated him cordially; but the reason was clear to me now. It was not my pride that he had hurt in not recognizing me. It was my anger that he had stirred—that he should have forgotten me so completely. It looked so much like the due corollary of his old conduct that I had taken fire.

And now I found he had not forgotten me at all; and knew that I had won my little victory over him because he remembered me so well.

It was a surprise and a shock; but nothing like the shock it gave me to find how elated and delighted I felt at the fact. For a time I could scarcely hold that delight in check. It took the bit in its teeth and ran away with my sober common sense. My thoughts very nearly made a fool of me again; and I am afraid that I positively revelled in the new knowledge just as any ordinary girl might.

But, as I had told General von Erlanger, I was not a "usual person;" and I succeeded in pulling up my runaway thoughts in the middle of their wild gallop.

I was no longer in love with Karl. I had settled that years before. I was intensely embittered by his conduct; he had behaved abominably to me; had flirted and cheated and fooled me; and I had always felt that I never could and never would forgive him. His present condition was a fitting and proper punishment, and he deserved every minute of it.

My interest in him now was purely selfish and personal. I had only one thing to consider in regard to him—how I could make use of him to secure justice to my father's reputation, and punishment for the doers of that great wrong.

Moreover, even if he did care, or thought he still cared for one whom he had so wronged, and if I were an ordinary girl and magnanimous enough to forgive him, and if, further, I could save him permanently from the opium fiend, we could never be more than mere friends. There was an insuperable barrier between us.

I knew this from the papers which my father had left behind him. I had better explain it here; for I thought it all carefully over as I sat that morning in the Stadtwalchen.

There was the great Patriotic movement in the way, of which Karl's father, Duke Ladislas, was the head and front. The aim was nothing less than the splitting of the Austro-Hungarian Empire. Hungary was to be made an independent kingdom, and Duke Ladislas was to have the throne.

The time to strike the great blow had been decided years before. It was to be at the death of the old Emperor. The movement had the widest ramifications; and the whole of the internal policy of Hungary was being directed to that paramount object.

In one of his papers, my father had suggested that the secret of his ruin was part and parcel of this scheme. While Duke Alexinatz and his son, Count Stephen, lived, the right to the Hungarian throne would be theirs; and thus, Duke Ladislas, a man of great ambition and the soul of the movement, had every reason to welcome Count Stephen's death; and that death had occurred at a moment when the Austrian Emperor lay so ill that his death was hourly expected.

My father's intellect, impaired as it was by his solitary confinement, could not coherently piece the facts together. Synthetical reasoning was beyond him for one thing; and for another he could not bring himself to believe that the man whom beyond all others in the world he admired and trusted, Duke Ladislas, could be guilty of such baseness and crime as the facts suggested. Appalled, therefore, by the conclusions which were being forced upon him, he had abandoned the work in fear and horror.

I had no such predispositions or prejudices; but as yet I had no proofs. I could only set to work from the other end, and attempt to discover the agents who had done the deed, and work up through them to the man whose originating impulse might have been the real first cause.

But the solid fact remained that Count Stephen's death cleared the way to the new throne for Duke Ladislas and his sons; and therefore, if I were to succeed in killing Karl's opium habit, and even induce him to play the great part in life open to him, he would be the heir to the throne, when gained, and I impossible except as a friend.

Two days before, nay two hours before, I should have asked and desired no more than that; but after this talk with Karl—and at that moment I stamped my foot in impotent anger, and wrenching my thoughts away from that part of the subject, got up and walked hurriedly away in the direction of Madame d'Artelle's house.

I arrived as she was sitting down to lunch, and she gave me a very frigid reception. I saw that she had passed a very uncomfortable morning. She had been weeping, and having found in her tears no solution of the problem I had set her, was sullen and depressed.

"You have been out, Christabel?"

"Yes, completing my plans."

"What a knack you have developed of making spiteful speeches! I had no idea you could be so nasty."

"What is there spiteful in having plans to complete?"

"I suppose they are aimed at me!"

"My dear Henriette, must I not be careful to have some place to go and live in? Be reasonable."

"You always seem to have some undercurrent in what you say. It's positively hateful. What do you mean by that?"

"Some of us Americans have a trick of answering one question with another. I think I'll do that now. What do you think I'd better do when you are gone?"

"I don't understand that either," she said very crossly.

"I mean to-morrow."

"I am not going anywhere to-morrow." She could lie glibly.

"That may be nearer the truth than you think; but you have planned to go away to-morrow—with Count Karl."

"Preposterous."

"So I think—but true, all the same. You are very foolish to attempt to hoodwink me, Henriette. You are thinking of trying to deny what I say. I can see that—but pray don't waste your breath. I told you this morning that in an hour or two I should know everything. I do now."

"Have you seen Count Karl?"

"Do you think I should tell you how I find out things? So long as I do find them out, nothing else matters. But I will tell you something. You will not go, Henriette. I shall not allow it."

"Allow?" she echoed, shrilly.

"I generally use the words I mean. I said 'allow'—and I mean no other word. I shall not allow it."

She let her ill temper have the reins for a minute, and broke out into a storm of invective, using more than one little oath to point her phrases. I waited patiently until her breath and words failed her.

"I am glad you have broken out like that. There's more relief in it than tears. Now I will tell you what I mean to do—and to do to-day. I have had inquiries made in Paris for M. Constans, and a wire from me will bring him here in search of you. You know what that means;" I added, very deliberately, as I saw her colour change. I guessed there was ground for the bluff that I knew much more than my words expressed.

"I don't believe you," she managed to stammer out—her voice quite changed with fear.

"Your opinion does not touch me. In your heart you know I never lie, Madame—and for once you may trust your heart. If you force me, that telegram will go to-day. Nor is that all. I will go to Duke Ladislas and tell him the story of the lost jewels, and who instigated the theft and received the stolen property."

"They have been given back; besides, will he prosecute his own son?"

"The theft shall be published in every paper, and with it the story of how Count Karl has been ruined by opium drugging. By whom, Madame—by the secret agent of the French Government, the ex-spy of the Paris police—Madame Constans? You can judge how Austrian people will read that story."

She had no longer any fight left in her. I spoke without a note of passion in my voice; and every word told. She sat staring at me, white and helpless and beaten.

"More than that and worse than that——"

"I can bear no more," she cried, covering her face with trembling fingers.

I don't know what more she thought I was going to threaten to do. I knew of nothing more; so it was fortunate she stopped me. She was in truth so frightened that if I had threatened to have her hanged, I think she would have believed in my power to do it.

"Why do you seek to ruin me? What have I done to make you my enemy?" she asked at length.

"I do not seek to ruin you, and I will be your friend and not your enemy, if you trust instead of deceiving me. I will save you from Count Gustav's threats."

"How can you?"

"What matters to you how, so long as I do it?"

"He knows all that you know."

"What, that you are here to betray the leaders of the Hungarian national movement to your French employers and their Russian allies?"

"Nom de Dieu, but how I am afraid of you?" she cried.

"If I tell him that how will it fare with you?"

"No no, you must not. I will do all you wish. I will. I will. I swear it on my soul."

"Tell me then the details of the elopement to-morrow. I know enough to test the truth of what you say; and if you lie, I shall do all I have said—and more."

"I will not lie, Christabel. I am going to trust you. It is arranged for to-morrow night. I leave the house here at nine o'clock in a carriage. At the end of the Radialstrasse Count Karl will join me. We drive first to a villa in Buda, behind the Blocksberg—a villa called 'Unter den Linden.' We are to be married there; and on the following day we cross the frontier into Germany and go to Breslau."

She said it as if she had been repeating a lesson, and finished with a deep-drawn sigh.

"Is he coming to-day?"

"No."

"To-morrow?"

"No."

"Ah. That is to convince me that all is broken off?"

"Yes." She was as readily obedient as a child.

"Count Gustav is coming to-day?"

"Yes. This afternoon at four o'clock. To settle everything."

"Good. You will see him and be careful to act as though everything were as it was left when you saw him yesterday."

"I dare not."

"You must. Everything may turn upon that. You must."

"But if he suspects?"

"You must prevent that. I shall see him afterwards. If you let him suspect or if you play me false, I shall know; and the consequences will not be pleasant for you. You will tell Count Gustav not to see you to-morrow, because you are afraid I shall guess something; and that if he has to communicate with you, he must write. It is the only way in which I can save you from him."

"And what am I to do afterwards?"

"I will tell you to-morrow. Be assured of this. I and those whose power is behind me will see not only that no harm comes to you, but that you are well paid."

"I am giving up everything."

"It is no time to bargain. What you are giving up in reality is the risk of a gaol and the certainty of exposure and ruin—and worse."

"Mother of Heaven, have mercy on me!" she cried.

I did not stop to hear her lamentations. It was two o'clock already. I had still many things to fix, and I must be back in the house soon after Count Gustav reached it. The fur was to fly in my interview with him; and I must have all my claws sharp.

I did not make the mistake of underestimating his strength as an adversary. I should have to use very different means with him from those which had sufficed to frighten Madame d'Artelle; and I must have the proofs ready to produce. I was going to change his present half-contemptuous suspicion into open antagonism; and that he could and would be a very dangerous enemy, I did not allow myself to doubt.

My first step was to find the house in Buda of which Madame d'Artelle had spoken. It was a bright pleasant house in a pretty, carefully kept garden; not more than a mile from the villa I myself had just rented. But to my surprise it was occupied: a girl was playing with a couple of dogs on the lawn. My first thought was that

Madame had misled me; my second, to try and ascertain this for myself.

I entered the garden and walked toward the house, and the dogs came scampering across barking. The girl turned and followed them.

"Your garden is beautiful," I said, with a smile. "If the house is as much beyond the description of it as the garden, it will suit me admirably."

"You came to take the house?" she asked.

"Yes, I have a letter here—let me see, oh, this is my list—ah, yes—'Unter den Linden.' Is not that the name?" and taking a slip of paper from my pocket I pretended to consult it.

"Yes, this is 'Unter den Linden'—those are the trees;" and she pointed to the limes which gave the name. "But I am afraid you are too late. I think it is let."

I was overcome with disappointment; but perhaps she would ask her mother. We went into the house and she left me in the dining-room. Presently the mother came; a tired looking creature who had once been pretty, like the girl, but was now frayed and worn. She was very sorry, but the house was let. I was just too late. It had only been let the previous day. Did I want it for long?

"Not more than twelve months certain," I told her.

She threw up her hands. "Just my ill-luck," she cried, dismally. "I have let it for two months, and we go out this evening. But perhaps I could get out of it."

"That is not worth while. I should not want it for a month yet, and perhaps could wait for two. Could I see over the house?"

In this way I was taken into every nook and corner of it; and enabled to fix every room and passage and door in my memory. And then I inspected the garden and outside places.

"Do you leave your servants?" I asked, at the end of a number of questions.

"We keep but one. My daughter and I live alone, and do most of the work when we are at home. And the servant goes away with us."

"An excellent arrangement. I have my own servants. I wonder now if we could induce your tenant to let me have the place in a month. Who is he?"

"It is taken for Count von Ostelen—but I do not know him. The agents have done everything. I could ask them."

"Do so, and let me know;" and I jotted down at random a name and address to which she could write, and left.

I had done well so far; and I drove rapidly to my own house in good spirits over my success.

There was only one point which puzzled me. Why had that

name, Count von Ostelen, been used? Was it merely as the name in which Count Karl usually travelled incognito? Just as he had used it in New York? Or had his brother some other motive?

It was only a trifle, of course; but then, as I have said, I am accustomed to take some trifles seriously.

If I could have seen a little farther ahead, I should have taken this one even more seriously than usual; and should not have dismissed it from my thoughts as I did when I reached my house and was kissing Gareth in response to the glad smile with which she greeted me.

My next step concerned her.

CHAPTER X

A DRAMATIC STROKE

"Have you any news for me?" was Gareth's eager question, natural enough under the circumstances, and her delicate expressive face clouded as I shook my head.

"We could scarcely expect any good news yet, dear."

"I suppose not; but I am so anxious."

"It will all come right in time, Gareth." But that very trite commonplace had no more soothing effect on her than it often has on wiser folk.

"I suppose I must be patient; but I wish I could do something for myself. I hate being patient. Why can't I go out myself and search for him? I put my hat on once this morning to start."

"I told you before the risk you would run."

"Oh, I know all that, of course," she replied, petulantly. "I've been with you nearly two days and you've done nothing. Two whole long days. And it's so dull here. It's worse than at Sillien."

"Would it have been better had those men taken you?"

She threw her arms round my neck then and burst into tears. "I know how ungrateful I am. I hate myself for it, Christabel. But I did so hope you had brought some news. And I am so disappointed."

I let her cry, knowing the relief which tears bring to such a nature as hers. She soon dried her eyes, and sat down and looked at

59

me, her hands folded demurely on her lap—the picture of pretty meekness.

"How pretty you are, Gareth—with your lovely golden hair, your great blue eyes, and pink and white cheeks."

"Am I?" she asked artlessly, smiling. "Karl used to say that; and I used to love to hear him say it. I only cared to be pretty because he liked it. But I like to hear you say it, too. You see I'm not a bit clever, like you; and one must be either clever or pretty, mustn't one? Karl's both handsome and clever. Oh, so handsome, Christabel. You'll say so when you see him. I wish I had a likeness."

This gave me an idea. "Couldn't you draw a likeness of him, Gareth, for me? You see it might help me to recognize him."

Her face broke into a sunny smile. "I can draw a little; I couldn't do him justice, of course—no one could do that. He's too handsome. But I could give you an idea of what he's like."

We found paper and pencil. "Do the best you can and then put my name on it, and sign it Gareth von Ostelen, and put the date to it, so that I can have it for a keepsake."

"Lovely," she cried, merrily; and set to work at once.

I watched her a few moments, and when she was absorbed in the task, I went off saying I had some directions to give about house matters.

It was part of my plan that John Perry and his son, as soon as the latter returned, should go to the house "Unter den Linden." I might need them for my personal protection.

I told John Perry now, therefore, that he was to hire a woman servant to come and help his wife in waiting upon Gareth. He was then to purchase a carriage and a pair of good horses, and procure uniforms for himself and his son. He was to act as coachman and James as footman; and everything must be in readiness for him to carry out instantly any orders he received from me. I should either bring or send the orders on the next afternoon.

I explained that in all probability he would have to drive to the house "Unter den Linden," stable the horses there, and dismiss any men servants he might find about the house; and I suggested that he should go first to the house and find an excuse to learn his way about the stables.

When I returned to Gareth she had finished the drawing and had added a clever little thumb-nail sketch of herself in the corner, where she had written her name and the date. The drawing really merited the praise I bestowed upon it.

"I could do much better if I had not to hurry it," she said, self-critically.

"Do another while I am away, then," I urged, thinking it would

60

fill out the time for her. "And now there is one other thing. Could you give me a paper or letter with his signature—I might be able to trace him through some of the public rolls."

There were no such rolls of course; but she did not know this, and thought the idea so clever that she gave me one of the two letters from him she had with her; and kissed me and wished me good luck as I drove away.

Although there was not much risk of my movements being traced, I thought it best to dismiss my carriage before I crossed the Suspension Bridge, and to finish the journey to Madame d'Artelle's in another.

As the minute approached for the trial of wits and strength with Count Gustav, my confidence increased. Every fighting instinct in my nature was roused; and the struggle was one in which I took a keen personal pleasure. His hateful treatment of the girl who had trusted him filled me with indignation and resentment; and the hope of forcing him to do justice to her was one of the sharpest spurs to my courage. He should do that or face the alternative of having his double treachery exposed.

I was a little later than I had intended in reaching the house, and I asked the servant somewhat anxiously if any one had yet been for me.

"No, miss, no one."

"I am expecting a Colonel Katona to call, Peter," I said, giving him a gold piece; "and I do not wish any one to know of his visit. I shall be with Madame probably; so when the Colonel arrives, make up a little parcel and bring it to me, and just say: 'The parcel you asked about, miss.' Put the Colonel in the little room off the music room, and tell him that I will see him as soon as possible. You understand this?"

"Yes indeed, miss," he answered with a grin as he slipped the money in his pocket.

"Where is Madame d'Artelle?"

"In the salon."

"Alone?"

"No, miss; Count Gustav is with her. He has been here about a quarter of an hour."

I went straight to the salon. Madame was sitting on a lounge, her face full of trouble, and Count Gustav was pacing up and down the room speaking energetically with many forceful gestures. He stopped and frowned at the interruption; but his frown changed to a smile as he held out his hand.

He opened with what, as a chess player, I may call the lie gambit.

61

"I have been endeavouring to cheer up Madame d'Artelle, Miss Gilmore," he said lightly. "I tell her she takes the postponement—or if you like, the abandonment—of the marriage with Karl too seriously."

"Is it abandoned?" I asked.

"Did she not tell you?"

"Yes; but I could scarcely believe it, seeing how much you have counted upon the marriage. The abandonment is a tribute to your influence. But why have you given it up?"

"I given it up? I? What can it be to me?" he laughed. "It is not my marriage, Miss Gilmore. I like my brother, of course, but I am not in love with him so much as to want to marry him."

"All Pesth knows how much you love your brother," said I, drily.

"I should not come to you for testimony, I think. I am afraid it would not be favourable. I am glad you are not the majority."

"Probably I do not know you as others do, or perhaps others do not know you as I do. But why have you abandoned the project of the marriage?"

"You insist on putting the responsibility on me," he said with a touch of irritation beneath his laugh.

"I can understand that the question is awkward."

"Not in the least. You see, you raised most unexpectedly the point about the admirable and excellent gentleman who was Madame's husband; and it must perforce be postponed until the proofs of his death are forthcoming. Thus it is rather your doing than mine;" and he shrugged his shoulders.

"You have found them more difficult to manufacture than you anticipated, I presume?"

"That is a very serious charge, very lightly made, Miss Gilmore." His assumption of offence was excellent.

"I am not speaking lightly, Count Gustav. When we parted last time you said that the proofs of the death of Madame's husband should be produced. Within a few hours I heard that the marriage had been postponed; you now say it was because those proofs cannot be produced. There must be a reason for such a sudden change of front; and I have suggested it. If you prefer, we will leave it that the proofs cannot be found or fabricated in time to suit you."

He heard me out with darkening face, and then crossed to Madame d'Artelle and offered her his hand.

"I think, Madame, it will be more convenient for me to leave now. With a lady we cannot resent an insult; we can only protect ourselves from further insult by leaving."

I laughed with ostentatiously affected hilarity, and sat down.

Madame d'Artelle gave him her hand nervously, and he turned from her and bowed stiffly to me.

"I think I should not go, Count, if I were you," I said, smoothly.

"Your attitude makes it impossible for me to remain, Miss Gilmore."

"Of course you know best, but I should not go if I were you."

He was uneasy and hesitated; went toward the door and then paused and turned. "If you wish to say anything to me and can do so without insulting me, I am willing to listen to you—as a friend of Madame's;" and he waved his hand in her direction.

"I've a great deal to say and I'm going to say it to some one. Of course if you go, I must say it to some one else."

"And what am I to understand by that?"

"You haven't decided yet whether to go or stay. Now, I'll be much more candid with you than you are with me. It's just a question whether you dare go or not. Your start just now is what we Americans call putting up a bluff. But you can't bluff me. I hold the cards—every one of them a winning card, too. If you go, you lose the game straight away, for I shan't be many minutes in the house after you. You're going to lose anyhow, for that matter: but—well, as I tell you, you'd better not go."

"I'm not versed in American slang, Miss Gilmore, and it doesn't lend itself to translation into German," he sneered.

"Then I'll put it plainer. Go, if you dare, Count Gustav;" and I challenged him in look as well as words.

"I am always anxious to oblige a pretty woman, Miss Gilmore," he said, with one of his most gracious glances.

"That's very sweet of you, Count. But the question is not my looks; it's your reputation and position."

At this point Madame d'Artelle made a diversion.

"I am not feeling well, Christabel, and am going to my room to lie down," she said, rising.

"That's just what I would have suggested, Henrietta," I answered, fastening on her action. "It's just as well. I have to say some things to Count Gustav that he might not care for even you to hear."

He made a great show of opening the door for her to pass and used the moment's delay to think.

Just as she went out the footman came to the door, carrying the parcel.

"Do you want me, Peter?" she asked.

"No, Madame, Miss Gilmore. The parcel you asked for, miss." I took it and he went out and closed the door.

"I have resolved not to stay longer, Miss Gilmore. I would do

63

much for any friend of Madame's, but I cannot with self-respect suffer your threats and insults."

I thought of a little dramatic stroke.

"One moment, Count, this parcel concerns you." I half tore the wrapper off and handed it to him.

He would not take it, waving it away contemptuously.

"You had better take it. It is from—Sillien, Count," I said, very deliberately.

His eyes blazed with sudden anger.

"I don't understand you," he cried; but he took it and tore off the covering to find a blank sheet of paper.

"This is another insult. I would have you beware."

"Not an insult—a message. To have been properly dramatic this should have been inside it—" and I held up before him the little sketch which Gareth had made for me with such laughing earnestness.

"The message which that parcel brings is—that Colonel Katona, Gareth's father, is here in the house waiting to see me. Now, do you wish to go?"

The suddenness of the stroke was for the moment irresistible.

The colour fled from his face as the laughter had died from his lips. White, tense, agitated and utterly unstrung, he stood staring at me as if he would gladly have struck me dead.

I had every reason to be contented with my victory.

CHAPTER XI

PLAIN TALK

That it was chiefly the stunning unexpectedness of my stroke which overwhelmed Count Gustav was proved by the promptness with which he rallied. Had I given him even a hint of my information or prepared him in any way for the thrust, I am sure he would have met it with outward equanimity.

My probe had pierced the flesh, however, before he had had a moment to guard himself; and he had flinched and winced at the unexpected pain of it. But he soon recovered self-possession.

"You have a dramatic instinct, Miss Gilmore, and considerable inventive power. You should write for the stage. The essence of melodrama is surprise."

"I could not hope always to carry my audience away so completely, Count."

He laughed. "I am afraid I have not done you justice hitherto. I have not taken you seriously enough. I think you are right in another thing—I had better not go yet. Our chat promises to be interesting. I should very much like a cigar. I wonder if Madame would object." He spoke lightly and took out his cigar case.

"It would be very appropriate," I said. "There is one character in a melodrama who always smokes."

"You mean the villain?"

"The hero rarely has time—after the first act, at any rate. He is generally being arrested, or hunted, or imprisoned, or ruined in some way—sometimes drugged."

He had struck the match and at my last word paused to look at me. He favoured me with such a stare that the match burnt his fingers, and he dropped it with a muttered oath which I affected not to hear. It was a very trifling incident; but he was so unusually careful in such matters as a rule that it offered another proof of his ill balance.

"I burnt my fingers and forgot my manners," he said lightly. "I beg your pardon, Miss Gilmore."

"You mean that you wish to have time to recover from the surprise. Pray wait as long as you please—and think. I have no wish to take any fresh advantage over you—at present."

"Oh no, thank you," he cried, airily. "We will talk. Now, we must know where we stand, you and I?"

"At the moment we are in the salon of Madame d'Artelle, who was your instrument and tool."

"That 'was' sounds interesting. Is that your number one?"

"Yes."

"Very well, then, we'll take her as finished with. I don't care much about her. She has disappointed me. She is pretty; beautiful even: but no brains. She has let you guess too much. I'd rather deal with you direct. What is number two? And how many numbers are there?"

He was so light in hand, took defeat so easily, was so apparently ready for a complete change of front, and spoke with such an admirable assumption of raillery that I had difficulty in repressing an inclination to smile.

"You admit your defeat, then?"

He spread out his hands, waving one of them toward Gareth's drawing, and shrugged his shoulders.

"I am not a fool, Miss Gilmore."

I had expected anything except this instant surrender; and it caught me unready to state my terms. I could not go into the question of my father's wrongs, because I did not know enough of the matter.

"The terms will be heavy," I said, slowly.

"One must pay a price for folly; and I shall at least have the compensation of pleasing you."

"You will make Gareth your legal wife?"

He drew two whiffs of his cigar, took it from his lips, and looked at it thoughtfully.

"I would much rather marry you," he said with sudden smiling insolence.

"Do you agree?" I asked, curtly.

"That's number two, is it? Is the list much longer?"

"You will abandon the attempt to ruin your brother?"

"That's number three—number four?"

"There is no number four at present."

"What, nothing for yourself? Then you are a most remarkable young lady. Oh, but there must be."

"You are wasting time, Count Gustav, and Colonel Katona may grow impatient," I answered.

"Give me time. I am lost in amazement at such altruism—such philanthropy. You come to Pesth to push your fortunes; chance and your clever little wits put a fortune in your grasp, and—you want nothing for yourself." He shot at me a glance of sly mockery. "Perhaps Miss von Dreschler seeks something? The other Christabel, you know."

"I have stated my terms, Count Gustav."

"My answer is that I accept all of them—except the last two;" and the laugh at his insolence was one of genuine enjoyment.

"Then there is no more to be said," I declared, rising.

"But indeed there is. Pray sit down again. We are going to talk this over frankly. There is always an alternative course in such affairs—that was why I was anxious to know your motive. Will you sit down?"

"No. I have said all I wish."

"Well, you gave me a surprise. I will give you one. You are Miss Christabel von Dreschler; or at all events you were, until you inherited your uncle's money and took his name with it. He was John P. Gilmore, of Jefferson City, Missouri. Now, allow me;" and he placed a chair for me with elaborate courtesy, while he regarded me with an expression of great satisfaction and triumph.

I sat down and he resumed his seat.

66

"By the way," he said, as if casually, "we are likely to be engaged some time, hadn't we better let Colonel Katona go?"

"I may still have to speak to him," I answered, drily.

"I don't think so, when he knows that you are Colonel von Dreschler's daughter—if I should have to tell him, that is—he will not be very friendly toward you. He will not, really. He is a very singular old man." The art with which he conveyed this threat was inimitably excellent.

"The truth when he knows it, will tell with him, no matter from whom it comes."

"Yes, but he may not have to know it. You may persuade me to marry Gareth—in reality, you see. Besides, your object in bringing him here has already been achieved; you made your coup, and it was successful. Why keep him? You can just as easily tell him all another time—if you have to; while if I agree to do now what you wish, you will only have to put him off and send him away. I really think he may go. I have very little doubt we shall come to an understanding."

I thought a moment. "Yes, he may go. I will tell him so."

"I will go with you to him. He has a great regard for my family. We will tell him you are indisposed, or anything you please. I can satisfy him more easily than you can, perhaps."

"I will go alone."

He shook his head and smiled. "Do you think that quite fair to me under the peculiar circumstances? I wish to be quite sure that what you say is discreet. I must make a point of it that we go together, really I must."

But I recalled my impersonation of the giggling miss, and was not willing that the Count should know of that.

"I will go alone to him, or he must remain," I said.

"I will go to him alone, then. You may be sure I shall not betray myself."

I let him go. I saw no risk in so simple a step, and was glad to be relieved from the interview. I read his act to be a confirmation of his words—that we were likely to come to an understanding, and in that case there would be no need for Colonel Katona ever to know that Gareth had been betrayed.

I was a little uneasy, however, when some minutes passed and the Count did not return, but he explained the delay by saying that the Colonel was a peculiar man, and had plagued him with many questions difficult to answer.

"I told him you were not well, and would find means to see him as soon as necessary. And now, to resume our conversation, Miss— von Dreschler."

He spoke as airily as if it were a game of cards which had been interrupted.

"You take that for granted; but it scarcely helps matters."

"Permit me to indulge in the rudeness of a contradiction. I think it does. It gives me the clue to your motive—an essential matter to me. You are an American, young, wealthy, very pretty, and undoubtedly clever. Why then do you masquerade as an adventuress? You may have one of two motives—and there is a very improbable third. As Miss von Dreschler, my brother paid you great attentions in New York; the matter being broken off suddenly, in obedience to the protest of one of the friends with him, who reminded Karl that what was going to happen here made it impossible for him to marry a private individual."

He was very quick to see the surprise with which I heard this, and paused to emphasize it.

"You are surprised. I always have thought that Karl's conduct was indefensible. You ought to have been told the real reason; and it was only a flight of romantic fancy for him to prefer to pose as a mean fellow, willing to win your affections and then run away. That was his deliberate decision, however. He believed you would get over the affair all the more easily if you thought him a scoundrel."

He glanced up again to judge the effect of his words as he paused to pull at his cigar; but I was on guard and gave no sign at all. It was, however, an unpleasant experience to have the other side of my chief life's story revealed by a man whom I knew to be false; and told with a purpose, in a tone of half sardonic raillery, and as a carefully calculated bid for my silence about himself. Heart dissection is a trying process under such conditions.

"You will see from this that Karl was—excuse me if I put it plainly; it is all necessary—was intensely devoted to you. He returned home profoundly unhappy and very love-sick—his is a nature which takes such things seriously—and to this hour he has never recovered. To forget you and the way he had treated you, he plunged into wild excesses which in a couple of years gravely impaired his health; heavy drinking was followed by the present passion for opium. In a word, you have seen for yourself what love has done for my brother."

"You have helped him downwards," I put in.

"He needed no help from me, but——" he waved his cigar expressively and jerked his shoulders. "And that brings us to chapter the second. For our purposes here, a dipsomaniac with a love craze and the opium habit is no use. You are Colonel von Dreschler's daughter, and may know something of the Patriotic Hungarian cause——" he paused to give me a chance to speak.

"The movement in favour of independence, you mean?"

"I thought you would know it;" and he nodded as if it were of the most trifling consequence. "Well, then, you will know that Karl became impossible. Yet he is the elder son and my father's heir; and some of us Hungarians are almost fanatics on the subject of succession. Everything was in danger; and as he has always refused to be set aside in my favour, there was nothing to do except to make him legally impossible. Another surprise for you now"—he spoke as indulgently as if he had been throwing me a candy. "The marriage with you became desirable; so Fate turns her wheel, you see; and I sent to New York to search for you, and we took infinite trouble in the vain endeavour to trace you. It was very unfortunate;" and he spread out his hands again.

I made no comment, but just kept my eyes on him, waiting for him to continue.

"Pardon me if I am personal again. You would have suited our purpose admirably. I suspected you were the daughter of Colonel von Dreschler; and as your father's reputation was—was what it was and is—Karl's marriage with you would have been absolutely fatal to his chances here."

"My father's reputation was the result of vile treachery," I cried indignantly. And I saw my blunder instantly in the start of satisfaction he gave, but instantly repressed. He smoked a couple of moments in silence.

"We will deal with that presently—but I thank you for that admission, although I am surprised you did not see the trap I laid to obtain it. Your natural indignation, no doubt. Well, as we could not find you, we had to obtain an understudy—Madame d'Artelle." His tone was contemptuous here. "And I think, now, you understand chapter two. You must admit I have been frank; and my frankness is a tribute to your perspicacity."

"You have no comments," he said, still lightly and airily, when I did not speak. "Very well, then, we'll go to chapter three. That concerns the future—and your part in it. What do you mean to do, or, in other words, why did you come here? You are an interesting problem. You may have come to try and clear your father's name; or to punish in some way the man who treated you so badly: clever and pretty women have done that before, you know. Or—and this I referred to as the really improbable motive—you may still wish to marry my brother. But whatever your motive and object, I pledge you my honour—the honour of the son of the Duke Ladislas and future King of Hungary—that I will help you to the utmost of my power. But you must also help me; and for your first object you must be content to wait a year or two, until my father's death."

"And Gareth?" I asked, after a pause.

A frown darkened his face and his eyes clouded. He rose and took a couple of turns across the room.

"Would to God I could undo that business!" he cried, either with deep feeling or an excellent simulation of it. "You can't understand what this is to me! I am not a man capable of deep love, but I care for Gareth beyond all women. It was a midsummer madness; and if I could repair the injury to her, I would. But the prospect of the throne is between us—and shall I give that up and wreck the whole of this great national movement for her? I would do anything else on God's earth for her—but that I cannot. It is impossible."

"And her father?"

"I know what you mean. He would plunge a knife in my heart or send a bullet crashing into my brain, if he knew. He is desperate enough for anything. But he must not know. You must never tell him."

"You have the hardihood to do the wrong but lack the courage to face the consequences," I exclaimed, bitterly.

"I was not thinking of that. I am not afraid of mere death, I hope," he cried contemptuously. "I am thinking of the millions of Czechs, men, women and children, whose hopes of liberty are centred in my life. Beside that, all else is as nothing."

"It is a pity you did not think of this before."

"A man is a man and will act as a man at times. I have done a wrong I cannot undo; and it only remains to limit its mischief."

"A convenient code."

"Where is Gareth?" he broke off.

"Not where you intended those miscreants of yours to place her."

"Oh, so that was you also, was it?" he said, understanding. "You are making yourself very dangerous. Do you persist in threatening me?"

"What if I do?"

He paused as if to give emphasis to his reply.

"Those who oppose a national movement, Miss von Dreschler, must not be surprised if they are crushed under its wheels. As the daughter of your father, your mere presence here might be a danger to you."

"You threaten me?"

"I warn you—and that is the same thing. But a way is open to you. Marry Karl and take him away."

"You are a coward!" I cried, the burning red of anger flushing

70

my face as I remembered his former taunt that such a marriage would degrade his brother sufficiently for his purpose.

"Cold facts not hot words will alone serve here," he replied. "What do you mean to do?"

"You can let your brother marry Madame d'Artelle. He is nothing to me."

He bent a sharp, piercing look upon me. "You mean that?"

"If I had influence with him it would be used to thwart your schemes. Keep him away from me, therefore, lest I tell him who I am and pit that influence against yours."

He paused and his brows knitted in thought. "What you mean is that you are willing to use Madame d'Artelle to revenge your own wrongs upon him. Then the third motive, the improbable one for your presence here, is the real one."

"If he will marry her, let him," I cried indignantly.

"You mean they are to carry out to-morrow's plan?"

"Yes."

"You amaze me. But then one never can understand a woman. And as for the rest?"

"I must think. It is a tangle. I shall probably tell Colonel Katona."

"It will be his death warrant. A hint that my life is in peril from him and a hundred knives will be out of their sheaths in my defence. And those who would defend me against him would be ugly enemies of Colonel von Dreschler's daughter. You do not understand us Magyars. You are raising a storm whose violence may overwhelm you."

"I will say no more now. But you shall do Gareth justice."

"Do you set that before the clearing of your father's name? That is the problem for you, and it is so searching that I can be sure you will not act in a hurry. But in any case, I do not fear you, Miss von Dreschler, nor anything you can do. I shall see you to-morrow, and by then you will have decided whether my brother is to marry Madame d'Artelle."

"I have decided. That is what I wish," I answered, firmly.

In his perplexity he stared hard at me and then bowed. As he was leaving the room he turned.

"I don't understand you; but I shall be sorry if you make yourself my enemy and drive me to any extremes. I respect you; and repeat, I shall be sorry."

I made no answer; leaving him to think I had spoken my last word as to Karl.

CHAPTER XII

HIS EXCELLENCY AGAIN

If the truth must be confessed I had surprised myself quite as much as Count Gustav in declaring my wish that Karl should marry Madame d'Artelle. I had spoken in response to the feeling of hot resentment he had roused by his bitter taunt that a marriage with me would prove an effectual disgrace for Karl.

And what stung me was the obvious truth of it all.

My father was the proscribed murderer of the man who, had he lived, would have been the future occupant of the new throne; and for Karl to marry such a man's daughter must mean absolute death to his chance of succeeding to that throne.

The gall and wormwood of that thought were intolerable. Madame d'Artelle, ex-police spy as she was, bigamist as she would be, and with a past that would not bear investigation, was a suitable and eligible match compared with me! And the torture I suffered as this conclusion forced itself home, is not easy to describe.

One thing was clearly borne in upon me. I would not marry either Karl or any other man until that slur was off my name. I would not rest until that was done. The wish to clear up the mystery which I had at first felt mainly for my dead father's sake, now quickened into a passionate resolve on my own account. For my own sake I must and would get to the bottom of the mystery; and the risk of neither my fortune nor my safety should be allowed to come between me and it.

I had called it a tangle; and what a tangle it was! Whichever way I moved there were difficulties that seemed insuperable. In one direction Gareth's pretty, smiling, trustful face blocked my path. Unless I broke my pledge to her, I could not open my lips to her father. And if I did not tell him, I might get no farther forward to my end. If he held the key to the mystery, it was only too probable that, as Count Gustav had implied, he could not speak without accusing himself. It was therefore useless to deal with him until I had found the means of compelling him to say what he knew.

Count Gustav himself knew of my father's innocence, and had pledged his honour to help me to clear it; but even if I trusted him, which I did not, the price was connivance in his schemes—in Gareth's fate and Karl's undoing. That door was therefore shut in my face.

There remained Duke Ladislas, General von Erlanger and Karl

himself. The Duke was hopeless, so far as I was concerned. The General most unlikely to help me. As for Karl, I doubted whether he knew anything, or even if he did know, whether he possessed a spark of the energy necessary to help.

Could I infuse that energy into him?

As the question leaped into my mind, I began to think earnestly of the means to do this. If Count Gustav was right in what he had said in his jeering, flaunting way about Karl's feelings for me, I might indeed have much power over him. Up to this point I had been stumbling at random and in the dark in regard to Karl. I had had an indefinite plan to secure his influence by saving him from the ruin which others threatened. But now a much clearer path opened.

And then I saw how my impulse of anger could be used for my purpose—the impulse which had led me to agree that the plan for the marriage with Madame d'Artelle should go forward.

My original plan had been to let the elopement take place and then go to the house, "Unter den Linden," and by exposing Madame d'Artelle, frighten her away and at the same time establish my influence with Karl.

I saw a better plan, however, into which all the preparations I had made would fit admirably. There was risk in it and danger to my own reputation; but I could take care of that. I was too desperate to be scared by any fear of consequences. What I thought to do now was to play Madame's part in the business, and to take her place in the carriage with Karl. I guessed that Gustav would see to it that he was stupefied with either drink or drugs, when the crisis came; and in a dark carriage, closely veiled, I could trust myself to maintain the deception successfully.

I knew that Gustav was to bring his brother to the carriage; and in this way I could delude him as to my own movements. That was as essential to my plans as it was that I should have free and full opportunities of exerting my influence upon Karl.

I had to think also of my personal safety. I did not under-rate the risk which I was now to run on that account. In pitting myself against Count Gustav I was fighting the whole influence which his father wielded. The Duke had not scrupled to sacrifice my father; and was not likely to be less drastic in dealing with me if I stood in his way. And one word from Count Gustav would be enough to bring the whole force of his anger upon me.

I was deliberating what steps to take when a note was brought to me from General von Erlanger, asking me in somewhat urgent terms to go and see him.

I was glad of the chance. I might find out from him how far the

73

Duke would have power to threaten my safety should Count Gustav obtain his help.

But I found his Excellency very far removed from an inclination to discuss serious matters seriously. I saw at once that he had dressed himself with more than usual care; he was wearing a number of the orders he had received in the course of a successful diplomatic and political career; and he welcomed me with genial smiles and quite unnecessary warmth. He held my hand so long indeed, as he greeted me, that his two daughters noticed it. I saw them nudge each other and snigger, and I had to give quite a tug to get it away.

He insisted upon my staying to dinner, all unprepared though I was; and when I pleaded that I had no dinner costume, he declared that I was never anything but charming; and that he would take no excuse.

The girls carried me away to put my hair tidy, and then gave me their confidences about their father and the new governess. She was a "beast," it seemed, according to Charlotte; and the General wished me to return.

"Father misses his chess with you," she said, with the ingenuous directness of her age: "that is why he wants you back. We think he's going to make you his secretary as well. He talks an awful lot about wanting help."

"He took over an hour dressing himself when he knew you were coming," chimed in the younger, Sophia; "and he made Charlotte go and tell him if his hair was parted straight."

"He's always talking about how well you play chess, and how clever you are."

"And he never puts those orders on unless somebody awfully particular is coming!" They rattled on in this way at considerable length; and during dinner watched the General's conduct to me very closely, nodding and smiling significantly at me, and winking at each other.

I had remained a week in the house after my coming to an understanding with him, and before I went to Madame d'Artelle's and during that time we had had more than one confidential talk.

When an old man yields to the influence of a very young woman, it is often a considerable surrender. It had been so in his Excellency's case; and I was quite conscious that I could do a great deal with him. Vivien could with Merlin; and a Minister of ripe and long experience can make a very interesting Merlin.

In those talks of ours he had sometimes forgotten the difference of forty years in our ages, and more than once had paid me compliments which might have been almost embarrassing had I been minded to take them at all literally.

The girls' chatter had therefore prepared me in a measure for what might be to follow when they had been sent away and we two were once again face to face over the chess board.

"I have missed my chess very much, Miss Gilmore. I can't tell you how much."

"You should teach Charlotte to play."

"She would never learn. She is just a child, no more."

"You are not playing well yourself, to-night."

He laughed. "That's what I like about you. You blurt the truth out with delightful frankness. I don't want to play to-night."

"Is that why you say you've missed your chess so much?"

"I've missed your white hands moving among the men, more than the game itself." He spoke very quickly, and fumbling nervously among the men upset two of them.

I made a move then that was not chess. I'm not sure that it was quite fair to him indeed. Pretending haste in picking the pieces up, I touched his hand and glanced at him. Our eyes met; and withdrawing my hand quickly, I upset some more men, with a suggestion of agitation.

"I beg your pardon," I stammered. "I'm afraid I don't remember how they stood. I—I think I'm a little confused."

"Why should you be?" he asked, with a glance.

"I don't know. It's very silly. I don't understand myself. I—I believe I'm nervous."

"I can't imagine you nervous—er—Christabel." It was very daring of him; but he tried to say it as if it was his rule to use my name.

I cast my eyes down and sighed. "I think I'll go now," I said after a pause; "if you don't mind."

"But I do mind, very much. Don't bother about the game. I don't care where the men were."

I smiled. "Possibly; but I think I was going to win. I began to see mate ahead."

"I wish I could," he declared.

"General!" I cried in protest; to let him see that I understood. I had given him the opening intentionally, but had scarcely expected he would take such immediate advantage of it.

We both laughed; he with a suggestion of triumph.

"If I am not to go, we had better set the men and start a new game," I said, and began to arrange the pieces for the game.

"I don't wish to play. I wish to talk," he declared, and then very

75

abruptly he got up and began to walk about the room, until he stopped suddenly close to me. I knew what was coming then.

"Do you know why I wished you to come here to-day?"

"Yes, I think so—but don't ask it." I was very serious and met his eyes frankly.

"How quick you are, and how daring. Any other woman would have been afraid to say that—afraid of being thought conceited. Why shouldn't I ask it?"

"I don't want to lose one out of the only friends I have in Pesth, perhaps the only one, General. And—other reasons."

He looked down at me and sighed. "Just now——" he began, when I interrupted him.

"I did it intentionally, thinking this thing should be settled at once, better at once—and for always, General."

"I have found out since you went what I never suspected before. I am a very lonely old man, for all my wealth and my position."

"We can still play chess—if not to-night; still on other nights. To-night, I too want to talk to you."

He made no answer, but moved away and walked about the room again in silence; throwing himself at length into a lounge chair and staring in front of him blankly and disconsolately.

After a time he roused himself and gave a deep, long sigh.

"Very well. We must leave it there, I suppose."

"No, we can't leave it there, General. I told you I wanted to talk to you." I left my chair and taking one close to his side, I laid my hand on his. "I need a friend so sorely. Won't you be that friend?"

His fingers closed on my hand, and he held it in a firm clasp.

"With all my heart, yes," he answered. "What is the matter?"

His ready assent moved me so that for the moment I could not reply.

"If I tell you all my little story, you will hold it in confidence?"

He looked up and smiled. "I would do much more than that for you, Christabel," he answered, simply, using my name now without any hesitation, and in a quite different tone from that before. "You may trust me implicitly, child, on my honour."

"I am going to surprise you. The name I bear is not my father's. I took it when my uncle, John P. Gilmore, died and left me his fortune. He made me a wealthy woman. My father was of Pesth, Colonel von Dreschler. I have come here to seek justice for his name and mine. I see how this affects you. If you cannot help me, I will say no more."

He released my hand to press his own to his eyes; and when he withdrew it he gazed at me very earnestly.

"You are his child! Gott in Himmel, his child."

"I did not hide my name because I was ashamed of it," I said.

"You have no need, Christabel. It was a damnable thing that was done. He was my friend, and I will help you all I can."

Then without reserve I told him everything I had learnt and all that I had done. He let me tell the story without interruption, and put his questions at the end.

"I cannot tell you you are not in danger from Count Gustav and his father. Your very name is a source of danger; and were you another woman I should counsel you with all insistence to give this up and go away. But you will not do that. I know you too well. I must think how to protect you. You have set me a very difficult task; but it shall not be impossible. Yet I dare not let my hand be seen in it. I will think it all over until I find a way. Meanwhile, trust me as your father would have done; and let me hear something of you every day. I shall know no ease of mind if I do not hear, every day. A note or message, saying all is well with you, will be enough. And if you find yourself in any trouble, let me know of it—I shall guess it, indeed, if I do not hear any day from you. And I will pledge myself to get you out—even if I have to appeal to Vienna on your behalf."

"I need no more than the knowledge that your help is behind me. But you think the danger is really serious?"

"If you threaten Count Gustav, you threaten the whole Patriotic cause; and if I could tell you the things that have been done to build up that great national movement even you might be daunted and turned from your purpose."

"Not while I live," I cried, resolutely.

"You are your father's child. He was as staunch and brave and fearless as any man that ever drew breath, but he was broken, and was but one of many victims. A policy of this stern kind has no bowels of compassion for man, woman, or child. Pray God you may never have to look in vain for that compassion."

"You almost frighten me," I said. His earnestness was so intense.

"No, nothing can do that, I am sure. If I could indeed frighten you out of this purpose of yours, I would; but instead, I will help you. I have many means, of course; and will exhaust them all. Go now, and let me think for you."

As we rose he stumbled against the table on which stood the chess board. He turned to me with a smile.

"I am afraid it will be some time before we play again. But the day will come, Christabel. It shall, or I am no player at this other game."

And with this note of confidence we parted.

CHAPTER XIII

GETTING READY

I don't like having to own that General von Erlanger went a little too far in saying that nothing could frighten me. The terms in which he had spoken of the Patriotic movement and his reference to its compassionless sacrifice of victims disturbed me profoundly.

I passed a sleepless, tumbling, anxious night; and if it be fear to conjure up all kinds of possible horrors, to shrink at the thought that even my life might be in danger, and to lie wincing and cringing and shuddering at the prospect of cruelty and torture, then certainly I was horribly frightened.

I was a prey to bitter unavailing regret that I had so lightly and thoughtlessly set out on a path which had led me to such a pass and brought me face to face with such powerful, terrifying, and implacable adversaries.

The temptation to run away from it all seized upon me with such force that I sought in all directions for reasons which would justify cowardice and clothe it with the robe of prudence. But my fears were confronted by the conviction that I had gone too far to be able to retreat without deserting Gareth; and at that my alarm took the shape of hot but impotent indignation at my lack of foresight.

Then my sense of honour and my fear had a struggle over that sweet, innocent, trustful, child, in which all that was mean and ignoble and cowardly in my disposition fought to persuade me to desert her; and before the night was half over had all but conquered.

I was tired of playing a man's part; and in those hours of weakness, the sense of responsibility was so cruelly heavy and the desire to be only a girl and just rush away from it all so strong, that once I actually jumped from my bed and began to dress myself with feverish eagerness to leave the house and fly from the city.

But I had not even the courage of my cowardice. The recollection of that sneer of Count Gustav's—that while my name still bore the stain I was not even the equal of such a woman as Madame d'Artelle stayed me. I tore off my clothes again and crept back into bed, to lie shivering at the consciousness that if I was afraid to go through with my purpose, I was even more afraid to run away from it.

I grew calmer after a while. I put aside as mere hysterical nonsense the idea that my life could be in danger. They had not even taken my father's life. If they found me in their way, they might devise some excuse for imprisoning me. That was probably the worst that could happen. It had been in General von Erlanger's mind; and he had promised to secure my liberty. I knew I could trust myself to him.

By reflections of this kind I wrestled with my weakness and at length overcame it; and in the end fell asleep, no longer a coward, but fully resolved to carry my purpose through and fight all I knew to win.

In the morning I began at once to carry out my plan. I sent a servant to ask Madame d'Artelle if she could spare Ernestine to come and help me.

Instead of Ernestine, Madame herself came—as I had anticipated, indeed. She found me in all the middle of packing; my frocks and things spread all over the room, and my trunks open.

"What does this mean, Christabel?" she asked.

"You can see for yourself. I have had enough of plots and schemes to last my life time. I jumped up in the night and half-dressed to run away. I was so scared."

"You are going away?" Relief and pleasure were in her tone.

I laughed unpleasantly. "You need not be glad."

"I am not glad," she replied, untruthfully.

"I am putting the work into stronger hands. That's all."

"You said you could protect me."

"I have done that. Count Gustav promised as much to me yesterday. You are free to leave Pesth at once if you like. You need not marry his brother unless you wish. And after to-day, not even if you wish. Is Ernestine coming to help me?"

"I wish you would speak plainly. You always frighten me with your vague speeches. You seem to mean so much."

"I do mean very much—far more than I shall tell you. You have been no friend to me—why should I explain? Take your own course; and see what comes of it. Is Ernestine coming, I say?"

"Yes, of course she can come; but I am so frightened."

"That will do you no harm," I rapped out, bluntly. "I wash my hands of everything."

"What am I to do?" she cried, waving her hands helplessly.

"I arranged yesterday with Count Gustav that the scheme for this romantic elopement should be carried out. You can play your part for all I care. The chief thing you can do for me is to send Ernestine here."

"But I——"

"Will you send her here?" and I stamped my foot angrily, and so drove her out of the room in the condition of nervous doubt and anxiety I desired.

With the maid's help my trunks were soon packed, and the work was nearly finished when Madame d'Artelle came back.

"Count Gustav is here," she said.

"Very well. You can close that box, Ernestine, and try to pack this toque in the top of the black one. You got everything I said for the voyage in the cabin trunk."

"He insists on seeing you, Christabel."

"I'll come down when I've finished." I spoke irritably. Irritation is the natural result of a couple of hours' packing.

Everything was ready when I went downstairs.

"I hear you are going away, Miss——"

"Gilmore," I broke in, giving him a look.

"I congratulate you on your—prudence." He too, like Madame d'Artelle, was obviously both relieved and pleased at the news.

"You need not smile at it. I am not doing it to please you, Count Gustav."

"I wish to ask you a question if Madame d'Artelle——" and he paused and looked at her.

"I don't see the need of all this mystery," she answered, tossing her head as she left the room.

"Please be quick," I said, snappishly. "I am both in a hurry and a bad temper—a trying combination even for a woman of my disposition."

"You have not slept well, perhaps."

"No. I had to think. What is your question?"

"About Gareth?"

"I shall not answer it," I said shortly, and frowned as though the subject were particularly unwelcome and disturbing.

"I think I can understand;" he answered believing he could read my mood. "And about Karl and Madame?"

"I have not forgotten your sneer. I will not disgrace him." I spoke with as much bitterness and concentrated anger as I could simulate, and was pleased by the covert smile my words produced, although I appeared to be goaded to anger by it.

"I will tell you one thing. She shall not either. By to-morrow some one will be here from Paris who will see to that."

"That may be too late."

"No. You dare not do anything to-day. You dare not," I exclaimed, passionately.

"You have told that to Madame?"

"No. She is nothing to me."

"You are very bitter."

"Again, no. You have only made me indifferent;" and as if I could bear no more, I hurried out of the room. I knew as well as if

80

he had told me that the effect of my words would be to drive him to use the time of grace I had left him.

I did not wait to see Madame d'Artelle, but had my trunks placed in a fly and, taking Ernestine with me, drove to the depôt. She took my ticket for Paris, saw to the labelling of my luggage, settled me in my compartment, and waited me with until the train started. I wished the proof of my departure to be quite clear.

But on the Hungarian railways the trains do not run long distances without stopping; and at the first station I got out and returned to Pesth. I was back in my house with Gareth before one o'clock, and had already seen James Perry, who had returned, and arranged one of my next moves.

A wire was sent to Paris to a friend of his requesting that a telegram be despatched as from M. Constans, saying that he would be in Pesth that evening at nine o'clock, and would come straight to Madame d'Artelle's house.

That telegram was the weapon with which I intended to frighten Madame away from Pesth in order that I might take her place.

I had one more preparation to make. I wrote out orders dismissing the men servants at the house, "Unter den Linden," and signed them "Karl von Ostelen," taking great care over the signatures. These I gave to Perry together with money for any wages they might claim, and instructed him to drive with his son to the house after dusk.

I told him I should arrive there later in the evening in a carriage; and that if the men in charge of it attempted to stable the horses there, he was to say that the Count's orders were that they should not remain. After that he and his son were to be in the house: to say nothing about me to any women servants, and to act just as I directed.

Poor little Gareth was more impatient than ever at the lack of news; but I pacified her by saying I expected to have some on the following day; and to escape her somewhat fretful questionings, I pleaded a bad headache and went to my room and lay down.

I needed rest after my broken night, and succeeded in getting to sleep for two hours. I awoke greatly refreshed; and although I was excited at the prospect of the evening's work, I felt very fit and ready to face any emergencies. I was quite able now to laugh at my cowardice of the previous night.

"What news is it you expect, Christabel?" was the question with which Gareth greeted me when I went down to her. "I have been thinking of it ever since you told me."

"To find Count von Ostelen, of course."

"How are you going to find him? Do tell me."

"I was governess to the daughters of General von Erlanger, his Excellency the Minister, you know, Gareth. I saw him last night: I was at his house; and I know he can find the Count if any one can. That reminds me. I was to write to him."

I had forgotten his Excellency's injunction to send him a daily message. I took a visiting card and scribbled on the back "Quite well" over my initials, and was giving it to James Perry to take when an extra precaution occurred to me.

"You will see the General yourself with this," I told him; "but you will not let his servants know from whom you come. I can't tell you everything; but something has occurred which makes it necessary for me to send a message every day to General von Erlanger. If I forget it, you must remind me; for you are always to carry it; and always to see the General yourself. Tell him to-day that I have arranged it so. And listen carefully to this—if anything should happen to me and you think I am in any great difficulty, or trouble, or danger—don't look scared: nothing may come of it all—but if I am, then you are to go at once to General von Erlanger and tell him all you know."

He was an excellent servant; but well trained as he was, he could not suppress his curiosity and surprise.

"We have always been faithful, miss; mayn't I ask whether——"

"No, not yet. If there is need, I shall tell you—because I trust you as fully as I trust your father and mother, and I have a very high opinion of your courage and ability. At present, you have only to remember what I have told you to do."

Gareth was very inquisitive about my movements when, as the dusk fell, I began to prepare for the work in hand. She plied me with prattling questions; why I was at such pains over my dressing; why I took a large cloak on a night comparatively warm; what the thick muffling veil was for; and she gave a little cry of terror when her sharp eyes caught sight of the revolver which I tried to slip into my pocket unnoticed.

"You are such a strange girl, Christabel," she said.

"Every one tells me that; but I generally get there."

"'Get there?' What is that?"

"An Americanism, dear, for gaining your own end."

"Are all American girls like you?" she laughed.

"Luckily for them, perhaps, no. I'm from the Middle West and we have more freedom there than in the Old World."

"Do you all go about in thick cloaks with heavy veils and carrying arms?"

"Gareth, no," I laughed. "We only do these things in fancy dress balls."

"Are you going to one to-night? Oh, I didn't know."

"It's only a masquerade to-night—and this is to be the cloak over my costume."

"Oh, Christabel dear, why didn't you tell me? But you've a walking dress underneath."

"I am going to start for the masquerade from the other house."

"Will there be dancing? Oh, I wish I could go."

"No, no dancing; but I guess the band will play."

"I love music," she cried, not understanding slang; and I didn't explain it.

"I wish you weren't going, Christabel," she said, kissing me when I was ready to start.

"It will be a long evening and I may wish that too before it's over," I replied, with a feeling that that might well be so.

"You will be here with the news at the earliest possible moment to-morrow, won't you, dear? I am so weary of waiting."

"I hope I shall be successful and have good news to bring you."

"I am sure you will. I have such faith in you, Christabel."

She kissed me and with my cloak on my arm and those words ringing in my ears, I set out upon the risky business before me.

CHAPTER XIV

I ELOPE

It was only to be expected that as I approached Madame d'Artelle's house I should be nervously uneasy lest the main foundation of my new plan should have collapsed.

I had built everything on the assumption that Count Gustav would induce his brother to carry out the original scheme of marrying Madame d'Artelle by stealth. I had threatened to bring her husband to Pesth on the following day; and since he knew as well as she seemed to, that M. Constans' arrival would put an absolute end to Madame's usefulness as a tool, I calculated that he would lose no effort to make use of her forthwith.

It was obvious, however, that my absence put an end to the

reason for secrecy; and it was therefore quite on the cards that Karl might have been brought to Madame d'Artelle's house and some kind of ceremony have been already performed there. I should look a good many sorts of a fool if I walked into the house to find them already married.

Peter opened the door and gave a great start of surprise at seeing me.

"Madame is in?" I asked, in as casual a tone as I could assume.

"Yes, miss. She is in, but she is going out. We thought you had left, miss."

"It's all right, Peter. I'll go up to Madame. She is probably in her room, dressing."

"Yes, miss; with Ernestine; but——"

"Don't trouble. You need not tell any one I have come back;" and I gave him a golden reason for silence. "Hide the fact of my presence and do what I wish, and there will be several more of these to follow."

"I am always anxious to please you, miss."

"I wish to see Madame quite alone; can you make an excuse to call Ernestine downstairs?"

He was a shrewd fellow enough in his way. We went upstairs and I waited in an adjoining room while he called Ernestine out and the two went down together.

As soon as they had gone I opened Madame's door and entered.

"Come, Ernestine, I want you. What do you mean by going away like that?" she said crossly, not seeing me.

"Perhaps I can help you, Henriette. Ernestine is busy downstairs;" and I locked the door behind me.

"Christabel! You?"

"I have had to come back to keep my word and save you. You are in great danger. M. Constans must have picked up the scent of the inquiries I made recently. I have this telegram;" and I put into her hands the telegram which I had received from Paris.

I thought she was going to faint. The man must have had some great hold over her; for she was certainly overwhelmed with deadly fear. She stared with horror-struck eyes at the paper as though it reeked with the threat of instant death. Then she turned to glare at me, with not a vestige of colour on her face.

"Nom de Dieu, he will kill me. He will kill me;" she said, in a low, strained, husky whisper, as she fell into a chair, and began to gasp and choke hysterically.

"I know nothing about that," I said, callously; "but if you make a fool of yourself in that way, you will have no time left to get out of his reach. If you want to die, you had better faint now. However, I've done with you;" and I turned toward the door.

"Don't go, Christabel, for the love of heaven don't leave me. I can't think for myself. Oh, don't leave me," she cried. "What shall I do?"

"As he's your husband I should think you ought to stay and meet him. This was sent off from the railway station, you see, and I find his train reaches here just before nine. He'll just be in time for the ceremony to-night."

"Oh, don't, don't, don't," she wailed. "Don't mock me like that. Don't be so hard. Help me. Do, do! I tell you, he'll kill me. I know he will. He tried to once before. You don't want to see me murdered. You can't. Oh Christabel, dear Christabel, say what I had better do."

"If you'll be sensible, I'll help you. You can get away without the least difficulty. Luckily your trunks are all packed, and as the mail for Breslau and Berlin leaves at half-past eight, you can be away before his train arrives. But you must be quick. You have only half an hour, and had better get your luggage away at once with Ernestine."

"How clever you are," she cried; and forthwith began to finish her dressing with feverish haste, her one thought now to fly.

I called up Ernestine, who started on seeing me as though I were a ghost. I explained that urgent reasons had caused her mistress to change her plans; and before Madame d'Artelle had finished dressing, the baggage was on its way to the station.

"What will you do about things here, Henriette?"

"I don't know. I don't care. In face of this I can do nothing."

"Count Karl will be disappointed and his brother angry."

"My life is in danger, would you have me think of anything else? Mother of Heaven, do you think I will be murdered to please a hundred counts?"

"Some one must see to things."

"Let me only get away and I care for nothing else." This was precisely the mood I desired her to be in. She was literally fear-possessed, and flight had become the one all-absorbing passionate desire.

I said no more until we were in the fly hurrying to the station. I meant to see the last of her.

"What of to-night's business—Count Karl?"

"I care nothing. The carriage will come for me and can go away again. I value my life. Holy Virgin, how slow the cab goes. We shall miss the train; I know we shall. And then?" her fear passed beyond words, and the sentence remained unfinished. "If he finds and kills me, my death will be at your door. You have brought him here."

85

"Why are you so afraid of him? He may be only coming to make peace with you and come to an understanding."

"Peace? The peace a tiger makes with a lamb. I know him."

She did not quite fit my idea of a lamb—except in her terror, perhaps; and about that there could be no mistake.

"Shall you come back to Pesth?" I asked.

"Am I insane, do you mean, when he knows the very name I have here?

"What about the servants, then? Paying them, I mean?"

"Let them go to Count Gustav. Thank heaven, here is the station," she cried, and the instant the vehicle stopped she got out and asked excitedly for the mail to Berlin.

There were some five minutes to spare, but she had bundled Ernestine into the carriage and was following when I stopped her.

"One question, Henriette? How is it that as I was out of the way the ceremony fixed for to-night did not take place earlier in the day?

"Don't stop me, the train may start. He could not be induced to get drunk enough; that's all." She said it almost viciously as she scrambled into the carriage.

I waited until the train started and then drove back to the house. I had to settle matters there with the servants. It would not suit my plans for them to go to Count Gustav with the story of this hurried flight.

I took Peter into the salon.

"You are a man of discretion, and your mistress and I both rely upon you, Peter. You know that Madame was contemplating a journey and at the last moment her plans have been hurried by news which I brought her."

"It is not for us servants to ask what our employers do, miss," he said, very respectfully. Part of the respect may have been due to the fact that I had laid some notes and gold on the table.

"The house will be shut up for a month, Peter; and all the servants except yourself, will leave. And they will leave to-night. You understand—to-night. I trust you to see to this. Go and find out what wages are due. This money is to pay them double that amount. I will settle with you afterwards. I do not wish them to know I am in the house."

He scented more reward, and went off with the important air of a major-domo; and on his return I gave him the necessary money.

"I shall pay you what is due to you, Peter, and give you three months' wages in addition. You will see the house locked up to-night and send the keys to me to this address, and let me know where I can write to you. But you can take another situation at once if you wish;" and I gave him the address of the first house I had taken.

That I was able to think of all these small details at such a time has often been a cause of some surprise—and I think of satisfaction. I have always rather prided myself upon my capacity to concentrate my thoughts upon the matter of the moment: to think in compartments, so to speak: and to throw myself thoroughly into the part which I was playing for the time. I was just as cool and collected in all this as though the settlement of the servants' wages was the only thing I had then to do or think of.

"I think that is all, Peter; I am leaving directly. I have a carriage coming for me; and when I go, you will see that none of the other servants are about."

"The servants are already upstairs packing their things, miss," he replied. "I will watch for the carriage and let you know."

When he left me, I walked up and down the room in busy thought. So far as I could see, my preparations were now complete. Count Gustav believed I had left the city; I had frightened Madame d'Artelle away; I had cut off the chance of his discovering her absence; and the only risk of such discovery would be at the moment when he brought Karl to the carriage.

There would not be much risk then, if I did not give myself away. I recalled Madame's words about Karl—"He could not be induced to get drunk enough," for the matter to go through earlier in the day. He was thus to be drugged now; and when he joined me, would be too stupefied to recognize me.

Then a question occurred. What would Count Gustav do as soon as he thought his brother had gone? Had he planned a marriage ceremony similar to the farce he had played with Gareth? If so, did he mean to be present at it to make sure his plan succeeded? Would he enter the carriage with Karl to drive to the house? Or would he be content to trust the work to the man he might hit upon to play the part of priest?

Wait—would it be a real priest; and so was it a real marriage he contemplated? And I was puzzling myself with little problems of the kind, when Peter came to say the carriage was waiting.

Leaving all these difficulties to be solved as they arose, I arranged my thick veil and throwing the cloak over my shoulders, hurried out. A footman stood by the carriage door, and I was glad I had thought to put the veil on before leaving the house.

He touched his hat, closed the door, climbed to the box, and we started at a smart pace. For good or ill I was now committed to the matter, and there was no drawing back.

Nor had I any thought or wish except to go through with it. My heart was beating more rapidly than usual, and I was excited; but not frightened. On the contrary, I was full of confidence, full of belief that I was doing the right thing, let the risk to myself be what it might; and convinced that I was taking not only the surest but the shortest road to the end I had in view.

On one thing I was resolved. Count Gustav must not recognize me. That was all in all to me at that moment. If he did, I saw clearly the use he could make of that knowledge.

Not only could he blacken my reputation by saying I had run away with Karl; but he could also use the fact with telling force against Karl himself—that he had married the daughter of Colonel von Dreschler, the murderer of Count Stephen.

Such a thing would suit his plans far better than the complication with Madame d'Artelle, a mere adventuress, with whom no marriage was legally possible. If he but knew it, I was thus playing right into his hands. But then he did not, and should not know it, until it was too late to be of use to him. He would spread about the story of Karl's marriage to Madame d'Artelle, only to find that she was on her way hot speed to Berlin at the very time.

And when the time came for the truth to be told—well, I had my plans already laid for his own exposure; and they would keep him busy defending himself.

The carriage rattled through the streets, covering quickly the short distance to the rendezvous in the Radialstrasse; and when it drew up I peered out eagerly through the closed window, and then saw that which gave me a profound surprise.

A tall man sauntered past the carriage, scrutinizing it with great earnestness; and as the light from one of the lamps shone on his face, I recognized Colonel Katona.

What could be the meaning of his presence at such a time? Was it more than coincidence? It could not be that. He was a recluse, and rarely if ever left his house to walk in the city. Why should he choose such a night, and such a time, and above all such a place?

I shrank back into the corner of my seat perplexed and anxious—seeking eagerly but vainly for some reason for this most unexpected development. As I sat thus waiting, I saw him presently pass again, retracing his steps, and scrutinizing the carriage as closely as before. This time he came nearer to the window and tried to peer inside.

A minute afterwards I heard a name called in a brief sharp tone of authority; the footman jumped from the box and opened the door, and I squeezed myself as far from it as possible, as Count Gustav came up, his arm through that of Karl, who was very unsteady and walked with staggering lurching steps.

It was easy to see that if Karl was helpless with liquor, his brother was both pale and agitated. His face was very set; and as he approached, I noticed him glance sharply about him twice—the second time with a start of what I read to be satisfaction.

He made no attempt to enter the carriage, much to my relief: and not a word was spoken by any of us beyond a few guttural incoherencies by Karl, as with his brother's help he stumbled into the carriage and sat lolling fatuously, his breathing stertorous and heavy with the drink.

The door was slammed, the footman sprang up, and as the carriage wheeled round I saw Colonel Katona again. This time he came out of the gloom and spoke to Count Gustav.

I had no time to see more; but the list of surprises was not completed yet.

We had not driven a hundred yards before Karl sat up, seemed to shake off his stupor, and laughed lazily.

"Well, Henriette, here we are—off at last. But I wonder what in the devil's name is going to happen next?"

He was neither drunk nor drugged, then; but merely acting. I almost cried out in my astonishment and relief.

But what did it all mean?

CHAPTER XV

AN EMBARRASSING DRIVE

I was so astonished at this turn of matters that I squeezed myself up into as small a space as possible in the corner of the carriage, a prey to completely baffling perplexity.

The sense of shame with which I had followed his shambling, drunken movements, as he was helped into the vehicle, gave way to a feeling at first of relief, and then of pleasure—both feelings mingled with consummate dismay.

Now that he was in possession of his senses, how was I to act toward him? Under the influence of either opium or drink, he would have been easy enough to deal with; and I could have chosen my own moment to avow myself.

My crude idea had been to get him into the house, let him sleep away the effects, and leave him under the impression that while Madame d'Artelle had been with him in the carriage, I had contrived to get her away. I was not ready to show my hand yet; and a nervous embarrassing fear of what he would think of this act of mine began to possess me.

I was soon worried by another unpleasant thought. While he remained under the impression that I was Madame d'Artelle, I was just an impostor, spying upon the relationship between them, of all parts in the world the most repugnant for me to have to play with him.

"I suppose you're too surprised to speak?" he said presently. "Is anything the matter?"

I made no answer, except to draw even further into my corner. He noticed it and laughed.

"Bit afraid of me, are you? You needn't be. I'm not dangerous, even if I'm not drugged. But I have been any time during the last three-and-thirty hours. You see I haven't seen you, and I haven't touched it ever since yesterday morning."

There was a bitterness in his tone I had not heard in it before; but the words filled me with pleasure.

"Not since midday yesterday, Henriette. Three-and-thirty hours: nearly two thousand minutes: every minute like an hour of hell. You didn't think I'd got the strength, I know. Neither did Gustav. And I suppose I'm only a fool to have done it—an infernal fool, that's all. It's getting easier already; but I'd give ten thousand kronen for a taste now—one little wee taste."

He sat suddenly bolt upright, clenched his fist and flung it out in front of him, and groaned as if the fever of temptation had laid hold of him with irresistible force.

"You don't seem to care," he said, bitterly, turning to me: and then his voice became strained and tense. "But you'd better. You hear that, Henriette, you'd better. You keep it from me or as there's a sky above us I wouldn't trust myself not to kill you."

Impulsively I stretched out my hand and laid it on his arm, as if to calm him. But he shook it off impatiently.

"All that's passed," he cried. "Two thousand hours of hell can change a man. They've changed me. I can see things now, and mean to see more. That's why I've come on this business. That and——" his voice fell and his head drooped, and with his lazy laugh he murmured—"What a fool I am, just because a girl——" The sentence was left unfinished, and his fingers stole to the pocket as if in search of the drug.

"I must smoke or have it. Not 'her sake' nor a million 'her sakes' will keep me from it if I don't. I shall stop the carriage and get it."

He lit a cigar and held the match up, and peered closely at me until the little flame flickered out. Then he leaned back and puffed fiercely, filling the carriage with the smoke, and making me cough. At that, he let down the window on his side sharply and bent forward that the air might blow on his face.

By the light of the street lamps I saw that his face was drawn and lined as if with the pain and passion of the struggle through which he had passed.

"Have we far to go?" he asked, raising his voice in consequence of the noise from the open window. I did not answer, and he shrugged his shoulders. "You're a cheerful companion for a man in my mood," he cried, almost contemptuously, as he closed the window with a shiver of cold.

He leant back in his seat, drew his coat closely about him, and smoked in silence, but with less vehemence. Presently he found the silence oppressive.

"One of us must talk," he said then. "I wonder why I'm here and what the devil will come of it!" he exclaimed, laughing.

I wondered, too, what would come of it; but I held my tongue. I had resolved not to speak during the whole ride if I could avoid it, so as not to reveal myself. And if I could reach the house without his discovering my deception, I saw a way by which I could mislead him.

"What are you wrapped up like that for? Throw your cloak back," he said next, and put out his hand as if to do it. I drew it closer round me. "Then you're not deaf as well as dumb," he laughed. "What's the matter with you? I can find a way to make you speak, I think—or you've been just play-acting ever since I knew you."

He bent toward me until his face was close to my veil. "You're not generally afraid to show your face. And you needn't be, it's pretty enough. You can hear that I know. A pretty woman never had a deaf ear for a truth like that—and it is truth; no more, no less than the truth. It didn't need either opium or drink for me to know that, Henriette—though you plied me with plenty of both for that matter. Can you deny that?"

He paused for me to answer; but I did not; and he leant back in his seat again.

"Yes, you're a beautiful woman, Henriette, and Gustav's a very clever, long-headed fellow—but between you, you made a bad mistake. You should have known better than to conjure up that old past of mine. You shouldn't have had a friend about you with haunting eyes. Heavens, how they haunted me—aye, and haunt me now. Doesn't that make you speak? No? Then I'll tell you more. That girl's eyes killed at a stroke every thought in my mind about you. More than that—it's just for her sake, I've endured all these hours of hell. I can trust you not to tell her that—but it's true, Henriette, just as true as that you're a beautiful woman."

Evidently he looked for some sharp outburst from me, for he spoke in a deliberate, taunting way as if to provoke me. And when I made no sign, he was sorely perplexed.

"You are going to explain a lot of things to me presently—I've come for that and that only—but I'll tell you something first that you don't know. I met that friend of yours yesterday morning when I was riding in the Stadtwalchen. We had quite a long and almost intimate talk, and she took me right back across the years to the past; and by no more than a word, a touch and a glance, she put something between me and the devil I had loved, until I hated it and hated myself for having loved it. And for the sake of what she said, I've been in hell ever since. But she did it; she alone, and I've fought against the cursed thing because of her words and her eyes. God, what it has cost me!" He ended with a weary, heavy sigh.

That in my great gladness at hearing this, I did not betray myself was only due to the strong curb I had put on my feelings. But I had heard his secret by treachery, and now, more than ever, I was eager to keep my identity from him. I longed for the drive to come to an end, and I looked out anxiously to try and see even in the darkness that we were reaching our destination.

"Yes, Henriette, those haunting eyes of hers have saved me, so far," he began again. "Saved me, even when it seemed as if all the fiends in hell were just dragging and forcing me to take it. I didn't. More than once the thing was all but between my lips; but she saved me. But I must see her again, or I shan't hold out. I must hear her voice and feel the touch of her hand. Where is she, Henriette? Where is she? That's one of the questions you shall answer. Gustav says she has gone to Paris. They told me the same at your house to-day—I was there twice, though you didn't know it. And you'll have to tell me that among the other things. You can tell me that now," he said almost fiercely, as he bent toward me again and stretched out a hand as if to seize mine.

I gave up my secret for lost; but the carriage slackened suddenly and with a quick swerve drove into the gates of the house.

Karl let the windows down and peered out curiously; and when the carriage door was opened by the footman, he got out and stood offering me a hand to alight. But I gathered my cloak carefully about me and springing out ran past him and fled into the house and upstairs as fast as I could, whispering to James Perry who had opened the door to come after me presently.

I chose a room at random and locking the door behind me, I flung myself on the bed in the dark, face downwards, and burst into a tempest of hysterical tears.

They were tears of neither pleasure nor grief. They were violent but without passion; and came rather as the swift loosening of the pent strain of excitement during the drive from the city. At least so I thought.

I do not think I had shed a tear since my uncle's death until that moment; and although they gave me intense relief, I remember feeling almost ashamed of myself for my weakness. To cry like a hysterical woman was so out of character with my resolve to play a man's part in this struggle!

The tempest was soon over, and I sat on the side of the bed and took off the veil and threw aside the cloak which had been so valuable a disguise, and was drawing the pins out of my hat when I remembered that I must be careful not to disarrange my hair. I was going to pretend to Karl that I had been in the house all the time; and my appearance must bear out that story.

I groped my way to the dressing-table by the window and fumbled about for a match to get a light of some kind; and finding none, drew up the blind. The moon had risen, and this gave a faint light; but it was not enough for my purpose, so I pulled back the curtain, glancing out as I did so.

The window looked upon the garden in the front, and I stood a moment recalling the plan of the house as I had fixed it in my mind when I had gone over it.

I remembered then what for the instant I had stupidly forgotten; that the electric light was installed, and I was turning away to find the switch, when I caught sight of a man moving in the shrubbery.

I thought at first it might be Karl, smoking, or Perry or his son on watch; but it was not. The figure was much too tall for either of the Perrys; and the movements too stealthy and cautious for Karl.

The light was not sufficient for me to get anything like a clear view of the man; yet as he moved there was something about him that seemed familiar. I watched him with growing interest; and presently, having apparently made sure that he was unobserved, he crossed the moonlit grass quickly to the window of the room that was directly underneath mine.

I recognized him then. It was Colonel Katona.

I threw open my window noisily; and he darted away under the shadow of the trees and hurried out of the garden.

It was no mere chance then that he had been in the Radialstrasse at the moment when the carriage was to be there.

Some one had brought him there to be a witness of Karl's escapade. Who had done so, and why? Not Karl; nor Madame d'Artelle; and no one else had known of it but Gustav and myself.

I had seen him speak to Gustav as the carriage wheeled round— wait, I recalled the two furtive glances which Gustav had cast about as he had come up to the carriage with Karl; and the expression of satisfaction after the second of them.

This was Gustav's work, then. And why had he done it? Why had he brought Colonel Katona, of all men in Pesth, to see Karl run away with Madame d'Artelle? Had any other man been picked out, I would have said it was merely that there might be an independent witness. But Colonel Katona—and then the reason seemed to flash into my thoughts, suggesting a scheme subtle and treacherous enough to be worthy of even the worst thoughts I had ever had of Count Gustav.

I thought rapidly how I could put this new idea of mine to the test, and how use it for my own purposes. But before I could decide, I heard hesitating steps in the corridor outside my room. Some one knocked gently at the doors of other rooms and then at mine.

"Are you there, miss?"

It was James Perry's voice. "Yes," I answered; and closing the window and drawing down the blind, I opened the door.

"The gentleman is asking for Madame d'Artelle, miss," he said. "What answer am I to give him?"

"I will take it myself," I replied. I switched on the light and made sure that my hair was all right. "What about the servants, James?" I asked.

"There are two woman servants only, miss; and my father and myself. We did as you said, and sent away a footman who was here."

"You have done very well. If you are asked any more questions about Madame d'Artelle, say that she left the house the moment after the carriage arrived, and that I have been here some hours."

"Yes, miss." He was very perplexed and, I think, troubled. We went downstairs, and he showed me the room where Karl was. It was directly under that in which I had been.

It was to the window of that room, then, I had seen Colonel Katona cross in the moonlight.

CHAPTER XVI

A WISP OF RIBBON

Karl was sitting in an attitude of moody dejection; his elbow on the arm of the chair, and face resting on his hand; and he turned slowly as I opened the door. The look of gloomy indifference vanished, and he rose quickly with a glance of intense surprise.

"Chris—Miss Gilmore!" he exclaimed.

"You asked for Madame d'Artelle. I have come to say she has left the house," I said in a quite steady tone.

"But you—how do you come to be here? I don't understand."

"I thought you knew I was Madame d'Artelle's companion."

"But they told me you had gone away—to Paris."

"I did start, but I came back."

"I have been twice to-day to her house to ask for you. I was very nearly rushing off to Paris after you. I'm glad I didn't." He said this quite simply, and then his face clouded. "But if I understand all this, may I—may I take to opium again?" His eyes cleared, and he smiled as he spoke the last words.

"I hope you will never do that," I replied.

"No, I shan't—now. Do you remember what I said to you in the gardens yesterday? Yesterday—why it seems twenty years ago."

"You mean that you would hate me if I stopped you taking it?"

"Yes, that's it. I have hated you too, I can tell you. I couldn't help it—but I haven't taken any since. It's cost something to keep from it; but I've done it. And I shall be all right—now. I nearly gave in, though, when I heard you'd left the city."

"I knew that you had the strength to resist when I spoke to you yesterday," and I looked at him steadily. He returned the look for a moment.

"It's wonderful," he murmured. "Positively wonderful." Then in a louder tone: "I think you must have hypnotised me."

"Oh, no. I only appealed to your stronger nature—your former self. You have the strength to resist, but you let it rust."

"I wonder if you would like to know why?"

"No, thank you," I cried rather hurriedly.

My haste seemed to amuse him. "Well, I don't suppose it matters. Then you're not going to Paris?"

"Not yet—at any rate."

"Then I shall see you sometimes. I must if I'm to keep from it, you know."

"Yes, if possible and necessary."

"It is necessary, and I'll make it possible. You don't know the responsibility you've taken on yourself so lightly."

"Perhaps I have not taken it lightly, but intentionally."

"You can't be here intentionally," he said, with a start. "You can't, because—do you mean that you know what I'm supposed to have come here for?" Half incredulous, this.

"Yes, quite well."

"That they want to drive me to marry Hen—Madame d'Artelle? And that my brother will be here with a priest in half an hour or so?"

"I did not know your brother was coming," and the news gave me a twinge of uneasiness. "But my object was to prevent the marriage taking place."

"Why?" he asked, somewhat eagerly.

"Her husband is still living."

"I mean, why did you wish to prevent it?"

"I will tell you that presently."

"Tell me now."

"No."

"Yes—I insist."

"That is no use with me."

"Isn't it? We'll see. You know what I carry here;" and he slid his fingers into the pocket from which I had before seen him take the opium pills. "I shall take it if you don't tell me."

"You must do as you please. But you have none with you."

"How do you know?"

"You told Madame d'Artelle so, in the carriage."

He laughed and took out a little phial half full of them, and held it up. "She is stupid. Do you think I should regard it as more than half a victory if I didn't carry this with me? Will you drive me back to it now?"

He took out one of the pills, held it up, and gazed at it with eyes almost haggard with greedy longing.

"This is childish," I said.

"No, it's a question of your will or mine. Will you tell me or shall I take this? One or the other. You can undo your own work. I can scarcely bear the sight of it."

"I accept the challenge," I answered after a second's pause. "It is your will or mine. Rather than see you take that I will tell you——"

"I knew you would," he broke in triumphantly.

"But if I do, I declare to you on my honour that the instant I have told you, I will leave the room and the house, and never see you again."

The look of triumph melted away slowly. "I don't want victory on those terms. You've beaten me. Look here." He opened the long French window, flung the pill out into the night, and then emptied the phial. "Rather than—than what you said;" and he looked round and sighed.

"Thank you," I said.

In the pause the sound of horses' hoofs on the hard road, reached us through the open window.

"Here come Gustav and the priest, I expect."

I bit my lip. "I don't want him to see me," I said, hurriedly.

"What does it matter?"

"Everything."

He closed the window. "What will you do?"

"I will lock myself in one of the rooms upstairs and tell my servants to say Madame d'Artelle is too ill to see him."

"Your servant?"

"Don't stop to ask questions. I can explain all presently. Do as I wish—please. He thinks you are—are drugged——"

"Not drugged—drunk; but how do you know that?"

"Madame d'Artelle thought so at first." The horses were now so near that I could hear them through the closed window. "You can still pretend. Lie on the sofa there. For Heaven's sake be quick. There are but two or three minutes at most now."

"Oh, I'll get rid of them."

I took this for assent, and hurried out of the room as the carriage stopped at the door. Calling James Perry I told him what do to and ran up again to the room where I had been before.

I would not have a light but sat first on the edge of the bed, wondering what would happen, whether I should be discovered, how long Count Gustav would stay, and how Karl would do as he had said.

The house was badly built, and I could hear the murmur of voices in the room below. I slipped to the floor and lay with my ear to the ground in my anxiety to learn what went on. I could hear nothing distinctly, however. The murmurs were louder, but I could not make out the words.

Then I remembered about Colonel Katona, and crossing to the window pulled the blind aside and looked out wondering whether he was still near the house.

The moonlight was brighter, but the shadows of the trees thicker and darker; and for a long time I could distinguish nothing. The carriage remained at the door; the jingling of the harness, the occasional pawing of the impatient horses, and the checking word of the coachman told me this.

If the Colonel was still there, the presence of the carriage no doubt made him keep concealed.

Presently other sounds reached me. Some one unfastened the windows of the room below and flung them wide open. A man went out and I heard his feet grate on the gravel.

"It's no use. He's dead drunk. We may as well——"

It was Gustav's voice, and the rest of the words were lost to me, for I shrank back nervously.

Then an instinctive impulse caused me to lay my ear to the ground and listen for the window to be shut. I heard it closed; but there was no sound of the bolt being shot.

Dark as it was and alone though I was in the room, I know that I turned deathly white at the possible reason for this which flashed upon me in that moment; and when I passed my hand across my forehead the beads of perspiration stood thick upon it. I felt sick and dazed with the horror that was born of that thought; and my limbs were heavy as I dragged them back across the room to the bed and sat there, listening intently for the sounds of Count Gustav's departure, and ready to rush downstairs the instant he had gone.

There was no longer any need for me to stare vaguely out into the garden. I knew now that the watcher was there, and why he was there. I had guessed the secret of that noisily opened window, of the loudly spoken words, and the closed but unbolted casement.

The carriage went at last, after I had heard Count Gustav's voice in the hall below speaking to some one who answered in a lower and indistinct tone.

While the two were still speaking, I unlocked my door softly and crept out to the head of the stairs; and even as the front door was shut by James Perry and the carriage started, I ran down.

"Go in there at once, James, fasten the bolt of the big window, and if the blind is up, draw it down. Quick, at once," I told him, and followed him into the room.

Karl was still lying on the couch.

"Leave the window open, you," he said. "I like the air."

"I told him to shut it," I said, as I entered and James went out. "I can't stand the draught and can't bear the look of the dark."

He sat up when he heard my voice and stared at me.

"You afraid of the dark? You?"

"Have you been lying on the couch all the time?" I asked.

"Yes, Gustav fooled me about and tried to make me get up, but I wouldn't, but what has that to do with anything? You do nothing but bewilder me—and Gustav too, for that matter."

"It's time that some things were made clear," I replied. "How did you prevent them coming in search of me?"

98

"Very easily. I told him Madame had gone to bed, ill—ill with temper, because I was drunk, and swore I would do her some damage if she came near me. By the way, what are you going to do?"

"I don't know. I've succeeded already in the chief part of my purpose, and am not ready yet for the next."

"What is your purpose?"

"I am going to tell you. One thing was to prevent your marrying Madame d'Artelle."

"You said that before when you wouldn't tell me the reason. What is the reason?"

"Because I know why the marriage was being forced."

"So do I—but it doesn't interest me. Although I meant to make Madame tell me many things."

"Probably I can tell you all you wish to know."

"Why do you think I was to marry Madame d'Artelle?"

"To complete your ruin in the eyes of the country, to make you impossible as your father's heir in the event of the plans of the Patriots succeeding. Such a mésalliance, added to the reputation for dissoluteness and incapacity which you have made for yourself recently would have completed your overthrow."

"You don't spare me," he said, slowly.

"There is no need. I am speaking of—the past."

At the emphasis on the word his face brightened with almost eager delight. "What power you have to move me!" he exclaimed. "Yes, it is as you say—the past. And why are you doing all this?"

"You remember what you said yesterday in the Stadtwalchen— that probably I had a motive? You were right. I have."

"Tell me."

"Yes. I came here to Pesth for a purpose which has become all in all to me. I looked round for the best means of accomplishing it. First I went to General von Erlanger—thinking to work through him. Then I saw and recognized the woman who was reputed to have so much influence over you—Madame d'Artelle. I knew I could get her into my power, and said to myself 'I can save Count Karl from her;' and I went to her. At her house I learnt the rest; that the plan was to force you to one side in favour of your brother. I said to myself again: 'If I save him from that scheme, he will have the power I need, and in common gratitude will be impelled to help me.' I had not seen you then."

He listened attentively, but his look grew gradually solemn and gloomy; and he shrugged his shoulders as he answered: "I see. You are like the rest. Timber to hew and water to fetch—for yourself. Well? What difference could it make whether you had seen me or not?"

99

His manner nettled me. Why, I know not: but I replied sharply: "Did you think I was a philanthropist—with no other thought but to help you? Or that you were so weak and helpless that out of sheer pity a stranger would be drawn to help you?"

He bent his head upon his hand and sighed dejectedly. "Go on," he murmured. "If I'm disappointed, it hurts no one but myself."

"If I had seen you, I should not have attempted it. Of that I am quite sure."

"What a contemptible beast I must have seemed to you! I suppose you know how you're hurting me? Perhaps you have another motive. If I had——" and he slid his fingers into his pockets as if in search of his little phial.

"It's very brave, isn't it, to threaten me like that?" I said, curtly.

He drew his fingers out as though they had touched fire, and glanced up hurriedly at me.

"You don't know what a coward it makes of a man," he sighed. "You're making it harder for me. You're killing hope. A dangerous experiment with a patient like me. There's only a very short bridge between me and the past."

"A bridge you will never recross," I said, firmly.

He looked up and met my eyes. "Not if you'll stand between it and me, and help me a bit now and then. I'm going to play my part—but you mustn't kill my hopes, you know!"

"I shall help you all I can, because you cannot help me unless you do play it."

He frowned. "I'll play it, if it's only to help you. What is it you want?"

"A thing that may be very hard to do."

"I'll do it. I swear that. It will be an incentive to feel I can help you. It gives me a glimmer of hope again and strength, the mere thought of it. You don't know how I'd like to please you."

For a moment I was silent; and in the pause, my ears, which are very quick, caught a sound which made my heart beat rapidly. The faint crunch of a footstep on the gravel outside the window.

He heard nothing, but saw the start I gave. "Why did you start?"

"Nothing," I said, with an effort to keep my voice steady. "I will tell you what I want. Years ago a great wrong was done to a very close and dear relative of mine here in Pesth. I came here to seek justice for his name—for he was left to die in shameful exile, with the wrong unrighted."

"I looked for anything but that; but I'd do more than that for you, much more. Who and what was he?"

He had no suspicion of the truth yet; and when I paused, he misunderstood my hesitation.

"You don't doubt me?"

"No; but——" I hesitated; and then there came another sound from without. A hand pushed the window frame; and this time Karl heard it.

"What was that?" he asked, and rose from the couch.

"The wind—nothing else."

"There's no wind," he said. "I'll see."

I put myself between him and the window. "No, don't open it. I'll"—I started and stopped abruptly. I saw something lying on the sofa.

It was just a wisp of faded ribbon. But it was the favour which he had begged of me that night years ago in New York. So he carried it with him always. The colour left my face and I caught my breath.

"You are ill? What's the matter? You're not frightened?"

I stretched out a hand and took it up quickly. I was trembling now. He tried to intercept me and to reach it first.

"You must give that to me, please," he said shortly, almost sternly. "It is mine. It must have fallen out when Gustav was trying to drag me up."

"It is nothing but a wisp of ribbon," I replied, lightly.

"I'll give you anything but that," he declared, again sternly.

"No, I will have this. I have a right to it."

He grew angry and his face took a look of such determination as I had not seen on it before. "No. Not that—at any cost." His voice was hoarse, but his manner very firm.

Our eyes met. His hard and stern; mine all but smiling.

"I tell you I have a right to it," I said.

"What do you mean?"

I paused.

"That it is mine."

He knew then. His eyes opened wide and his hands clenched as he stepped back a pace, still gazing full at me; and his voice was deep as he answered—

"Then you—my God—you are Christabel?"

"Yes. I am Christabel von Dreschler—it is my father's name that has to be cleared."

He made a step toward me, stretching out his arms.

"No, not while that stain remains—if ever."

He stood, his arms still partly outstretched, and gazing at me in silence.

At that moment the pressure of a hand on the window was repeated, and the frame was shaken.

He turned to it again. "I must see what that means," he exclaimed.

"Not if you value your life, or believe that I do."

For a moment he challenged my look, but then yielded.

"As you will, of course—now; for all this is your doing;" and with a smile and a sigh he let me have my way.

CHAPTER XVII

IN THE DEAD OF NIGHT

I had resolved what to do, and I lost no time.

"You are going to trust me in this and do what I wish?" I asked Karl.

"Yes, of course. You have a right to no less. But what does it mean?"

"You heard the noise at the window?"

"Yes."

"It was not the wind. Some one was attempting to open it. I am going to find out who it is and why they are there."

"How?"

"By stratagem. I wish you to go upstairs and remain there until I call you."

"Why should I do that?" he asked, hesitating and perplexed.

"Because I ask you. You will do it?"

"I don't like it—but if you insist, I promise."

"Before you go I wish you to lie on the couch there while my servant comes here and does what I will tell him; and you will act as though you were bidding him good-night—but as if you were still drugged."

"Hadn't you better tell me everything?"

"There is no time. Will you do this? Please."

He shrugged his shoulders and lay down on the couch.

I went out and called James Perry and instructed him what to do.

He went into the room, crossed to the window and stood there a moment with his shadow showing plainly on the blind. Then he pulled up the blind, and turned as if in obedience to some order from Karl. Next he threw the large window open and stepped out on to the gravel, and stood there long enough for any one who might be watching to have a full view of the interior of the room.

"No, sir, it is not raining," he said, and came back through the window making as if to close and fasten it. He stopped in the act of doing this, and partly opened it again, as if obeying orders from Karl.

"No, it's not cold, sir, but it will be draughty," he said.

Then with a shrug of the shoulders he left it open and turned away. Taking a rug from one of the lounges he threw it over Karl, taking pains to tuck it in carefully; and then stood back as if asking for any further orders.

"Good-night, sir," he said, and crossing to the door, he switched out the light.

Immediately this was done, I ran in again, hurried Karl out of the room, laid a sofa pillow on the couch, and arranged the rug over it as James had done. Then I recrossed the room and waited, my fingers close to the electric light switch, to see if the trap was laid cleverly enough to deceive the man I was expecting. I stood in a dark corner by the door, partly concealed by a screen, where I could see the whole room and all that occurred.

My eyes soon grew accustomed to the comparative darkness. The moon was shining brilliantly, and the slanting rays through one of the windows fell right across one end of the couch on which Karl had been lying. They revealed the lower half of what appeared to be the huddled figure of the sleeper, the upper half being wrapped in deep shadow.

The house was all silent. I had heard Karl go upstairs, James Perry being with him; and had caught the latter's careful tread as he came down again to the hall where I had told him to wait, in case I should need and call him.

The night was very still. I could see right out into the moonlit garden, and as the window was partly open, could trust my ears to catch the faintest sound. But scarcely a leaf moved. The dead stillness was almost oppressive.

The suspense began to affect me soon. I have not the slightest fear of the dark; but as minute after minute passed and no result followed my careful preparations, I began to think I had failed. The net must have been set too conspicuously; and so set in vain.

To pass the time I began to count my pulse beats. One, two, three—to a hundred. Again one, two, three—to a second hundred; and a third, a fourth and a fifth. Then the counting became mechanical, and my thoughts wandered away. It became difficult to remain still.

An impulse seized me to cross the room to the window and look out, and I had to fight hard to restrain it.

Then I caught a sound in the garden. The rustling of a bush. I held my breath to listen. There was no wind stirring to account for it. Not a leaf of all those full in view moved. It was a sign therefore that the patience of some one beside myself had begun to give out.

I braced myself for what was to come, and in a second my wits were all concentrated and every nerve in my body thrilled with expectation, quickening to eager anxiety.

I had not long to wait.

There was another rustle of bushes, and a bird startled from its roosting perch, flew chirping its alarm across the lawn. The sharpness of the noise made me start.

Another pause followed; then another sound—this time a slight grating on the gravel; almost immediately a head showed at the window pane; and a man peered cautiously through the glass into the room.

I crouched closer into my hiding place as his face turned and the eyes seemed to sweep in all directions to make sure that no one else was there to see him.

Stealthily and silently his hand was stretched out, felt the heavy frame, and pushed it open sufficiently to let him enter. The window gave a faint creak in opening; and he stood as still as death lest it should have been heard.

I held my breath now in my excitement. What was he going to do? It was Colonel Katona. I could recognize him by the moonlight; and a moment later his purpose was clear.

He changed something from his left hand to his right. The glint of a moonbeam on the barrel showed me it was a revolver.

I had read the signs aright. He had been tricked into the belief that Karl was the man who had betrayed Gareth, and had come now to do what he had swore to me he would do to any man who harmed her—take his life.

He must surely have had some apparently overwhelming proof given him before he would go to this desperate extreme; and I would know what that proof was, before the night was much older. Already I had a strong suspicion.

These thoughts flashed through my mind in the moment that the Colonel stood hesitating after the noise made by the creaking window; and the instant he moved again, I had no eyes but for him, no thought except for what he proposed to do.

His next act surprised me. He closed the window softly behind him and drew down the blind. The noise was much greater than before, but he paid less heed to it. He pulled it down quickly, shutting out the moonlight; but there was enough dim light through the blind for his purpose.

I could just make out that he held the revolver ready for use as he stepped to the couch and stretched out his hand to seize and wake the sleeper.

I chose that moment to switch on the light and step forward.

He whipped round and levelled his weapon point blank at my head.

I had no fear that he would fire, however. "Good-evening, Colonel Katona," I said, in as even and firm a tone as I could command. "That is only a dummy figure which I put there. I was expecting you."

He lowered the weapon and stared at me as though he could scarce credit his eyes.

"You!" It was all he could get out for the moment.

"Yes, of course, I. Gareth's friend, you know. You see, there is nothing but a sofa pillow here with a rug over it;" and with a show of unconcern, I pulled the rug away.

"You!" he said again, adding: "You who know my child's story. If you have tricked me in this, I will have your life as well."

"If I had tricked you, I should deserve nothing better. You have not been tricked by me, but by others. You may put that revolver away; you will not need it here."

"Why did you say you would send me the news you had promised, and then send me that letter and tell me of this house where he was to be found, and what was to be done here? You are lying to me with your smooth tongue," he burst out fiercely. "You saw me come, or guessed I was here, and you are lying to shield him—the villain who wronged Gareth and would now wrong you."

"If you believe that, kill me. I will not flinch, and you will live to find out the horrible crime you would commit. You will have murdered one who saved and befriended Gareth in the hour of pressing need. It would be a fitting climax that you who helped to drive to a shameful death your friend, Ernst von Dreschler, should now murder me, his daughter."

"Ernst's child! You, his daughter?" he murmured.

"Yes, I am Christabel von Dreschler."

So overwhelmed was he by the thoughts which my avowal caused that he could do little but stare at me helplessly; until he sank down into a chair, as though his strength failed him, and, laying the revolver on the table, leaned his head upon his hands.

I thought it discreet to pick the weapon up and put it out of his reach; and then sat down near him and waited while he recovered self-possession.

His first question was a natural one. "Where is Gareth?"

"Safe, and in my care."

"You can take me to her?"

"She is within an hour's drive; but there is a difficulty in the way. She believes in the honour of—of her husband——"

"Husband?" he burst in eagerly.

"She believes him to be. There was a ceremony of marriage; and believing in him, she would not let me bring her to you, because he had made her take an oath not to do so."

"The villain!" he exclaimed with intense passion.

"I fear that the reason is what you think."

"You know who he is?" The hard eyes were fierce and gleaming as he asked.

"I know who it is not," I answered.

"You know who it is, then?"

"You must not ask me. I cannot tell you yet."

"You shall tell me."

"If you think you can force me, try;" and I faced him, with a look to the full as resolute as his.

"Why won't you?"

"For Gareth's sake. I am thinking of what, in your present desperate mood, you cannot—her happiness."

"I am thinking of her honour."

"No. You are thinking of murder, Colonel Katona. You came here to do it, believing that you knew who had betrayed her."

"He shall pay for it with his life."

"There may be a heavier penalty to exact than that."

"Show me that, and as there is a God it shall be exacted."

"I will show it you, but at my own time and in my own way. No other."

"You are playing with me, and shielding the villain here."

"I am doing neither. The man you seek is not Count Karl."

"You are lying," he cried again vehemently. "See this;" and he drew out a crumpled letter and thrust it toward me.

But I would not look at it and got up. "If I am lying, there is no longer need for you to speak to me of this. If I am not lying, you are a coward to insult me so, even in your passion. Leave the house as you came and probe this for yourself. My servants are within call, if you do not go." I picked up his revolver and handed it to him. "Here is your weapon."

He made no attempt to touch it but looked up at me. "You are a daring girl," he muttered.

"Ernst von Dreschler's daughter does not lie, Colonel Katona," I answered, with deliberate emphasis.

"Forgive me. I spoke out of my mad misery. I will not disbelieve you again. God knows, I am not myself to-night."

"You can trust me or not, as you please. But if you trust me, it will have to be absolutely. I believe I can see a way through this trouble which will be best for Gareth—best for all. It is of Gareth I think in this. She would trust me."

"Let me go to her," he cried.

"Yes, but not yet. It would not be best. She is quite safe, and if you will but have a little patience, I will bring you together and all may be well with her."

"You talk to me of patience when every vein in my body runs with fire."

"I talk to you of Gareth's happiness, and how possibly to spare her—the only way and that but a possible one," I answered, as I put the letter he had offered me in my pocket.

He pressed his hand to his head. "My God, I cannot be patient," he cried, vehemently.

"You could show patience in the slow ruin of your friend, Colonel Katona. Must I remind you of that? I am here to avenge that wrong, and seek tardy justice for his name and mine. You can help me to avenge the wrong and do justice to him, dead though he is. For the sake of my dead father no less than for that of your child patience is needed. I will have my way and no other."

"What do you mean that I can avenge your wrong?"

"You hold the secret that can do all."

"What secret?" And for all his wildness about Gareth and for all his mad rage, my words had touched a secret thought which drove the colour from his tawny face and brought a fear of me into his eyes—fear it was, unmistakably.

"It is enough that I know it," I answered, so curtly and with such concentration that he dropped his eyes as though I might read some secret in them.

I would have given all I was worth to have known what was in his mind at that instant.

In the pause that followed, I heard some one descending the stairs. I knew it must be Karl; and then a daring thought suggested itself.

"You must go, now; I will come to you."

He looked up at me searchingly and keenly, and rose slowly.

"I will go," he said. "I shall see you to-morrow. For God's sake."

"I will come to you. You trust me?"

"I am getting afraid of you—but I trust you."

"I will put that trust to the test now. Count Karl will go with you to your house until to-morrow."

His eyes blazed for a moment. "Do you mean——"

"If he had done you this wrong, should I propose it?"

"I don't understand you. I can't."

"It must be as I say. You will not even speak Gareth's name to him. Remember—not her name even—until I see you to-morrow. Your word of honour on that."

"Yes. I give you my word. But all must be made clear to-morrow. I cannot wait."

"I will go and tell him," I said; and with that went out of the room just in time to prevent Karl entering it.

CHAPTER XVIII

THE COST OF VICTORY

I led Karl into one of the other sitting-rooms.

"I am going to make an appeal to your generosity," I said.

"What has happened? Who was outside the house? What is the meaning of all the mystery? I was thinking myself mad up there and came down to see."

"It is good that you care so much. Two days ago you would have given a shrug of your shoulders, a toss of the head, a lift of the eyebrows, and with an easy smiling 'It doesn't matter,' have left any one else to do the thinking. Don't let your cigar go out; it probably helps you." He was holding a long black cigar such as he had smoked so furiously in the carriage.

"You have given me plenty to make me think," he answered. "But what has happened?"

"I told you—I am going to appeal to your generosity. Not to ask me to tell you everything, but just to accept my explanation."

"I was afraid it was something else."

"What?" I asked not thinking, and so falling into the trap.

"That you should keep what you have not yet returned; that little link with the past—the ribbon favour, Christabel." His eyes were very gentle as he spoke my name.

For a moment I wavered, lowering my head; then taking courage to face what must be faced by us both, I lifted my eyes and, firm in both look and voice, answered him—"It must not be a link. It is no more than a relic. There can be no connecting link with that old time for us two."

"You think that? Perhaps; but I don't;" and he shook his head. "You are very strong, Christabel; but not strong enough for that—not strong enough to change me, at least. It's the only thing in life I care about."

"It must be put aside," I declared.

"Your part is of course for you to decide; but mine is for me. You cannot take my share from me."

"I shall prevail with you. I must. You are going to take your rightful position as your father's heir. You know what is to happen here when the Patriots gain their end. You know what will be expected of you then; and you have to think, not of yourself, not of any mere personal desire, any smaller end, but of your country."

"'Mere personal desire,'" he repeated. "Is that how you read it?"

"It is what your countrymen would call it—your countrymen, who will look to you to do your duty. They must not look in vain."

He made no reply but sat smoking, his brow gathered in deep furrows of thought.

"There are two Count Karls," I continued. "The one who years ago lived a life which made men proud of him, and filled them with trust and confidence in his power and vigour. The real Karl; the man who at the call of patriotism and the counsel of a friend, was even strong enough to let himself be condemned in the eyes of the girl he cared for as cowardly, selfish, and false. That was the real Karl. The other was but an ignoble man; a purposeless parody of the real and true; and he, I thank God, exists no longer. But the noble Karl has to face again to-day the same hard problem he solved so roughly and crudely years ago. With this difference however—the girl knows all now and will help him."

The trouble in his face deepened and he shook his head slowly. "No, no. I cannot."

"Yes, you must. We must, Karl. We don't make our lives; we do but live them."

"I cannot," he repeated, heaving a great sigh.

"We have no choice. I have seen this throughout. If I have helped you—as I love to think I have—to tear aside the coils that were binding you fast to the wheels of ruin, I have done it in full knowledge of all this; of what must be; of what neither you nor I nor we two together, if we were true to ourselves, could possibly prevent. You must not, you shall not be false to your duty and your country."

"No, no. It is too much to ask."

109

"In so far as I have helped you, I have a right to ask you. I press that right with all my power."

His face changed and with a glance of resistance, he answered, quickly:

"It may be easy since you do not care——"

"Karl!" The cry stopped him. His look changed again, and he tossed up his hands and drooped his head.

"I am ashamed," he murmured. "Heaven knows, I have not your strength."

"Don't make that mistake. This is as hard for me as it can be for you. Harder perhaps, for to a woman her heart thoughts must be always more than to a man. Our lives are so much emptier. We need have no concealment now. When I first met you here, I thought—so little does a woman know her heart—that the old feeling was dead; that the long-nurtured resentment of the past had killed it. I was hot against you when you did not recognize me, and burned with indignation. But I did not know."

"Nor yesterday, when we spoke together?" he broke in, eagerly.

"Ah, yes, I began to know then, and to be glad. Not glad with the joy of expected happiness; but so glad that I had been wrong in the years between. But when, to-night, I found this"—and I took out the little ribbon favour—"then indeed I knew all."

He held out his hand. "Give it me."

"Better not, far better not. We must be strong; and this can only be a source of weakness. We will face together that which must be faced and destroy it."

"No," he cried, earnestly. "No. It is mine. I will keep it. Give it me."

"Of what use is it? A mere piece of tawdry faded ribbon when I have given you all my heart."

"Christabel!" His outstretched hand fell as he spoke.

I crossed to his chair and stood by him and laid my hand on his shoulder, looking down into his face. "You will be strong, Karl. I trust you to destroy it;" and I held it out to him.

Instead of taking it he seized my hand and pressed his lips upon it. "If I lose you, I shall go back to what I was," he said, holding my hand and looking up.

I shook my head and smiled. "I have not so little faith in you as that. I, like your countrymen, appeal to the real Karl, and I know we shall not appeal in vain. You have a noble part to play in life, and you will play it nobly as becomes you—and I shall watch you play it, proud to think that I have helped you to be worthy of it and of yourself."

"My God, I cannot give you up," he cried, desperately. "I cannot

110

go back to the lonesomeness of those years. You don't know what they have been to me—desolate, empty, mournful, purposeless. If you bring them back to me after this, I—Christabel, you must not."

"Is that weakness worthy of you or of me?"

"You don't understand. It was bad enough and black enough when my only thought was that I had had your love and had wantonly killed it; that was purgatory. But now, meaning to do well, what have you done but ill? You have shown me happiness, only to shut the gates upon me and drive me out into the black misery again. If you love me, you will never do that—you could not."

I went back to my seat. "You make this very hard for me—for us both. So much harder than it need be. You had better go now, and leave this where it is. Yet I had hoped."

"Hoped what?"

"That I could help you to be strong enough to do the only right thing. And you kill my hope by thinking only of yourself. I would have had you act from the higher motive; but if you will not, the fault is not mine. You force me to say what must be said. Decide as you will, it can make no difference. I can never be to you what you wish: and what, were things other than they are, I would wish with my whole heart. But I could have been your friend—and that you make impossible."

"Christabel!"

"I mean it. I could never be the friend of a man who would set a woman above his duty and his honour, even though that woman were myself. I thought so much better of you."

"You are hard and unjust to me," he cried.

"No no. I am hard to myself, but only just to you. But let it be as you will."

He rose and began to pace the room.

"You had better go. I have failed with you; and failing, must lose all I had wished to win—my own purpose and all. I shall not see you again. You have made it impossible. I shall leave Pesth to-morrow—with all my efforts failed."

"No," he burst out almost violently, stopping close and facing me. "If you go, you know how it will be with me."

I looked at him firmly, and after a pause said in a deliberate tone: "If you cannot rise to the higher life, what matters to your country if you fall to the lower. And as with your country, so with me."

The words cut him till he winced as in pain, and dropped again into a seat.

"Can you say that—to me?"

My heart was wrung at the sight of his anguish, but I would not let him see it. "You had better go—please," I said; for the silence became intolerable.

He paid no heed to my words, but sat on and on in this attitude of dejected despair; and when after the long silence he looked up his face was grey with the struggle, so that I dared not look into his eyes for fear my resolve would be broken and I should yield. For firm as my words had been, my heart was all aching and pleading to do what he wished.

"You need not turn your eyes from me, Christabel," he said, a little unsteady in tone. "You have beaten me. It shall be as you say; although I would rather die than go back to the desert. Pray God the victory will cost you less than it costs me to yield."

I think he could read in my eyes what the cost was likely to be to me: I am sure my heart was speaking through them in the moment while my tongue could find no words.

"I knew you would be true to yourself," I said at length.

"No, anything but that. No credit to me. I only yield because to resist means your abandonment of what you hold so dear. That must not be in any case."

"Whatever the reason, your decision is right. Your country——"

"No, that has nothing to do with it. Less than nothing, indeed. You and I must at least see the truth clearly. I have no sympathy with the Patriot movement. I have never had. That has always been the cause of dispute with my family. I hold it all to be a huge mistake and folly. I am doing this for you—and you only. Now, more than ever, I shall hate the cause; for it has helped to rob me of—you."

I had no answer to that—indeed, what answer could I have made except to pour out some of the feelings that filled my heart, and thus have made things harder for us both.

He sat a moment, as if waiting for me to speak, then sighed wearily and rose. "I had better go now, as you said. I suppose now you will let me see you again."

"Of course. To-morrow. Meanwhile, until I do see you, I wish you to go somewhere and not show yourself."

"All places are alike to me—again," he replied, with dreary indifference.

"I wish you to go and stay with Colonel Katona, and stay in his house until I send to you."

"Colonel Katona! Is he here? Why?"

"His daughter is my friend. It was he who came to the window to-night, seeking news of her."

"Has he a daughter? I didn't know. But why look for her here of all places in the world?"

"I will tell you the story another time. It is mixed up now with mine. But I do not wish you to speak of her to her father."

"She is nothing to me; I can promise that easily enough."

I touched the bell, and told James Perry to have the carriage brought at once to the door.

"When shall I see you? To-morrow, really? You know the danger."

"That danger is past," I said, firmly.

"You have more confidence in me than I have."

"After to-night I shall never falter in that confidence."

"I thank you for that, Christabel, I shall try;" and he smiled. As he withdrew his eyes they fell upon the wisp of ribbon lying on the table. He picked it up, gazed at it, then raised it to his lips and laid it again on the table. "You still wish this to be destroyed?" he asked, keeping his gaze averted.

Simple as were the words and the act, I could not find an answer on the instant. "It is best so," I murmured at length.

"Very well," and he turned away. "You are always right. Of course, it's only—folly and—and weakness."

We heard the carriage drive to the door then. He started and held out his hand; then as if with a sudden thought, he said; "I had forgotten about you. I am so self-wrapped, you see. What are you going to do?"

"I shall stay here to-night."

"Is it safe, do you think?"

"I have my servants here."

"Besides, you are so fearless yourself. Good-night. It is all so strange. I feel as if I should never see you again. And I suppose in a way that's true. As things are to be in the future, it won't be you, in one sense. You said there were two Karls—and now there are to be two Christabels. That sounds like a bad joke, but it feels much more like a sorry tragedy;" and he sighed heavily.

He went out then to the carriage, and I to fetch Colonel Katona to join him.

When they had driven off I went back into the room and sat down feeling dreary and anguish-sick. I was tired out, I told myself; but no bodily weariness could account for the ache in my heart. I had succeeded in all far beyond my expectations; had won my victory with Karl; I was almost within sight of the goal which had seemed impossible of attainment only a few days before. I had every reason to rejoice and be glad; and yet I laid my head on my arms on the table feeling more desolate, sorrow-laden, and solitary than ever in all my life before.

My servant roused me.

"What is it, James?"

"Is there anything I can do for you, miss? I knocked five times before you heard me. Can I get you something?"

"No, thank you, James. I am only tired and am going to bed. Stay up until your father comes back with the carriage. Then go to bed yourself, but let him sit up for the rest of the night. I shall sleep more soundly if I know some one is watching. You must be up early, as I shall need you."

I yawned as if I were very sleepy—one has to keep one's end up, even before one's servants—and bade him good-night. I was turning from the room when my eye chanced on the ribbon favour which Karl had left lying there.

Fortunately James had left the room; for the sight of it struck all thought of pretence out of my mind. I was very silly; but it seemed in an instant to rouse a vivid living consciousness of all that I had voluntarily given up, and yet might have retained by a mere word.

I was only a girl then indeed; and the tears came rushing to my eyes and set the little ribbon dancing and quivering and trembling in my sight.

I dashed them away and, thrusting the little mocking token into my bosom, I ran out of the room as hurriedly as though I were rushing to escape from the sad thoughts of that other Christabel of whom Karl had spoken.

CHAPTER XIX

A TRAGI-COMEDY

The following morning found me in a saner mood once more, and I lay for an hour thinking and planning.

I hold that there are narcotics for mental pain just as for physical; and if the mind is healthy and the will resolute, one can generally be found. I had to find one then.

I did not make the mistake of attempting to underrate my loss. I knew I had had to give up what I prized more than anything in life. I loved Karl with my whole heart; I knew indeed that I had never ceased to love him. The sweetest future which Fate could have offered me would have been to pass life by his side as his wife.

But the pain of knowing that this was impossible was now mingled with other emotions which tended to relieve it. There is always a pleasure in self-sacrifice, no matter how dear the thing renounced. I found a sort of subtle comfort now in the thought that I had been strong enough to do the right thing; to put away from me firmly the delights I would have given half my life to enjoy; to act from a higher motive than mere personal desire.

The sense of self-denial was thus my mental narcotic; and I sought with all my strength to dwell upon the intense gratification of the knowledge that I had been instrumental in helping Karl at the crucial crisis of his life. His country had need of him; and that he would now play his part manfully, would be in a degree my work. That was my consolation.

I could claim truthfully that no selfish motives had swayed me. The clearance of my father's good name had ceased now to be more than a solemn duty to him. The loss of Karl had rendered me indifferent to any considerations merely personal to myself.

In regard to Gareth, too, my chief desire was to see justice done her. Accident, or perhaps rather Fate, had put into my hands the weapons with which to fight the man who was menacing both her and me; and I could claim to have made no selfish use of them. The thought of her brought back with it the necessity to gather up the threads and carry my purpose to success. The end was not far off now.

I had first to anticipate what Count Gustav would do after the stroke he had meant to deal the previous night. I was convinced that he had plotted nothing less than that Colonel Katona should kill Karl under the belief that he had wronged Gareth.

I could follow the steps which had led to this. When, at Madame d'Artelle's, I had let Count Gustav see the Colonel alone, he had given a false message that I would send the information. Having thus prepared him to expect news, he had written him in my name that the man who had wronged Gareth was about to marry another woman, and had given such details of the elopement as would enable the Colonel to witness it and thus identify the man he sought.

This explained something that had puzzled me—why the pretence of the elopement had been persisted in when my apparent departure had destroyed the necessity for any such secrecy. The elopement had become a vital part of the subtle scheme to reveal Gareth's betrayer to her father.

Then to give countenance to it all, Count Gustav had sent as if from me the letter of Gareth's which the Colonel had brought with him and given to me. I read it now. It was to Count von Ostelen, of course; and in it Gareth poured out her tender heart to the husband she knew and addressed as Karl.

It was a cunningly planned scheme; and had Madame d'Artelle really come to the villa, it would almost certainly have succeeded. But the question now was—What would be Count Gustav's next move?

He would believe that Karl was dead—assassinated by the Colonel in his frenzy. That started another suggestion. If murder had been done, all in the house would have been implicated; and Count Gustav was quite capable of using the deed for a further purpose. He would have had the Colonel arrested for the murder and so prevented from causing further trouble; and he would also have got rid of Madame d'Artelle, the accomplice he had used for his brother's undoing, by charging her with complicity in the crime. His path would then have been free indeed.

He had frightened me away from the city, as he believed; and if I ever returned it would be only to find everything buried in that secrecy which those in power and high places know how to secure.

What would he do when he came to the house and found me there alone and helpless to resist him? I could not doubt for an instant. I should be arrested on some charge and shut up until I disclosed to him Gareth's whereabouts and everything I knew of the matter.

I would act on that presumption—except that I would force his hand in one direction and safeguard myself in another.

I rose and dressed myself hurriedly. I knew Madame d'Artelle's handwriting, and with great pains I imitated it as closely as I could in a brief, but to him very significant note.

"For Heaven's sake come here at once. A terrible thing has happened. I am beside myself with horror.

"HENRIETTE D'ARTELLE."

The writer's distracted state of mind would account for any discrepancies in the handwriting; and I succeeded at the third or fourth attempt in producing something like a resemblance to her signature.

This letter I sent by James Perry; and with it another to General von Erlanger.

I gave him the address, "Unter den Linden," and wrote:—

"I shall probably be in great danger here at about eleven o'clock this morning. Will you be near this house at that time so that at need the servant who brings this may find you and bring you to me. You will please know nothing except that you have been asked to come to your former governess who is in trouble.

"Your friend who trusts in you,

"CHRISTABEL VON DRESCHLER."

I told James to get an answer from his Excellency; and despatched him upon his errand at an hour which I calculated would bring Count Gustav to the house by about ten o'clock. I allowed an hour for the interview to reach the crisis to which I intended to work.

In the meanwhile, I told the elder Perry to drive to my own house and ascertain that all was well with Gareth.

Then I went into the room in which Colonel Katona had been and pulled down the blinds, closed the shutters and drew the curtains so that it should be as dark as possible; and coming out locked the door behind me and put the key in my pocket.

Having thus set matters in train I sat down and made an excellent breakfast, anticipating considerable enjoyment from the little comedy I had designed.

I was going to fool Count Gustav and then anger and mystify him. He was, I knew, a dangerous person to play tricks with; but I had no cause to be afraid of him. I was quite prepared to be arrested, and I wished to lull his suspicions and foster his over-confidence.

Thinking things over, another point occurred to me. If the two Perrys remained in the house, they would be arrested with me. Therefore, when the father returned with the good news that all was well with Gareth, I sent him home at once and told him not to come back.

James Perry arrived just before ten o'clock. He brought me a very satisfactory assurance that the General would do just as I asked; and said that the Count Gustav had told him he would come to the house immediately.

"Now, James, things are going to happen here this morning," I said, explaining an idea which had occurred to me. "I shall probably be arrested, and you will share that arrest if you are in the house. You are a very shrewd, quick-witted fellow, and you must manage not to be seen, but to remain near enough to the front of the house to hear a window broken. I may not be able to show myself at the window and signal to you; but I am sure to be able to manage to throw something through the window; and the moment you hear the crash of the glass, you are to fetch General von Erlanger to me, and then hurry off to my house."

I calculated that it would be a very simple matter for me to pretend to fly into a passion at the moment of any crisis, and to so work myself up that it would seem a natural enough thing for me to hurl something solid at Gustav and, missing him, to break the window. I looked round for a suitable missile, and selected a very solid glass ink bottle.

Count Gustav kept his word and arrived a few minutes after I had sent James Perry away. I had left the front door partly open, so that he might not have to ask for Madame d'Artelle; and he walked right in, tried the door of the room I had locked, and then entered that where I was waiting for him.

His surprise at seeing me was complete. Had I been a ghost, he could not have stared at me in greater amazement.

"Good-morning, Count Gustav, I am glad you have come."

"Where is Madame d'Artelle?" he asked, very sharply.

"It is scant courtesy not to return my greeting. You are probably so surprised as to forget your manners. You had better find her for yourself," and affecting irritation, I turned away and picked up a book.

"Good-morning, Miss—what name shall I use now?" he replied with a sneer.

"You may use either Gilmore or von Dreschler as you please. Names are of small account after what has happened here."

"Where is Madame d'Artelle?"

"She has done that which might be expected of her in a crisis like this—run away. She is probably across the frontier now."

"But I have just had a letter from her begging me to come here at once; written evidently in great agitation."

"There are enough hours in a night to allow of many short letters being written. She was intensely agitated when she fled!"

"You seem to be cool enough."

"My nerves are of a different order from hers. Besides, I have nothing to fear in all this."

"How is it that you are here at all?"

"I am not Madame d'Artelle, and therefore not accountable for my actions or movements to you."

"You left Pesth yesterday—when did you return?"

"If you consult a time table you can see at what hours the trains reach the city, and can judge for yourself which I was likely to be in."

"You can answer me or not, as you please," he said angrily; "but you will have to account for your presence here."

"Why?" and I looked at him meaningly. He passed the question off with a shrug of the shoulders.

118

"That is your first mistake, Count Gustav. You must keep your temper better than that, or it will betray you."

He affected to laugh; but there was no laughter in his eyes.

"Well, if Madame was only fooling me with her letter I suppose I may as well go again," he said lightly.

"You know that you have no thought of going. Why are you afraid to put the questions which are so close to your lips?"

I was getting my thrusts well home each time, and was goading him to anger, as well as starting his fears of me.

"Why was that letter written?"

"Because of what has happened here."

"What has happened?"

"Yes, that is one of the questions. I can tell you." I paused and added slowly: "The man you sent here came to do the work you planned."

He bit his lip hard, and his hands gripped the back of the chair behind which he stood. "You delight in mysteries, I know," he sneered.

"Your sneer does not hide the effect of my news, Count Gustav. You know there is no mystery in that for you—and there is none for me. Put your second question."

"What do you mean? I don't understand you."

"That is not true. You want to ask me where your brother is."

"I'll ask that or any other if you wish," he replied, attempting a jaunty, indifferent air. "Where is he?"

"God have more mercy on you than you had on him. You have already seen the answer to your question in the drawn blinds of the room where you last saw him alive."

Strive as he would he could not but shrink under my words and tone. His fingers strained on the chair back, his breath laboured, his colour fled, and his eyes—those hardy, laughing, dare-devil eyes—fell before my gaze. He had to pause and moisten his lips before he could reply.

"If you mean that any harm has come to him," he said, speaking at first with difficulty and hesitation, but gathering firmness as he proceeded; "there will be a heavy reckoning for some one. Who is in the house beside you?" He did not dare to look up yet.

"You coward!" I cried, with all the contempt I felt.

This stung him to fury. "If you have had a hand in this and seek to shield yourself by abusing me, it will not help you. I tell you that."

"Seek to shield myself! I should not stoop to seek so paltry a shield as you could be, whether you were white with fear or flushed with selfish purpose. I do not need a shield. I know the truth, Count Gustav. I know all your part in it, from your motive to the final consummation of your treacherous plan. And what I know to-day, all Austria, all the world, shall know to-morrow."

That was enough. He looked up then, his eyes full of hate of me. I saw his purpose take life and shape in his thoughts. If with safety to himself, he could have struck me down as I stood facing him, he would have done it; but he had what he believed a safer plan in his mind. To have me imprisoned and the secret buried with me.

His new purpose gave him clearer directness of thought at once, and he began to work toward it cunningly. "I can understand and let pass your wild sayings at such a moment, Miss Gilmore. Such a thing as this has, of course, unstrung you..."

"Oh, it is to be a madhouse, is it," I broke in, interpreting for him his secret thought. "I had expected only a prison. You cannot do it, Count Gustav. I am prepared."

But my jeer did not move him. The force of his first surprise was spent, and he was now close set upon the use he intended to make of my presence. He knew the peril which my threat held for him.

"It is singular under the circumstances that you regard yourself in danger of imprisonment, Miss Gilmore; I hope not significant. If you would like to offer any explanation, it is of course open to you to do so."

"I think it probable that there will be an explanation before you leave, Count Gustav; but what in particular should I explain now?"

"We shall require one of—what you say has happened here. Who is in the house?"

"Myself and the servants."

"The manservant was sent away and his place taken by another. By whose orders?"

"Mine."

"I shall need to see him."

"Like Madame d'Artelle, he has gone."

"He was here last night?"

"Certainly."

He shrugged his shoulders. The answer suited him admirably. "He was in your employ," he said, drily.

"I have nothing to conceal," I replied, putting as much doggedness into my manner as a guilty person might have used at the first glimpse of the net closing round him.

"It is a very grave case."

"I can see that—but I know who did what was done as well as who instigated it."

"You were a witness of it, you mean?"

"Of course I mean nothing of the kind. I did not see the blow struck; but I was not asleep at the time; and the instant the alarm was given I was on the spot, and I can identify all concerned."

"Who do you say struck the blow?"

"I did not say. But you know perfectly well the man you sent here to strike it. And so do I."

"You actually charge me with being concerned in having my own brother assassinated?" he cried with well assumed indignation. "It is infamous!"

"Infamous, of course—but true."

"I mean such a charge, madam," he declared, sternly. "I will speak no further with you. You will of course remain here until the agents of the police arrive."

"I have no wish to leave. I tell you I am innocent."

"You at least are found here alone; you admit having fled from the city yesterday and returned surreptitiously; you brought your own man here and sent my brother's away; you have a motive strong enough to account for all in your resentment of my brother's treatment of you; and you seek to put the foulness upon me with an elaborate story that you know the man who did this to have been brought here by me."

"It has a very ugly look, I admit—but there is a flaw in it, none the less."

"That is for others to investigate, madam. I will go to the room. It is locked. Where is the key?"

I took it from my pocket and handed it to him.

"Another significant fact," he said, as we went out of the room and crossed the hall. "I will go in alone."

"No, I have a right to be present."

"It is most unseemly; as unseemly as your smile. My poor Karl." He spoke as if he were genuinely dismayed at the blow, sighed deeply, paused to brace himself for the task, and then entered.

The room was gloomy enough to make it impossible to see anything clearly; but I had arranged the sofa pillow on the couch and covered it with the rug.

He was really affected; although not in the way he intended me to believe. He crossed slowly to the couch and stood by it, as if lacking courage to turn back the rug.

I went to the window and drawing the curtain let the blind up and the sunlight in.

He was now very pale, and his hands twitched restlessly.

"You do not dare to look on the brother whose murder you planned," I said, with cold distinctness.

"How dare you say that, at such a time, madam," he cried fiercely; and taking the rug he turned it back gently.

121

I laughed.

The laugh so enraged him that he tore off the rug and swore a deep, heavy oath.

"What does this mean?"

"That I think we may pull up the rest of the blinds and open the windows and let the fresh air in;" and with another laugh I did as I said.

I turned to find him overcome by the sudden reaction from the strain and the new problem I had set. He was sitting on the couch with his face buried in his hands.

CHAPTER XX

MY ARREST

I stepped out into the sunlight glad of the fresh air in contrast to the dismal closeness of the room. I was quite willing to give Count Gustav a few minutes in which to puzzle over the reasons for the trick I had played him.

He would be quite sure that I had some deep purpose in it all. You can always gamble on it that cunning people will credit you with cunning; and I had said enough to him to cause him profound uneasiness.

It took him longer than I had expected to decide upon his next step; for I had already anticipated what that step would be. He would go through with the plan of having me arrested. I was certain of that; because it was the only means, short of murdering me, by which he could ensure my silence.

But the pretext for the arrest was now so flimsy that in making it he would have many difficulties to face—especially when I brought General von Erlanger on to the scene of action. But before I did that, I had some very pointed things to say.

I was perfectly easy in mind now as to the result of the trouble. I was going to win. I felt it. I could afford to be confident; and I took great care that he should see this for himself.

I knew presently that he was watching me closely, so I began to sing light-heartedly. I flitted about from bush to bush and gathered a little bouquet of flowers; and spent some minutes in arranging them, holding them at a distance and viewing them critically with my head on one side—for all the world as though their arrangement were just the one thing that fully engrossed my thoughts.

Then I carried them into the room and touched the bell, telling the woman who answered it to bring me some water; and as I placed them in a vase I said, as if to myself, and with a nonchalant laugh: "They will brighten up my cell wonderfully."

The little prick of the words irritated him and he scowled.

"I am surprised people call you Gustav of the laughing eyes," I bantered. "You are very handsome, of course, but I have never heard you laugh really gaily."

He forgot sufficiently to swear; and I pretended to be greatly shocked. "I hope you are not going to be violent; but I thought it just as well you should know there is a woman in the house, and that she should see you. Have you got over your disappointment yet—or do you think the body is in the sofa pillow?"

It was aggravating of course; the truth, flippantly suggested, frequently is; and he was in that mood when small jibes galled.

"You are right in the suggestion—I am thinking what may have been done with my brother's body."

He thought this would scare and frighten me but I only laughed. "No you are not. You are thinking only how you can connect me with what didn't occur?"

"Where is my brother?"

"Didn't I tell you that Madame d'Artelle fled last night; and did I say she went alone?"

"I don't believe you," he growled, sullenly.

"'Of the laughing eyes,' indeed," I cried, with a shrug. "Your laughter seems to be dead, even if your brother is alive—perhaps it is because of that."

He very nearly swore again; but he was recovering his wits, if not his temper, and managed to sneer instead.

"The oath would have been more natural," I said, promptly. "But since you are shaking off some of your chagrin, you may be ready to listen to me. I have something to say—to propose."

"I ought not to listen to you."

"There is time—until the police come, at any rate. I will confess to one crime—forgery. I wrote that letter to you in Madame d'Artelle's name. I wished to bring you here at once; and I prepared, carefully, this little stage effect for your benefit. Shall I tell you why?"

He waved his hand to imply indifference.

"No, you are not indifferent, Count Gustav. I wished you to understand how really dangerous I am to you—as well as to witness

123

your brotherly grief at seeing Count Karl's dead body"—and I touched the sofa pillow.

He was able to smile now with less effort, and his lip curled contemptuously.

"I am dangerous—although I can jest. Your brother is safe, quite safe, where you will not think to look for him. I knew what you purposed to do, and I alone prevented it. You don't believe me. I will give you proofs. Two days ago when we were at Madame's house you went to Colonel Katona to tell him I was too indisposed to see him, and you came and told me you had said that. You did not say that. On the contrary you told him I would send him the information he needed of the identity of the man who had wronged Gareth."

"It is an easy tale," he said, with a shrug.

"Yes, easier than you frequently find it to tell the truth. You yourself sent in my name the proofs which the Colonel needed—one of the letters which Gareth—little, trusting Gareth,—had written to you, believing you to be your brother—Karl, Count von Ostelen."

"It is false."

"I have the letter;" and I held it up before him.

I got right home with that blow, and all the malignant cruelty in him was expressed in his eyes as he made a quick but futile attempt to snatch it from me.

"It is only another of your forgeries," he said.

"Gareth will not deny it;" and at that he winced. "You did not name your brother—that was too open a course for you—but you told Colonel Katona that the man was going to run away with another woman; and you named the hour and the place where he might be seen—last night in the Radialstrasse at nine o'clock—and that they were coming to this house—'Unter den Linden.' Do you still say it is false?"

He made no reply, but sat with a scowl tugging at his long fair moustache.

"When you led your brother to the carriage last night, you looked about you to make sure that the Colonel was there; and as the carriage started, he spoke to you and asked if the man he had seen you put in the carriage was indeed your brother Karl."

He shrugged his shoulders again. "You may as well go on."

"I am going on. Fearing lest, even at the last moment, the plan should miscarry, you came here yourself; and yourself, finding your brother lying nearly unconscious on the couch, opened the window so that the watcher in the garden might see where his helpless victim lay; and then—you left the window open to make his entrance easy and certain."

"You tell a story well," he said, when I paused. "I told you once before you should write plays. You have admirable imagination." He was quite himself again now. He spoke lightly, lit a cigar, and took a couple of turns across the room.

"It appears to have interested you."

"Naturally. I suppose now I can pick up the rest from what you said before?"

"Yes. The sofa pillow has done duty before."

"A very likely tale, of course—and your witnesses?"

"No one knows all this except myself."

"Very fortunate—for them, if not perhaps for you."

"There is nothing fortunate or unfortunate in it. It is the result of my intention. I alone hold the secret, and can make terms with you for keeping it."

"I had scarcely dared to hope that. What are your terms?" He put the question in a bantering tone.

"Last time I mentioned three conditions. Two of them are pointless now, because Madame d'Artelle has fled and your brother is aware of your—shall I term it, policy?"

"I am not much concerned at your phrases," he snapped.

"These are no mere phrases. The third condition stands—you must make Gareth your wife, legally."

"Well?"

"And the fresh condition is that the mystery of my father's ruin is cleared at once, and justice done to his name."

"And if I refuse, I suppose you are going to bring all these trumped-up charges against me. It is almost laughable."

"I do not think many people will see much humour in it."

"Possibly not—but then they may never have an opportunity of hearing the story. You have been very clever—I pay you that compliment—but you have also been very foolish. You should have made sure that there was more than your word for all this."

I gave a little half-nervous start, as though I realized my mistake, and then said, quickly: "I have evidence—this letter of Gareth's."

"You will not have it long, Miss von Dreschler. I could almost be sorry for you; in fact I sympathize with you deeply. Your belief in the imaginary story of your father's wrongs has, I fear, preyed upon your nerves until they have broken down. He deserved his fate, as the murderer of the young Count Stephen; and now you come here to threaten first my brother and then myself. As the daughter of such a man, it was perhaps to be expected; but it is quite sad."

"Are you not forgetting what you said when we last spoke of the subject?"

"Oh, no, not in the least. I said then that I would do my utmost to help you—knowing of course that no help in such a matter could be given. The truth can only be the truth; but I hoped that time and thought and kindness would lead you to see your delusion. I fear I was wrong."

I would have laughed, had I not known that I had now to show signs of nervousness.

"And Gareth?"

"You appear to have hidden that poor girl; but she will of course be found and then she too must be convinced of your unfortunate delusions."

"And will no appeal to your chivalry avail to make you do justice to her? You said you cared for her."

"I was anxious, and I think, rightly anxious, to soothe what I saw was a cause of serious and therefore dangerous excitement in you. She also has misled you; no doubt inadvertently; and your prejudices against my family have warped your judgment until you are really incapable of seeing anything but what is black in me. I am truly distressed for you, believe me." His assumption of pity was almost too much for my sense of humour.

"If by black you mean dishonour and cowardly treachery, I agree. I think you are one of the vilest men that ever lived."

He smiled blandly and spread out his hands. "I am afraid you do; it is very painful. Happily, others know me better."

I heard a carriage drive up rapidly, and understood that the crisis had come with it. I glanced at the clock. It was a quarter past eleven. I had timed matters aptly.

I rose, my hand on the inkstand which I had kept all the time in readiness.

"So far as we are concerned now and here, Count Gustav, there is no more to be said. I will take my story to those who will know how to investigate it."

"I am deeply sorry, but you cannot be allowed to leave the house. Those are the agents of the police."

Footsteps and men's voices were in the hall.

"They dare not keep me here!"

"While your delusions remain, I fear they will not let you go. But if you give me that letter, I will do what I can for you."

"If I could believe you," I cried with agitation; and I took another paper from my pocket.

"I should like to be your friend, and will," he said, hurriedly.

I gave him the false letter, and cried, "I can escape this way. Detain them here."

126

I ran towards the window, tripped intentionally, and half-falling flung the inkstand through the glass.

"Stop," cried Gustav, in a loud voice. "This is not what I want."

The crash of the glass brought the men into the room, and one of them ran and placed himself between the window and me.

Glancing out, I saw James Perry pass the house, running at full speed. My ruse had succeeded. The signal had been heard, although Gustav suspected nothing, and all I had now to do was to waste a little time while I waited for his Excellency.

I took advantage of my apparent fall to thrust Gareth's letter into my bosom. Brutal as the police might be, they still had women searched by women; and my one piece of tangible evidence was safe for the time.

I got up, holding my handkerchief to my hand, as though I had cut it in falling, and sitting down breathed hard, as one does in pain or agitation.

"This lady attempted to escape by the window, Lieutenant Varga, and has apparently hurt herself in consequence," said Count Gustav, to the man who was seemingly in charge of the party.

It was best for me of course to say nothing; so I just gripped my hand and swayed backwards and forwards in imaginary pain.

"It is a case for us then, Excellency?" asked the man.

"Let your men see that this lady does not leave the room, and I will explain the matter to you as we go over the house."

Nothing could have suited me better. The two left the room, and I threw myself on the couch. I did not care thirty cents what story he concocted.

They were absent a few minutes, and the official returned alone, bringing my hat and cloak.

"I shall have to ask you to accompany us, madam," he said, with some touch of pity in his tone. "I have no doubt all can be explained. But you have a letter I must ask you to give me."

"I shall not give it you. And I shall not go with you."

"You will only make my duty more painful by refusing."

"I can't help that."

He signed to his men, and as they came and stood by the couch I heard another carriage drive up to the door.

"On second thoughts, I will go with you," I said, and got up.

"I am obliged to you," was the reply, with a grave bow. He waited while I put on my hat. I was really listening for General von Erlanger's voice. I heard it at length.

"I am ready," I declared; and he opened the door, only to start back in surprise and to draw himself up stiffly as his Excellency entered.

"What is this?"

"Ah, I am glad your Excellency has arrived in time to see me being arrested as a lunatic," I said, sweetly, as I put my hand in his. "Good-bye."

The General gave me first a grim smile, and then glanced round at the police officials.

Count Gustav, not knowing who had arrived, came in then, and the General turned to him slowly, but with instant appreciation of the position.

It was indeed a very interesting situation; and Count Gustav looked exceedingly uncomfortable.

CHAPTER XXI

HIS EXCELLENCY TO THE RESCUE

I have said somewhere that I did not take General von Erlanger's importance at his own estimate of it; but what occurred that morning might well have induced me to reconsider that opinion. Certainly none of those present in the room shared it. They all, including Count Gustav himself, stood in considerable awe of him.

A slight wave of the hand sent Lieutenant Varga and his men out of the room; and until they had gone and the door closed behind them, not another word was spoken.

I threw my cloak over the back of a chair, sat down, and began to study Count Gustav's face. He stood leaning against a cabinet, alternately frowning and smiling as he strove to think what line to take.

"Miss von Dreschler is of course my friend." This use of my name chased the smiles away. "I know her to be anything but a lunatic—she is saner than a good many of us, indeed—so that I am sure you would wish to explain this, Count."

"You know her by that name, then?"

"Oh, yes. I know her history."

"Do you know what has occurred in this house?"

"She will tell me in a moment if I ask her."

"Certainly, I will—if Count Gustav desires it," I chimed in.

"She has preferred a very odious accusation against me, General, and has shown such a strange prejudice, as the result of certain delusions she entertains, that I deem it necessary for the state of her mind to be inquired into."

"What is the accusation?"

"Nothing less than that I have endeavoured to compass the death of my brother."

"Yes, that is grave enough and odious enough. To whom has the accusation been made?"

"To me, so far; but she threatens to make it public."

"Surely you do not take such a thing seriously. What could you have to fear from such a charge?" Cleverly said; as though the whole thing were just a monstrous absurdity.

"Nothing, of course; but——" he finished with a gesture to imply that such conduct could not be tolerated by an honourable person like himself.

"Surely you would not wish to shut up a lady in a lunatic asylum for fear she might utter impossible charges against you."

"I believe her to be insane—on that point, of course; however reasonable and clever she may be in other respects."

"My dear Count Gustav, can't you see the extraordinary unwisdom of what you proposed to do? Why, the first effect would be to make every one who heard the charge believe there was some ground for it, and that she was shut away because you were afraid to face the thing. Your high position, your well-known probity, and your acknowledged and admired honour and love of justice render you able to laugh at such a thing. It would fly off from you like a pebble flung at an ironclad and leave no more injury."

Very astute and extremely diplomatic. I had certainly done his Excellency much less than justice. He was making it impossible for my adversary to go any further; and at the same time showing his own admiration of the Count's qualities and his regard for the ducal family.

Count Gustav found himself very awkwardly placed. "That is no doubt true, but I cannot take the same lenient view of the matter. Such things are apt to do much harm in the present disturbed state of public feeling."

"Well, my loyalty to your father, the Duke, and your family are too well-known to be questioned, I hope; and of course, if the matter is pressed, we must do what you wish—have the thing threshed out to the last straw, and the truth proved even to my very wilful young friend here. I have too much faith in her powers of sound judgment to believe for an instant that she would not accept the proofs of truth and appreciate them."

"I wish no more than a full investigation," I agreed; my admiration of his diplomacy mounting. "I may have spoken in haste and may be entirely wrong; and I hope I know how to retire from an impossible position and to withdraw any mistaken statements."

It was admirable comedy. But Count Gustav did not admire it. He saw himself drifting nearer the rapids.

"Do you think you could ask for more than that, Count?" asked the General, blandly.

But the Count stiffened his back. "I have chosen my course and, with all deference to your Excellency, I shall persevere in it. This lady is not to be trusted to be at large."

The General turned to me with an apologetic air. "I am afraid under these circumstances, Miss von Dreschler, I can do no more for you. You will understand that a member of the Duke's family speaks with great influence and power. Let me appeal to you to withdraw these charges now and let the matter end at once."

"No," broke in my adversary. "It has gone too far to end here and now." The General's words had given him confidence.

"Your Excellency sees that a withdrawal would be useless," I exclaimed, with a shrug. "It is not that which Count Gustav desires. It is to shut me up so that I may have no chance of repeating elsewhere what I have said to him. He shrinks from any real investigation."

"Oh." His Excellency was quite pained as he uttered the protest. "Please, please, be careful what you say. There is no such thought in Count Gustav's mind. Everything you wish to say, every charge you mistakenly bring, shall be disproved to your entire satisfaction. You are maligning the most honourable man in Pesth, a member of the most illustrious family. Of course there shall be investigation. Is it not so, Count?"

"I have stated the course I intend to pursue," was the dogged reply.

"Do you wish Varga to deal with the matter?"

"Yes. I have explained it to him."

His Excellency threw up his hands and shook his head. "Dear, dear, I could almost wish I had not answered your letter so promptly, Miss von Dreschler. It is a very distressing matter."

"Oh, she sent for you?" exclaimed the Count, angrily.

"Yes, indeed. Scarcely the act of a lunatic, of course. It was very clever indeed, for it forces the thing to my knowledge. You see, Count, there is another very serious obstacle in your path. Miss von Dreschler is an American citizen—and you know what the Americans are when you twitch only a feather of the big bird. The eagle has a very loud cry, monstrously sharp eyes, and talons that dig deep in unearthing things."

I vowed to myself I would never again doubt his Excellency's shrewdness or his importance. I could have kissed him for the way he played that beautiful check-mate.

The Count was entirely nonplussed for the moment. He could only frown and repeat; "I have chosen my course, and even you cannot stop me, General."

"My dear young Count, you are making things exceedingly awkward. You see the affair is known to me officially; and that is everything. You are too young to appreciate all that this means; but when you are my age and have had my experience, you will see such a thing as I see it."

"I shall of course appeal at once to the United States Consul," I said, quick to take the cue thus indicated.

"You hear that. I was sure of it. No, believe me, Count, this is a matter to be settled in a very different way. You must not act in a hurry. I tell you what we must do. We must all have time to think things over; and to afford the necessary opportunity I will take Miss von Dreschler to my house until to-morrow; and if you will come there, say at noon, we shall no doubt have found a way out."

But this would not suit Count Gustav, I knew; and he held on to his resolve to pursue the course he had chosen.

"My dear Count, I know how your father would act in such a case. We really cannot run the risk of making it a cause of international complication. If you will not accept my suggestion all I can do is to send word to the American Consul and let him have the custody of this young lady. The people at the Consulate will then of course go fully into the affair, everything will be made public, and heaven knows what trouble will come out of it. But it would simply ruin me at Vienna if I were to consent to your wish. It is only a matter of a few hours. Miss von Dreschler will no doubt consent to do nothing for that time; and meanwhile, if you wish it, you and I can go to the Duke."

"There is another way," said the Count, suddenly. "We will go at once to my father and lay the matter before him. He can decide what should be done, and take any responsibility off your shoulders, General."

It was a shrewd move, but the check was obvious. "I agree to that readily, with but one condition—the American Consul must be present to protect me."

His Excellency gave me a quick glance of appreciation. "Oh, yes, of course. The Count will not object to that."

"But I do object. We want no more in this than there are at present."

"Then as an American citizen I claim my rights and the protection of my flag."

"Will you remain here a few minutes?" asked the General; and he led the Count out of the room. They were absent nearly half an hour, and then his Excellency returned alone.

"I have prevailed upon the Count to take my view of what should be done; and if you will give me your word to say nothing of these matters until twelve o'clock to-morrow, you will come with me to my house and remain there until then."

"Then we shall have another game of chess much sooner than we anticipated, your Excellency," I said lightly.

"You play too much chess, young lady, and far too daring a game. I may give him your word?"

"Oh, yes. I have done all I wished here and am ready to go."

"You'll make no effort to escape?" he asked with a twinkle in his eyes. "You are to be a prisoner, you know."

I nodded and laughed, and a few minutes later he handed me into his carriage to drive back to the city.

He was more disposed to think than to talk during the drive, and several times I caught a furtive smile flitting over his face and drawing down the corners of his mouth.

"I'm afraid I have a dangerous prisoner. You have already given me one awkward corner to turn this morning; and I see others ahead."

"I never knew what diplomacy meant until this morning," I replied; "and the cleverness of it quite fascinated me."

"Diplomacy often consists in helping a friend to do what he doesn't wish to do," he said sententiously.

"I suppose, by the way, I am only a prisoner on parole?"

"If you take my advice you will not stir out of my house until we have had the meeting to-morrow."

"Why not?"

"I cannot talk easily in a carriage," he answered, with a glance which I understood to mean that he had strong reasons he preferred not to explain.

I said no more until we reached his house and he took me into his library.

"I cannot give you more than one minute, and therefore cannot wait to hear your story. I have pressing matters that will keep me all the afternoon."

"I have no clothes, your Excellency," I cried, with a little affectation of dismay.

132

"Which means you wish to go out in order to carry on the scheme with which your busy little brains are full. You cannot go out, Christabel—I have said that you will remain here. Understand that, please." He spoke almost sternly; but the twinkle came into his eyes as he turned away and added: "As for your clothes, I had thought of that difficulty, and I told that American servant of yours to call here this afternoon on the chance that you might need him."

I laughed and was running out of the room, saying I would go and find the girls and tell them I had come to spend the rest of the day with them, when I stopped and went back to him. "I haven't thanked you," I said.

"It is not to me that any thanks are due—but the Stars and Stripes. They gave us the mate."

"But it was you who made the move; and it is you I thank."

"The game is not finished yet, Christabel. We'll wait for that."

"I see the combination that will win it."

He took my hand and pressed it. "You deserve to win; but the stakes are almost tragically high, child."

"In chess there is always a king without a throne."

CHAPTER XXII

COLONEL KATONA SPEAKS

I wrote a short note to Colonel Katona saying that circumstances prevented my going to his house that day; but that I had something important to say to him, and wished him to come to me to General von Erlanger's at once.

Next, an equally brief one to Karl:

"DEAR FRIEND,

"I cannot keep my word to see you to-day. I have been compelled to come here, to General von Erlanger's house, and must remain until to-morrow. But to-morrow I shall see you. Please me by staying where you are until then. Colonel Katona is coming here, and will bring you a message from me saying where we can meet to-

133

morrow. I am sure you will do this as you have done so much 'for her sake.'

CHRISTABEL VON DRESCHLER."

Then a letter to Gareth followed:

"I am now confident that I shall have great news for you to-morrow. I have been working hard for you all the time, and success is in sight. But we cannot gain it unless you will now do your part and help me in all my plans for to-morrow. I wish you to remain in your room to-morrow morning, and not to leave it under any pretext whatever, until I myself come to you. You will of course be very curious to know the reason for this: we women can't help that. And I will explain it all to-morrow. You have trusted me so far. Trust me in this also—for I tell you frankly that if you do not, everything even at the last moment may be ruined. Keep a brave heart, for I am very hopeful happiness is in sight for you.
"Ever your friend,
"CHRISTABEL."

Lastly I drew up a concise statement of the whole facts of the case, giving as full details as were necessary to enable any one to understand it clearly, as well as my position in regard to it. This was for James Perry to take to the American Consul if any danger threatened me. I took this step, not because I doubted my friend the General, but lest he should find his wish to help me thwarted by those above him.

I had my papers ready by the time James Perry arrived. I explained first what he was to do with the paper for the Consulate, and added: "Your father will know where to take the letters for Colonel Katona and Count Karl, James, because he drove them home last night. Send him off with them the moment you get back. Give this letter to the Countess von Ostelen; and this list of clothes to your mother. You are to bring them back here to me."

"Yes, miss," he said, as he pocketed them.

"And now I am going to set you a difficult task. You have done me splendid service so far—but you are now going to play me a treacherous shabby, cowardly trick."

"I hope not," he said, noticing my smile.

"You will need all your wits; because a great deal hangs upon how you act—all my plans in fact. You took a letter from me this morning to Count Gustav. Did you see him?"

"Yes, for a moment. He took the letter, laughed and seemed rather pleased, and then gave me the message—that he would go to the house at once."

"You think he would know you again?"

"Oh, yes, I am sure of that."

"Good. Now, you are going to betray me to him. He is desperately anxious to know the whereabouts of the Countess von Ostelen, and you are going to be scoundrel enough to take advantage of my absence from home to tell him where to find her. It will be hard for your mother's son to be a scoundrel, James, I know."

"I hope so, miss, with all my heart."

"But as scoundrels can play at honesty, there's no reason why honest men shouldn't sometimes get a bit of their own back by playing at villainy. You are deeply interested in the troubles of the Countess von Ostelen; you have been shocked by my rather cruel treatment of her; you have heard her ask me again and again to let her leave the house; and your chivalry is roused because I keep her locked in her room. Realize that part of your feelings, and think it over, because that is the sly hypocrisy on the surface of your conduct."

"I am afraid I am a bigger rascal than I thought," he said.

"I am sure you will be to-morrow when you see him. Of course you have another motive—which you understand will be dragged out of you when the Count, who will be suspicious, begins to question you. You want money and a place in the household of the Duke, his father. The dollars will be the main thing. Half the sum down before you open your lips: the rest when you complete the work. That is, the Count is to give it to you when you let him into the house to fetch the lady away."

"What sum should I name?" he asked with a grin.

"I don't think a thousand dollars would be too much for such information; but this is a poor country, so we'll put it at about half that—fifteen hundred gulden. Your honour is worth more than that, James; but, as good Americans, we must gauge the conditions of the market. Take those letters now, and when you come back I will have ready for you a letter in bad German, which you will copy—telling the Count you are my servant and have something pressing on your conscience—hypocrites always have bulging consciences, James— that it concerns a lady who is a prisoner in my house, and that you will pay him a visit to-morrow at half-past eleven. He has a serious appointment here at twelve; but when you tell him that you can get him into my house just after that hour, he will prefer to keep the appointment with you instead of coming here."

"I think I can do it all easily. But what am I to do when he comes?"

"I shall be there to welcome him, James. You must contrive so

135

that you do not reach the house until half-past twelve. You can be a quarter of an hour late in going to him; the interview will last quite half an hour—you will be agitated over your villainy, you know, and will have to drive your bargain; and the ride with him to the house will take another quarter of an hour or twenty minutes. Put him into the small drawing-room which looks on to the garden behind and come to me."

I sent him away then, telling him to think it all over and to ask me any questions necessary when he returned with my clothes.

I drafted a carefully mysterious letter, such as I deemed a scoundrel would write, making much of my conscience, but hinting unmistakably at a money reward; and when he came back we discussed the whole plan in considerable detail.

We were still occupied in this way when Colonel Katona's card was brought to me. I found him looking very haggard and worn with the emotions and incidents of the preceding night; but he held my hand and pressed it very warmly, and the hard eyes as he gazed at me were more like Gareth's than I would have deemed it possible for them to be.

"You have news for me, Miss von Dreschler? It is of my child?" he asked eagerly.

"Yes, it all concerns Gareth, Colonel."

"You are going to take me to her?"

"I hope so—but it will depend upon you."

"Then it is settled—there is nothing I will not do for that;" and he sighed deeply. "Tell me what you wish."

"You find me in a different mood from that of last night. Then I was thinking mainly of Gareth and a little only for myself. Now I am thinking only of myself."

"You saved me from a terrible mistake last night."

"To which you had been tempted by the man who has wronged your child. I sent Count Karl away with you that you might see how deeply you had wronged him in your suspicions."

"I saw that—afterwards; and saw, too, why you knew he was innocent. He speaks of little else but you."

"Count Karl knows the road which duty compels him to take, and he will follow it to the end. He is a changed man."

The Colonel looked at me earnestly for a moment, his expression inscrutable. Then he nodded.

"Yes, he is a changed man; thanks to your influence—only that."

"The cause is of no consequence; it is only the fact that matters."

"You are very strong—for such a child."

"I have a strong purpose, Colonel Katona. I am going to be true to that purpose now with you."

"I am afraid I know what you are going to say."

"To ask plainly whether you will do justice to my father and tell me the whole story of that cruel wrong."

"The whole story?" he asked, anxiety in both look and tone.

"The whole story—nothing less will satisfy me."

He paused in evident distress, and pressed his hand tightly on his forehead. "It cannot be. It is impossible. Count Karl urged me— he of all men—but I told him what I tell you—it is impossible."

"Then you will never see Gareth again." I made my voice as hard and cold as I could.

"I have feared this," he murmured.

"And I, Colonel Katona, have worked for it."

"I cannot, I cannot," he murmured again, love and fear doing desperate battle in his mind. "You are not so cruel."

"I can be as hard as steel in this cause. Hear what I have done. I know, of course, where she is. I know the man who has done her this wrong. I have to-day so planned matters that to-morrow he shall know where to find her. If you do not speak now to help me, I declare to you that to-morrow Gareth shall be again in his arms."

A groan escaped his lips at this, and he bowed his white head as if in an agony of shame.

"Have you no mercy?" he whispered, at length.

"I am thinking of my father and his shame and ruin. You helped to kill his honour and blight his life. You were his friend. Had you mercy then, that you would ask it now of his child?"

"They told me he was dead. I swear that. I did not know the truth until years afterwards—when he had escaped. It was then too late, too late. My God, you know not what this is that you ask me to do."

"I ask for the truth. He trusted you. He has left it on record. You betrayed that trust—for your employers. You set their favour then before your friend's honour, just as now you set it before even the honour of your child."

Every one of my biting violent words went right home. He winced under the pain of them; and when I paused and he glanced up, his face could not have been more stricken had I been his judge sentencing him to death. Nay, I think he would have faced death with far less agitation.

"From you, his child, this is terrible," he murmured. "I have been very guilty; but not as you think. I was not false to your father like that. I will tell you all so far as it touches me. I know now that it was resolved that the young Count Stephen should die; and a quarrel was purposefully caused between him and your father. I was used at first only as a tool in the work. I had reason to know that the Duke Alexinatz was so incensed against your father, that it would go hard with him if he remained in Pesth."

"I know that it was at your persuasion that he made ready to fly from the city."

"It was true what I told him—Duke Ladislas wished him to leave, as otherwise the Duke himself might have been involved in the quarrel. He sent me direct to your father. Up to that point I was true to my friend. I would have given my life for him cheerfully—then."

"And after?"

"Count Stephen did go to your father's rooms in search of him, his blood heated with wine and the lies told by others; and it was there he was shot."

"You knew of this?"

"Nothing, until the next day; and then the story was told me that the two had met and quarrelled fiercely; that my friend had been killed; that the matter must be hushed up in the interests of Duke Ladislas; that he had in reality instigated it, and that loyalty to him made it impossible to speak the truth. Your father had been secretly buried, I was assured."

"I am waiting, Colonel Katona," I said, presently.

"From that point on I was guilty. My silence then was the first act of treachery; and others soon followed. I could not bring the dead to life, I was told, but I could help the living; and in helping them could save from ruin the cause to which I was pledged. The confession by your father was found and used—and I stood by and suffered his name to be dishonoured. For that I can plead no excuse."

"And when you knew that my father had not died but had been imprisoned all those years, and had escaped—what did you do then?"

"I know. I know," he exclaimed, wretchedly. "I did nothing. They came to me——"

"Who came to you?"

"Those who had done it all; and with them Count Gustav to whom all had then been told. They appealed to my loyalty to the cause, to Duke Ladislas, and to my country—and I yielded."

"Count Karl, too?"

"No. He knows nothing of it. Nothing."

"If he had known of all this and you had found the news which you thought had come from me to be true—that the man for whose family you had sinned in this way was the same who had wronged Gareth, what then?"

There was such a glitter in his eyes as they met mine that I almost feared he had read the thought and intent behind my words.

"I would have had his life first and"—he checked himself with sudden effort.

"And what?" I asked.

"I would have killed him," he murmured, doggedly.

"The rest is your secret?" I hazarded. He made no other answer than to glance at me quickly.

"If I tell you to-morrow where to find Gareth, will you make public what you have told me to-day and denounce the men who were concerned in my father's ruin?"

At the direct question he was profoundly agitated again. "Is there no other way?"

"No. None. I am pleading for my father's honour."

"I will do it," he said, with a bitter sigh.

"On your word of honour, Colonel Katona?"

"Yes. On my word of honour. God help me."

I drew a deep breath of relief. I needed no further assurance. I had seen enough to know that what I still had to tell him—that Gustav was the man he sought—would suffice to change any lingering remnant of indecision into grim set purpose.

I told him I would send him word on the following morning where he and Count Karl were to come to me at about noon.

"You will give me your hand, Christabel?" he asked, hesitating, as we were parting.

"Yes. I trust you now to undo the past."

He held my hand a moment and seemed much affected.

"I had meant to speak to you about Count Karl. He——"

"Please!" I broke in.

"If I could help your happiness it would be some recompense for my wrong to your father."

"You cannot do that."

"You care for him?"

"Please," I said again.

"I know. He has told me what stands between you. I am glad now that you made me speak—although your words stabbed me to the heart. But I am glad now—and perhaps I can help you. It should not be all tragedy for you two. But heaven knows it is tragedy whatever happens."

I was glad to be alone. The interview had tried me. I endeavoured to analyze my feelings; and I am afraid I realized that while I was jubilant at the prospect of success, the knowledge that it brought nearer the parting from Karl made me almost wish for failure.

That was rank treachery to my purpose and my dear father's memory, I know. But then, I was only a girl; and after all, even in the strongest of us, the heart will have its way at times. Mine took it then for a desolate half-hour, until I was roused by the two chattering girls who came romping in to take me away to dress for dinner.

CHAPTER XXIII

A GREEK GIFT

At dinner his Excellency was thoughtful and taciturn, and we had a rather dismal meal. He noticed my dress when we met, however.

"You have your clothes, then?" he said in his dryest manner.

"Yes, my servant came to arrange the things I needed."

"I don't wish to know," he exclaimed, promptly, with a glance which showed me that he understood I had not been idle.

But after that he scarcely spoke. The girls chattered to me, chiefly making fun of the new governess before her face in the most impudent manner; but I was too busy with my own thoughts to pay much heed.

Something had happened since the General and I had parted; and I was sure it concerned me; so I waited and watched until either he should tell me or I should find it out for myself.

He sent the girls and their governess away almost before they had finished eating, and took me at once into the little salon where we usually played chess.

"Is it a compliment to me that you have arrayed yourself so?" he asked.

In that moment I seemed to guess what was in his thoughts. "It is perhaps a coincidence," I said with a smile.

"Why a coincidence?" He was puzzled.

"Because I had not expected to see any one but yourself."

He nodded. "That instinct of yours always interests me."

I had gone to the chess board and taken two or three pieces out

140

of the box. I put them back. "So we are not to play chess to-night. Who is it?"

"No, there you are wrong for once. We are to play. I have spoken of your chess-playing powers to a very old friend of mine, and he is coming to see us play."

I shook my head. "Your Excellency means that the game is to be a pretext. What is his name?"

"I am not 'your Excellency' to you, Christabel. It is General von Walther—an old comrade of mine."

"I am getting interested in him already—an old comrade whose unexpected visit made you so thoughtful during dinner that you could scarcely speak a word. On my account, too. The only time you spoke was to express satisfaction that I was dressed well enough to receive him."

"You are building a palace with match boxes, Christabel. You had better set the men."

I set them and we began to play. I made two or three egregiously bad moves; and he did not notice them. The "old comrade" was evidently still absorbing his thoughts; and began to fill mine too.

"Hadn't we better have something more like a real game when he comes in? It should at least look like serious chess," I said, and was making some impromptu changes in the positions of the men when General von Walther was announced.

I shut down the smile which followed my first glance at him. It was too bad of his Excellency to try and deceive me. I had seen the "old comrade" before, however; and I was not likely to forget him. It was Duke Ladislas himself.

They both played up to the arranged parts, and of course I did my best to help them.

"Come in, old friend," said his Excellency, genially. "This is the chess prodigy. My old friend General von Walther, Miss Gilmore."

"His Excellency always flatters me, General, because on one occasion I was lucky enough to beat him."

"I am delighted to meet you, Miss von Dreschler," said the "general," so occupied in giving me a sharp look that he did not notice he had used the wrong name. "You are a great favourite of my old friend."

I made an appropriate reply, and for some minutes we chatted about chess, and the weather, and what I thought of Pesth, and so on—anything except what he must have come to speak about; whatever that was.

Then I challenged him laughingly to a game; but I suppose he

141

was in reality no player at all, for he got out of the challenge by saying he would rather look on.

So we went on with our game again and had made some half a dozen moves, when a servant came to say that Count Somassy, the Minister of Justice, wished to speak with his Excellency. He pretended intense regret for the interruption to our game, begged us both to excuse him for a few minutes, and then the "old comrade" and I were left alone. I knew of course that this had all been arranged; and that we were now to come to the real business of the meeting.

"You are staying some time in Pesth?" he opened.

"I scarcely know. You see I am a foreigner now, and an American citizen is never long away from the States without a heart ache."

"You say 'now,'" he commented, as I had intended. I thought he would appreciate the word.

"Yes. I am Hungarian by birth—but a naturalized citizen of the United States. Here, of course, I am only a girl; but at home, in Jefferson City, Missouri, I am quite a person of importance. I inherited my uncle's fortune, and over there you know we reckon importance by dollars. You would be astonished at the consideration I receive in my travels from all our representatives, consuls, and even ambassadors."

This was not strictly accurate; but the point had to be driven home that he could not play monkey-tricks with me. He did not like this any more than I thought he would, and paused so long that I said: "Shall we not have a game, General, while his Excellency is away? It looks as if his sudden appointment might last some time."

I think he began to gather in that I was not quite fooled by the little entertainment.

"I think not, thank you. The fact is I wish to speak to you on some matters."

"Connected with America?"

"Well, not exactly. Rather of a private character."

I froze instantly and was appropriately dignified. "I don't think I quite understand. In Missouri we don't discuss our private affairs with strangers."

"This is not Missouri," he said, dropping for the moment the "old comrade" tone and using the brief curt note of authority. As an American citizen I resented the tone and rose.

"I am not a school girl, sir, having a lesson in geography." It was intentionally pert and flippant, and I made him a bow and moved toward the door.

"I am sorry. Pray forgive my manner. An old soldier, you know, drops now and again into the drill manner."

"American women do not take kindly to drilling, General."

"No, no, Miss Gilmore; you must acquit me of any intention to offend you. I wish to speak to you seriously. Pray sit down again."

I should have been intensely sorry to have ended so promising an interview, so I sat down and stared stonily at him. He was one of those vulture-faced old men, with a large hook nose, a wide mouth, and a small square chin, which when he spoke suggested irresistibly the moving lower bill of the bird. He had dark, piercing, beady eyes, rather deep set under prominent eyebrows, and a waxen white forehead, rounded like a bird's poll.

"I wish to speak to you about Count Gustav."

"Yes?"

"I am a friend of his and his family, and possess their confidence, and being also a friend of General von Erlanger's, I thought it would be desirable for me to speak with you."

"Yes?"

"As a mutual friend, if I may say so, and an old man of long experience of the world."

"Yes?" I said again, maintaining the same stony stare.

"Count Gustav has told me the facts, and as it is generally the case in these exceedingly private and painful matters a solution satisfactory to both sides can be found by a third disinterested person—where there is a mutual desire to find one, of course—he deemed it best, and I agreed with him, that I should see you and speak plainly and frankly to you."

This time when he paused I bowed merely and said nothing.

"I may take it that you do desire some arrangement? You are silent, but I presume it; because I am convinced so charming a young lady as yourself could not harbour any personal malice against the Count. That would be a monstrous thought. And further, you are so capable, so exceptionally capable and clever, that you cannot have disguised from yourself that to attempt to harm a member of the Ducal family, whatever the motive or supposed facts, would not only end in failure, but also in personal inconvenience, to use no stronger term, to the person making the attempt."

I kept my eyes fixed steadily on him; and my stare and silence began to tell on his temper. I was rather glad to see that.

Getting no reply, he made another long speech about his amiable intentions, my many excellent qualities, his extreme reluctance to see me come to harm, the impossibility of my hurting Count Gustav, and the necessity for an amicable settlement. But he made the threat a little more unmistakable this time—owing possibly to his anger at my stony reserve.

He paused, and we looked at one another in silence.

Then as if he had done with preambles he said: "And now, what is it you want? I invite you to speak frankly."

"'Frankly'?" I repeated, with a nasty little accent on the word. "May I put two questions to you?" He bowed and waved his hands. Like the rest of him they were bird-like and suggested talons. "Do you come to me from Count Gustav or from the Duke himself?"

"I speak for—both," he answered, not without hesitation.

"Then please tell me what is behind your threat of 'personal inconvenience'? What do they intend to do, if I refuse to come to an arrangement? What can they do to me?"

"They are strong enough to frustrate any attack of the kind from you or any one else."

"But what can they do? You are a mutual friend, you know, General;" and I gave him one of my sweetest smiles.

"I have no hesitation in saying you might be in great personal danger, Miss Gilmore."

"I have already reminded you that I am an American citizen."

"You may take it from me that you will be prevented from taking any action of the hostile kind you contemplate."

I smiled again. "I am not in the least frightened, General. I am smiling because you come to me to speak about a mutual arrangement—when you have made up your mind that the only arrangement to be thought of is unconditional surrender on my part. And to force that, you threaten me with unspeakable penalties. We shouldn't call that any sort of arrangement at all, in the States, but merely—pardon the word—bluff."

I was gaining my first point rapidly. He was getting very angry at my opposition and the way I put it.

"I was prepared to find you a very daring young woman; but this thing shall not be allowed to go farther. You reckon on General von Erlanger's help; but he will be powerless here."

I indulged him with a third smile. "You are not quite right there. I have done something else. Knowing the Duke's power and influence might prevent his Excellency from protecting me, I wrote out an account of the matter and have arranged that—if anything unforeseen should happen to me, to-night, for instance—it shall be placed to-morrow morning in the hands of the American Consul. And even against the Ducal family, I will back my Government to keep its end up."

I paused, but he had nothing ready to answer that with; so I continued: "I think you'll agree that that foresight of mine cancels your threat, and that we can start in again on equal terms."

His talons having failed to grip me now gripped one another, and with considerable tension too. His right hand fastened like a vice on his left wrist.

"I did not threaten you, I only warned you. What is it you want?"

"In the first place, fair play—and it is not playing fairly for Duke Ladislas to come to me in the disguise of a mutual friend."

"You know me, then?"

"As well as you know me. Inadvertently, when you entered, you called me by my name—von Dreschler. You know, also, one of the objects I seek—justice for my father's name. That it be cleared from the shame and disgrace foully and treacherously put upon it in the interest of you and your family—the responsibility for a deed of blood of which he was innocent, but which you, or those promoting your interests, instigated, planned, and carried out."

"'Fore God, you speak daringly, madam."

"I speak the truth, my Lord, just as I demand to have justice done. Not demand only, but command it shall be done—for the power to command has been put into my hands by the perfidy and wickedness of your son, Count Gustav."

I looked for an outburst from him in response; but none came. He sat silent, the right talon still gripping the left as though he wished it were my throat.

"I do not know with what motive you came to me," I said after a pause; "unless it was to try and frighten me into silence. But I will deal more frankly with you than you with me. If you have come to offer me less than justice to my father's memory, we are only wasting time; and the interview, painful to both, may as well end right now."

"I offer you that and no less," he answered, and he loosed his wrist to wave his hand as if with a gesture of compliance.

It was my turn to be surprised now; but I was sceptical at so ready a surrender after his threats. "That is glad news, indeed. When will the truth be made known?"

"At once. I will see that it is done. As others have done, you have misjudged me. I see that of course. I have been secretly deemed, I know, to have had some guilty connivance in the death of the young Count Stephen; and in that, have had to bear the blame for the acts of my too zealous adherents. My family profited by their rashness; and so the world held, as it will, that advantage and guilt went hand in hand."

"I seek in that awful matter only justice for my father's memory.

Restore his good name, and who else loses or gains, is nothing to me."

"I pledge myself as to that. The facts shall be drawn up and made public; and further, I will interest myself to secure that the title he held, Count Melnik, shall be restored to you, together with the estate which was confiscated. Full justice shall be done."

"Thank God for that!" I exclaimed, intensely moved.

"To-morrow, my son Gustav is to come here to you, and he shall bring with him full confirmation in writing of what I have now promised you. On that I give you my word."

I leant back in my chair overcome. The knowledge of what I had gained mingled with the poignant regret that my dear father had not lived to share the joy of his vindication brought the tears to my eyes. I could not speak, so mastering was the emotion.

"I will leave you now, Miss von Dreschler," said the Duke as he rose. "When we next meet you will be the Countess Melnik—not that I think you will value such a title except for what it means—the full restitution of your dead father's honour."

He held out his hand, and I rose and gave him mine in silence.

When he had gone I sank back in my chair, elation at my success still battling with that vehement but useless regret that my father had not lived to see that night; and the battle was still being waged when his Excellency entered.

I dashed away my tears.

"I have won," I said, smiling. "I am sure I owe it chiefly to you. The Duke has given me a solemn promise that my father's name shall be cleared."

I looked for a sign of congratulation; but instead, my old friend glanced at me slowly and very shrewdly, and moved on to his chair.

"You are an excellent linguist, but probably do not know the dead languages, Christabel. There is an old tag of Virgil's for instance: 'Timeo Danaos et dona ferentes'."

"I know what that means, at any rate," I cried. "'I fear the Greeks even when bearing gifts.'"

He turned and looked at me again very thoughtfully. Then nodding his head he answered with slow emphasis; "It is possible to learn the meaning of it—even in Pesth."

"You think this is a Greek gift?"

"I think—we may still finish our game of chess, Christabel;" and he came over to the board and examined the position of the men.

CHAPTER XXIV

WHAT THE DUKE MEANT

"There is always this about chess," said his Excellency, when I had taken my place opposite to him; "you cannot play it unless you detach your thoughts from all other matters."

"I don't wish to detach mine," I returned.

"Then I shall certainly beat you; for I intend to detach mine, at all events for a few moves. Now study this position;" and he insisted on talking chess for some minutes, and then we played. Gradually the fascination which the game always had laid hold of me, and, concentrating my thoughts upon it, I began to play very carefully, until I caught my old friend's eyes studying my face instead of the game.

"I think you are playing earnestly now, so that we may as well stop and talk. While I light a cigar, think back to your conversation, and then tell me your impressions."

He was unusually deliberate in choosing and lighting his cigar, and leaving the chess table threw himself into an easy lounge chair and smoked for a while in silence.

"Well—what are the impressions?"

"You have disturbed them and me," I replied.

"Intentionally."

"Just as you intentionally misled me about your 'old comrade'."

"He made me do that; but I knew you would see through it; and I had no scruple."

"But he was surprised when I told him who he was."

"No man likes to have his incognito fail him. But your impressions."

"I think he will do what he said—and what I wish. You know what he promised?

"Oh yes, that of course."

"He did not come prepared to do it."

"No. You have made another convert, Christabel. He is charmed with you. You are a wonderful little lady."

"I did not exert many charms. I was just as hard as a stone, and then said things that made him look as if he would gladly have taken me by the throat with those talon hands of his."

"It was that daring of yours that won him round. I don't know all you said; but from what he told me, I should think he was never

147

spoken to in such a way before by man or woman—or child; for you are really little more than a child."

"What do you think he meant to do in coming here?" I asked.

"That was what made me so thoughtful during dinner."

"You are keeping something from me."

"I?"

"Well, you mean that he is?"

"I know him. It would be very remarkable if he were not."

"But you agree that he will do as he promised?"

"'I fear the Greeks even when they bring gifts,'" he quoted again. "At least, I should if I were you. His influence is great; and in a week or so I should think you will be Countess Melnik. I don't think anything you can ask him for will be refused. You will be as much honoured as your father was the reverse."

"The scent is too cold. I do not understand," I said, after a pause.

"You are not meant to—nor will it affect you. You have been threatening a good many plans, little lady. I like to see you at fault. It is a rare pleasure."

"It cannot be about Colonel Katona's daughter. If he knows of that he knows what I told Count Gustav. He will not deem me likely to desert her. Yes, I am at fault."

"You have not told me yet what passed at that house where I found you to-day."

I told him everything, except as to what had passed between Karl and myself.

"It is all grave enough," he said. "A secret is very much like dynamite—unless there is great care, the explosion may hurt the holder. I have told you often enough how great a favourite Count Gustav is; not with his father only, but with us all."

"'Us'?" I repeated.

"I am one of the Patriots. Count Karl lacks both force in himself and support outside."

"He is not understood."

His Excellency's eyes brightened. "Is that why you have not told me what you and he may have said to one another?"

I felt the colour steal up into my cheeks. "It was not necessary."

"No, Christabel, that is just the word—not necessary." He glanced at his watch. "Dear me, it is quite late. I must send you to bed."

"You have not shown me the scent," I cried, with a little shrug of irritation; as I began to pack away the chessmen.

He regarded me with the old amused twinkle in his eyes, and then with a glance at the chess-board, a thought struck him and he

148

crossed to me. "You are fond of chess problems, by the way. I'll set you one."

He swept all the black pieces off the board except the king and one pawn, and then left the white king and five white pawns, two of the latter so placed that but one move for each was necessary for them to become queens.

"Could you win that game if you were white?" he asked.

"It is but childish; of course these pawns become queens."

"Exactly. In chess any pawn that can get far enough can be a queen—but not in life, you know. Good-night, Christabel."

I scarcely heard his good-night, but sat staring down at the little pieces where he had placed them.

"You think that any such thing was in his thoughts?"

"What I think is—that orange-blossoms have a very charming scent, Christabel, and Count Gustav is the hope of the Patriots. Again, good-night, child. You have won your victory—by your own wits mainly, although other things have been fighting for you. Go to bed and dream of it, and remember—the first obligation of a conqueror is magnanimity. No—no more to-night, child, except— God bless you and give you happiness."

I lay a long time thinking over the events of that full day, and wrestling with the problem which his Excellency's last words had set me: "The first obligation of a conqueror is magnanimity."

So that was the secret. I had won in the struggle. Not only was my father's fame to be righted, but I was to be honoured, not from any recognition of justice, but in order that I might be a fit wife for a duke's son.

Then I was to be "magnanimous," too; which meant that I was to consent to acquiesce in the family arrangement by which Karl was to be set aside in favour of Gustav; and to cease all my efforts against him.

I had beaten them in all other respects; and now they had seized upon Karl's old feelings for me, and had somehow divined mine for him; and the two were made the subject-matter of this new bribery-bargain.

The shame of it made my cheeks burn and flush in the darkness; and I winced and cowered at the humiliation as the bitter thoughts crowded thick and fast upon me. I recalled what had passed between the Duke and me, and reading it all now by the light of this later knowledge, my pride was stabbed and pierced by a hundred poisoned darts that rankled and festered with cruel pain.

He had come to view me as a possible wife for the son whom he designed to disinherit! My love for Karl was to be made a stake in the game of injustice he would play! I was to be tossed to Karl as a sort of compensation for his wrongs; and I was to be "honoured" that I might be duly rendered fit for the position! The show of reparation to my father was a mere sham and pretence to tinsel another wrong! My duty to the dead, the solemn charge laid upon me, was to be a lever to force me to consent to it! And this was my victory!

Is it to be wondered at that the ashes gritted my teeth; that in my hot indignation, I spurned the whole transaction as base and ignoble, and that I vowed rather to forego my supreme purpose than gain it at such a price. My father's honour was dear to me; but he would never have me win it for him at the price of my own.

The whole bargain was dishonourable alike to the dead and to me; and the mere proposal should harden my heart and stiffen my resolve to go through with my task in my own way.

I grew less passionate when I had settled this resolve firmly; and was able to reflect upon the probable result of the Duke's intention to my plans. They were now in danger of being badly broken up. If he kept his word and sent Count Gustav to me with what he had termed the written confirmation of his promise, it was clear that the scene I had planned to take place at my house would be prevented.

The Count could not be in both places at once; but would he come to me, if James Perry played his part well? I had to risk everything on my judgment of his action. Long and anxiously I weighed that problem; and at length decided he would not come to me, if once he was persuaded that he could get hold of Gareth in despite of me.

He knew that she was the key to everything for me. If he could whisk her away from my care, my power over him was gone. I might accuse him to Colonel Katona as the man who had wronged her; but if she was bestowed safely in his charge, he could laugh at the accusation, and could challenge me safely to produce any proofs of it.

Moreover, I had so planned that he would feel safe in testing the truth of the story which James Perry would tell him; and would see that if he found it false, he could still come to the meeting, scarcely an hour behind his time. For such a delay, a hundred excuses could be pleaded; and he was not the man to be at fault for some plausible one.

He would test it, I felt confident. He had everything to gain by doing so, and nothing to lose. At least so he would reason. Success would mean all in all; failure no more than the need to invent an excuse.

I determined to go on, therefore; and fell asleep at last in complete assurance that on the morrow matters would go as I had planned before the Duke had seen me.

In the morning General von Erlanger greeted me with even more than his usual kindliness.

"You have not slept well, Christabel," he said. I suppose my face showed this.

"I had to think."

"What are you going to do? You know all that I meant in what I said at parting last night?"

"I am going to wait for the meeting at noon."

"And then?"

"If no one comes I shall go away."

"There is of course something behind that. But Count Gustav will come. His father will see to that."

"Are you against me, too, in this development?"

"I should never be against you. But I wish you to be on our side."

"If I can no longer tell you all that is in my thoughts, do not blame me. Let us wait for the meeting. I am afraid, if I were to speak, some of my chagrin might show itself."

He made a gesture of disappointment. "I have lived too long in the world, Christabel, to look for either schemes or counsels of perfection. Life must always be a compromise. I will not counsel you now; I will only hope."

"That is at least left to us all—even to me in this."

He gave me a sharp look, threw up his head slightly, and said: "Remember, Count Gustav is necessary to the country."

"It is an unfortunate country, then," I retorted, rather tartly; and we said no more.

Soon after breakfast James Perry came. He told me that he had written the letter; and I gave him his final lessons, and said that his father, who was waiting close at hand—was to take a letter which I had written to Colonel Katona, and then to be at the door with the carriage for me at twelve o'clock to the instant.

In the letter to Colonel Katona I merely gave him my address, and said I would be there within half an hour of midday to meet him and Count Karl.

When I had arranged those details, I had nothing to do except wait for the time of the meeting with such patience as I could command.

I did not know that two hours could possibly contain so many weary dragging minutes as those. I resorted to every device I could think of to use up the time. I walked up and down the room counting my steps. I tried to read; only to fling the book away from me. I repeated a quantity of poetry, from Shakespeare to Walt Whitman. I got the chess board out and tried problems; only at last to give it all up and just think and think and think.

At eleven o'clock I went to my bedroom and put on my hat in readiness, although I was not to leave until an hour later. Then to find something for my hands to do, I unpacked my trunk and tumbled all my clothes in a heap; and began refolding and repacking them with deliberate care.

I was in the midst of this most uninteresting task when a servant brought a message that General von Erlanger would like to see me.

I bundled everything back into the trunk anyhow and anywhere, locked it and went down. It was half-past eleven by the great hall clock as I crossed to the library. James Perry was just about making his entrance as traitor.

His Excellency was fingering a letter as I went in.

"I am anxious to have a last talk with you before Count Gustav comes, Christabel. There are some things I wish you to see quite plainly."

"We have only half an hour," said I.

"No, we may have longer. I have a line from the Count to say that an unexpected but very pressing engagement may prevent his being quite punctual; and he begs me to explain this to you."

"Oh, General, what perfectly glorious marguerites!" I exclaimed, enthusiastically, turning to point to the flowers in the garden, lest he should see my face and read there the effect of his words. Count Gustav's engagement was with James Perry; and my heart beat fast as I saw victory ahead.

His Excellency crossed and stood by me. "Yes, they are beautiful. I pride myself on my marguerites, you know. But—isn't it a little singular they should appeal to you so strongly at this particular moment?"

"I love marguerites," I replied, with a smile. I was master of my features again then.

"So do I. To me they stand for simplicity, truth, trust and candour, especially between friends—such as, say, you and myself, Christabel."

We exchanged looks; mine smiling; his grave, very gentle, and a little reproachful.

CHAPTER XXV

ON THE THRESHOLD

His Excellency had at times some very pretty ways. He stepped through the window now, and, plucking three or four of the finest marguerites, offered them to me.

"You will accept them—in the sense I have just indicated?" he asked.

"You punish tactfully, General. I suppose you think the rebuke is warranted. I would rather you gave them to me—to-morrow, say;" and I turned from the window and sat down.

He laid the blossoms on the table. "We will leave them until our chat is over. I hope you will take them then."

"I think not. There is only half an hour, you know."

"You are resolved not to give Count Gustav the grace he asks? You believe there is some purpose behind this note?" and he held it up.

"That is one of the marguerites, and must wait—until to-morrow."

"You shut me out, then? You are a very resolute, self-reliant little person, you know, Christabel. Is even this letter your doing too?"

"I told you we would wait for the meeting."

"Umph!" he nodded. "Then I suppose it's not much good for me to say anything. I am sorry," and he sighed.

"I should like to tell you something," I said; "but it might make you angry; and you have been so kind to me—so much more than kind."

His look relaxed. "You will not make me angry. I am too old to heat quickly."

"I think you should not have been a party to this Duke's scheme. It is not honourable to any one concerned—and to me, dishonourable in the extreme."

"You don't think I would do anything dishonouring you? Why, I would have—but you remember the question you would not let me ask."

"Is it honourable to me to make a pretence of granting the justice I seek for my father's memory, while in reality using that very thing and—and my own feelings, merely as a means of doing yet another wrong to another man? To fool me thus and make a

153

sport of me for these wretched, sordid policy purposes? Why, you yourself spoke of it contemptuously as no more than a Greek gift."

He showed no irritation at my warm words, but on the contrary smiled and pressing his finger tips together said: "I suppose it will sound strangely to you—but I can still, from my side, offer you those marguerites in the sense I indicated."

"Candour?" I almost threw the word at him.

"Are we not at a little disadvantage? We are not calling spades, spades. May I do that?"

"Certainly, so far as I am concerned."

"Then I will. Count Karl has loved you ever since he knew you in New York. You love him now—yes, don't protest; it is quite true. He wishes above all things in the world to make you his wife. The Duke knows this and he consents to the marriage. The Duke knows and consents because—I am going to surprise you—Count Karl himself told him and asked his consent. The Duke came yesterday to see you for himself: deeply prejudiced against you, because of Count Gustav's misrepresentations: but you conquered him; as I told you last night you had. He resolved to grant you what you desired, to have your father's title revived——"

"As a bribe," I burst in impulsively.

"And justice done, that the way might be clear for the marriage. That he told you the truth in regard to Count Stephen's death is itself a proof that he means to keep his word. Now, what is there dishonourable to you in that?"

"What of the Greek gift?" I quoted against him.

"You should look at that dispassionately. Count Karl is impossible as the leader of the Patriots. You tell me he is misunderstood; and very possibly you may be right. But the fact is what I say—the Patriots would not follow his lead: and thus only Count Gustav remains to us. It may be unjust; but there is always some injustice in popular movements. What then remains? Either the whole movement must be wrecked, or Count Gustav must be brought through this trouble. That was the Greek gift."

"And I and my feelings are to be used as a pawn in the game."

"That is the view of a very clever but very young lady who sets great store upon having her way in her own way. But it is not Count Karl's view, Christabel."

"And Gareth?"

"Ah, there has been most extraordinary bungling over that."

"Bungling?" I cried, indignantly, almost contemptuously. "Would you offer me these while speaking in such terms of her?" and I picked up the marguerites and tossed them again down nearer to him.

"Almost you hurt me there," he said with a sigh. "The thing is full of thorns; but of this you may be sure. You would not be asked by me to desert that poor child. What is to be done must be done in the open; but what is best to do—where best seems to mean worst for some one—cannot yet be decided. Frankly I do not yet see the way."

"Does the Duke know of her?"

"I think not—-I almost fear not. His faith in Count Gustav is surprising for a man of his experience. But then he is his father."

"He is a sorry, shoddy hero for the Patriots," I exclaimed, with such bitterness that His Excellency lifted a hand in protest.

"He is the only possible leader after his father, Christabel; and for that reason I am going to ask you to hold your hand. I can offer you these now, may I not?" and he held out the marguerites to me with a smile.

"Yes—but I cannot take them yet."

His face clouded. "You have something in your thoughts, yet."

"It is close to twelve o'clock and he has not come," I replied, significantly.

He lifted the letter from Gustav. "We have this. You will wait— after what I have said?"

"Not a minute unless you make me a prisoner."

"Don't, Christabel. That is unjust. Where are you going?"

"To my own house."

"Who is there?"

"At present, Gareth—only."

"Whom do you expect?"

"Count Gustav——and others."

"For God's sake," he cried, more disconcerted than I had ever seen him; and his white shapely fingers twisted the flowers nervously during the pause that followed. "You have frightened me," he murmured at length.

"The deeds are not of my doing," I said slowly.

"Where is your house?"

"Why do you wish to know?"

"That I may follow you there presently," he answered.

"You have twisted those blooms and wrecked them. Is candour wrecked with the petals, General?"

He looked up and I saw by his glance that he knew I had read his intention.

"You did not mean to come alone," I added.

"It is a case for the Duke himself. You must not take this responsibility alone, Christabel; you must not. The issue of everything is in the balance."

"I may be wrong. Count Gustav may not come."

"You have probably made sure of him. Give me the address. We must know it. You see that, I am sure."

I thought earnestly. "If I give it you, will you wait at home here and do nothing for an hour; and if you bring the Duke will you promise to tell him first of Gareth? I may be back within the hour with nothing done."

"Yes, I give you my word on both points. It will be a trying hour."

I wrote down the address then and handed it to him. "It is twelve o'clock. I must go. If I do not return, I shall look for you in an hour and a-half from now."

"I wish you would let us come at once," he said as he went out to the carriage.

"You might only witness my failure; and I am jealous of my reputation for succeeding."

"I have no smile just now to answer yours," he said, as he handed me into the carriage.

In some respects he had influenced me more than I had let him see during our conversation. Indeed, I scarcely cared to own to myself how differently I viewed the conduct and offer of the Duke.

I was in truth intensely delighted at the news that Karl had asked the Duke's consent to make me his wife. I had known of course that he was willing to set everything else aside if he could prevail upon me to marry him. He had told me no less than that. But I fastened upon this formal request for the Duke's permission almost greedily, as though it gave a fresh practical turn to the position. My heart was indeed only too willing to find any reason or pretext for playing traitor to my resolve.

I told myself over and over again during that drive that the facts were really just what they had been before his Excellency had spoken to me; and that the view which I had taken in those hot, restless, angry hours in the night was the one which I must take.

But I found it increasingly difficult to be consistent. My dear old friend himself would certainly be the last to harbour a single thought in any way dishonouring to me. I trusted him entirely; and he was on the side of my heart's desires. He had also declared dead against the abandonment of Gareth, and had stipulated that whatever was done for her should be done "in the open."

Could I ask more than that? It meant that Count Gustav should not of himself decide what was to be done; but that Gareth and her father should have their part in it. Was I to put myself in her father's place and usurp his duty, merely because I had a fanciful estimate of what was due to me and to my irresponsible opinion of my importance? Temptation can take very subtle forms.

Moreover, was that same estimate of my own infallibility to force Count Karl upon the Patriots when he was obnoxious to them—as his Excellency had declared? Was I to unsettle still further the political disturbances of the country, just because I thought duty required me to be self-denying and miserable and to lose the man I loved?

That such thoughts could occur to me will show in what a chaos of irreconcileable wishes, hopes, and intentions my mind was during that drive, and how my pride, prejudices, and judgment fought and wrestled with the secret desires of my heart.

I was in the worst possible frame of mind for the work that had to be done. Before his Excellency had spoken to me, my course had seemed quite clearly defined; but for the moment I was in that to me most contemptible of all moods—reluctant to go back and yet half-afraid to go forward. I was thus relieved to hear when I reached the house that Colonel Katona and Karl had not yet arrived.

I went up to Gareth. She was flushed with excitement; but when the colour died down, I could not but see how really fragile and delicate and ill she looked. She welcomed me with tears, and kisses and many questions. Why had I not been before? What had I been doing? Why had I wished her to keep in her room? What was the news I brought with me? Who was coming, and when? Was it her Karl? Had I told her to keep in her room for fear of being seen by him before I could prepare him for her presence?

Her own eagerness in putting the questions lessened my difficulty in answering them; and she fussed about me lovingly, making much of me, caressing me, and thanking me; chattering all the time like a child in her eager anticipation of coming happiness; so that my heart alternately glowed with pleasure that I had held on to my resolve and was heavy with fear lest a crushing disappointment was at hand to blight her love and shut out the sunlight from her bright young life for ever.

Her trust in Gustav was absolute, and her faith in his love unshakable.

"He will be so glad. Does he know yet I am here?"

"No, Gareth, not yet."

"I think I am glad of that," she laughed. "What a great start he will give, and how his eyes will open, and what a light of love will be in them when I run up and put my arms round him."

"Pray God he may," was my thought. I still nurtured the hope that what he had once said to me was true; and that so far as there was room for love in his selfish heart, Gareth filled it. It was largely on that hope, indeed, I was building.

"He will be so glad that—do you know what I have thought, Christabel?"

"No, dear."

"I am going to be very cunning. I am going to use that moment of his delight to urge him to take me to my father and tell him everything. Do you think he will do it?"

"It might be better——" I began, when I stopped suddenly as a new thought occurred to me.

"What might be better, Christabel? Tell me; I am so anxious about this. I have been thinking about it ever since I guessed what your news was, and that you were going to bring Karl to me. Tell me, what would be better?"

"I was thinking it would be better if you could first have done something for him; have won his own father to be reconciled to your marriage."

"Oh, I dare not do that," she cried, shrinking like a frightened child. "Besides, I don't know who is his father."

"I do. He is a very great man—Duke Ladislas of Kremnitz."

"I have never seen a Duke in all my life and couldn't speak to one to save it."

I scarcely heard her, for I was thinking what would be the effect of a meeting between this sweet simple-souled child, and that stern, hard-faced, eagle-eyed old man. I pictured the scene if, his Excellency having told the Duke of Gustav's marriage, I were to lead her in to him and say—"This is Gareth."

"You're not thinking a bit of what I'm saying, Christabel," she cried presently. "And you're looking dreadfully solemn. This might be a funeral, instead of one of the happiest days of my life. But don't let us talk any more about dukes—and such people. I couldn't do what you say without telling Karl first."

"Oh, by the way, that's a little mistake about his name you make, Gareth," I said, as if it were a very trifling matter. "He is not called Karl by his friends and his family—but Gustav. The mistake must have been made at first; and I expect he liked you to call him Karl, as the name you first used."

"What nonsense, Christabel. Why we were married as Karl and Gareth." She was almost indignant.

"I suppose he was just humouring you. But his brother's name is Karl. Perhaps they both have that name; and he liked you to call him by it, because no one else did."

For a moment a great doubt clouded her bright eyes. "Do you

think you have made a strange mistake, Christabel, and that it is not my Karl who is coming?"

"No dear, I have made no mistake. I could not do that. I only tell you this, that you may not be surprised if you hear others speak to him as Gustav, and look for you to do the same. If I were you, I should call him Gustav before others, and use the other name when you are alone."

"But it is such an extraordinary thing."

At that moment Mrs. Perry knocked at the door and called me.

"I must go now, Gareth."

Her eyes were shining and her face alight with love and nervous anticipation. "Is it Kar—Gustav?"

"No, dearest. Not yet. He may be some little time yet. You will wait here patiently till I come for you?"

"Not patiently," she cried with the rueful pout of a child.

I kissed her. "Courage and a little patience, Gareth," I whispered; my arms about her and her head on my shoulder.

"Yes. I'll try to be patient—but you don't know what it is to wait like this in such suspense."

"I'll come for you the instant I can," I assured her, and went out to Mrs. Perry.

"The two gentlemen are here, Miss Christabel."

"I'll go down to them;" and I ran down, with no very clear thought of what I was to say to either Colonel Katona or to Karl, until I knew for certain that Gustav would really come.

And there was no news yet from James Perry.

CHAPTER XXVI

FACE TO FACE

As I entered the room Karl came to me with both hands outstretched. Utterly regardless of Colonel Katona's presence, he exclaimed in a tone of intense earnestness; "Thank God, for a sight of you again, Christabel."

"Count Karl," I said, half in protest, as I put my hands into his nervously and glanced at the Colonel.

"Never mind the Colonel. He knows everything," he declared in the most unabashed manner, "even that I have come to recant. I must take back the promise I made the other night."

"Good-morning, Colonel Katona;" and I drew my hands away from Karl, who had held on to them with quite embarrassing pertinacity.

The Colonel's hard eyes were quite soft with the softness of Gareth's as he smiled. "You have a lovely garden here, may I go out into it?"

"Indeed you may not," I replied quickly. If Count Gustav caught sight of him he would be scared right away.

"Count Karl wishes to speak to you alone—that's why I asked," he replied in his blunt, soldierly way.

"I think I am too embarrassed to know what to say or do;" and I sat down helplessly. "I believe it would be best for us all if we were to talk for about a quarter of an hour of nothing but the weather."

Karl laughed. "I can say what I want to say before the Colonel, Christabel," he declared. But Colonel Katona read something in my manner which disturbed him, and he looked at me earnestly, with an eager appeal in his eyes.

"I hope with all my heart it will be fine weather," I said with a meaning look; "but fine or wet I am not yet ready to...." I could think of no word to fit the sentence, and came to an impotent stop.

"I can wait," declared the Colonel, in evident relief; and turning his back to me, he stared resolutely out into the garden.

I glanced at Karl, and was pained to see how really worn and ill he looked. The sunken cheeks, hollow eye sockets, and haggard, drawn features told their tale of the struggle through which he had passed.

He placed a chair close to mine and as he sat down he said, in a low voice: "I have kept my word so far, Christabel, but I can't go through with it. It will beat me."

"You must have courage."

He shook his head with a despairing smile. "You'll think me a miserably weak creature, but I can't help it. I broke down yesterday and I had to do something. I wrote to the Duke and told him how it was with me, and that he must give his consent; and that if he would, I'd give mine."

I didn't pretend to misunderstand him. "You should not have done that."

"If you wish to save me, you must give in, too—and marry me. I don't care about anything else. Gustav is the man they all want. Let them have him. I told you I had no sympathy with the whole thing. I only held out because somewhere in the back of my mind there was an idea that the thing was a mistake, and that if I insisted on retaining my heirship, I might stop it all. But that means losing you again. I can't do that. I can't."

He was so dejected, so worn with the struggle which he had made at my bidding and for my sake, that if I had been in a firmer mood I could scarcely have urged him. And if I tell the truth, I was in anything but that firmer mood. The gates of happiness yawned wide in front of me, and my heart was urging and spurring me to enter them. I was very weak just then.

"You are ill and not yourself," I said.

"Yes, I am ill—but worse in mind than in body. If I had known what it meant when you laid your hand on my arm that day in the Stadtwalchen and I gave that little bottle to you, I wouldn't have done it. I would do it again to win you, Christabel, but not to lose you."

"I saw the Duke last night—or rather he came to see me."

"My father?" he exclaimed, in great surprise.

"Yes, he wished to see what Colonel von Dreschler's daughter was like."

"Did he tell you I had written to him?"

"No. He did not mention your name—but he promised that my father's memory should be cleared, and even that his old title and his estate should be restored."

"Then I've done something to help you, after all, Christabel? I'm glad;" and he smiled. He had no knowledge of all that lay beneath the surface; and I did not tell him. "I wonder what he thought of you," he added, after a pause.

"I think I surprised him," I said, drily.

"I'm sure of that," he agreed in a pleased tone. "I think I see. If he consents to our marriage and helps to secure for you the old title, it will be the best proof he can give the world that he knows your father was innocent of everything. So you see you'll have to marry me, Christabel, if it's only to secure your own purpose. Thank God!" he exclaimed fervently.

"Do you mean you would give up your birthright merely for me?" I asked.

"Why, of course. That's just what I told him," he replied, simply.

"Do you think I would let you?"

He glanced at me with another smile. "I shall give it up in any case. You must do what you please, you can't prevent me. But I——" he hesitated and added hopefully: "I think I'm very sure of you."

"You can't be sure yet of the Duke's consent. There is more to come than you know."

He reached forward suddenly and seized my hand. "I don't care what's going to happen now. You love me. That's enough for me to know."

"You are very confident—almost audacious. Very different from what you were when—Miss Gilmore met you before."

"It's your doing—all of it. You've given me backbone enough to be resolute on one point at any rate—I won't lose you."

"You must wait to see what occurs here to-day," I said.

"I tell you I don't care. What is it?"

The answer came in a very unexpected form. The door opened and I snatched my hand from Karl's as I heard James Perry say: "Will you wait here a minute, my Lord?"

He had mistaken the directions I had given him about the room into which Karl's brother was to be shown; and the next instant, Count Gustav entered and was staring at us all in amazement.

James was a shrewd fellow, and having recognized his blunder did the best thing to cover it. He shut the door behind Count Gustav and thus made his retreat impossible.

"I am afraid you have mistaken the house, Count," I said, drily. "This is not General von Erlanger's. But pray sit down."

He was bitterly chagrined, and shot at me such a glance of hate that I knew he understood I had outwitted him. Then his devil-may-care nature reasserted itself, and he sat down and laughed.

"I suppose this is prepared for me?"

"Yes and no. My servant has mistaken the room into which you were to be shown—that is all. I meant to see you alone first. There will probably be some money to be returned to you—unless he has made another mistake as to that. I told him to be careful to insist upon part payment for his treachery in advance. I'll ring for him."

"What's this, Gustav?" asked Karl, as I crossed to the bell.

"Nothing to do with you," was the surly reply.

"Good morning, Count Gustav," put in Colonel Katona, "Miss von Dreschler, may I not now go and admire your garden?"

"No, Colonel, not yet if you please." At the answer, his face clouded ominously. He glanced from me swiftly to Count Gustav, and back to me with dark suggestiveness.

James Perry came in then.

"Did Count Gustav give you any money this morning, James?"

"Yes, Miss Christabel."

"Give it to me." He handed me a bundle of notes and went out. I passed them on to Count Gustav. "You have made a mistake, Count. American servants are not to be found on the bargain counter."

"There is something here to be explained," said Colonel Katona, abruptly.

"Count Gustav was to have come to me at General von

Erlanger's at twelve o'clock to-day; perhaps it might explain matters if he told us why he preferred to come here." I spoke very coldly.

He dropped his eyes to the ground, declining the challenge, and sat swinging his legs moodily in silence.

"What is it all, Christabel?" asked Karl.

"Trouble perhaps for us all, and probably very serious trouble. If Count Gustav will not explain, I will."

I stopped for him to speak.

"You know why I came?" he said.

"Your brother and Colonel Katona do not."

"Hadn't we better speak together alone first?"

"Yes, if you wish."

We went out together into another room.

"You have played me an ugly trick," he began.

"It is rather that you sought to play me one and failed. You came here to steal Gareth from my care."

"Where is she?"

"In this house here."

"My God!" There was no mistaking the intensity of his feelings. He threw himself into a chair and stared down at the carpet, his face wrinkled in lines of thought, perplexity, and fear. "Does Colonel Katona know?" he asked after a long, tense pause.

"Not yet."

"You mean to tell him?"

"I have brought him here for that purpose.

"He mustn't be told."

I raised my eyebrows and shrugged my shoulders, and left him to interpret the gesture as he pleased.

"You don't know what you are doing. My God, you don't; or you'd never dare. What are your terms now?"

"No more than they were before—and no less."

He took a paper from his pocket. "Here's the first of them—over my father's signature."

"Is this what you were to have brought to the General's house?"

"Yes," he nodded.

"It is not your doing, then, that part?"

"What else do you want?"

"You know quite well—that you make Gareth your wife."

"You're not so clever as you think you are," he jeered. This cheap sneer at me appeared to afford him some relief.

"Have you no thought for her?

"I don't wish to hear about her from you."

"Then her father and yours had better speak of her. The Duke knows the story by now; and the matter has to be settled somehow."

"You are brewing an awful mess and making any settlement impossible. But then you're a woman, and can be trusted to do that."

"Shall I send for Colonel Katona to come to us here?"

"No," he cried quickly, and then gave a desperate sigh.

"Yet you love Gareth," I said.

"I tell you I won't hear of her from you."

"And she has given you all her innocent heart, trusting you, believing in you, loving you, as only such a sweet pure girl as she could."

"I will not hear you," he cried again fiercely.

"If you will not, there is only one alternative." He was silent, so I continued. "I do not plead for her—don't think that. Her cause needs no pleading at my hands; because there are those who will not see injustice done to her. You know that—selfish, reckless, wicked and daring as you are. Her father is equally daring, and knows how to revenge a wrong done to her."

"What do you want to say, then? Can you see any way?"

"When you spoke to me that afternoon at Madame d'Artelle's house about her, I saw that you loved her; and what I would appeal to now is that love of yours for her."

"Go on," he said sullenly.

"You would be neither sullen nor indifferent if you could have seen her when to-day she knew you were coming. You know little of a woman's heart; but I know it—and all Gareth's was in her glad eyes at the thought of being once again with you. She is not well, moreover worried and harassed by suspense; ill with the fever of unrest. She has no strength for the part you have made her play, and the passionate desire to have this tangle straightened and peace made with her father is wearing her life away."

Whether he was touched by this, I cannot say. He gave no sign.

"You wish for a chance to checkmate me," I continued; "and here you can find one. I promised her happiness—you can give that promise the lie; you can break her heart and blight her life, and probably kill her. I have acted in the belief that you cared for her: you can sneer that belief out of existence, and win at least that one success over me. You would have a victory of a sort; but I would not envy your feelings in the hour of triumph."

He took this in silence also. I did not think he had even cared to listen.

"Have you anything more to say?" he asked after a pause.

"If your heart is dead to her, no words are needed—none can do any good. But it will not be well for you."

"Threats now?"

"I leave them for Gareth's father. You know what he can do?"

Something in the words touched him. He looked up with a new, sudden suspicion. "You know that, too?" he asked, sharply. "Is that why you've trapped me here like this?"

"That is not my part of it," I replied, ambiguously, leaving him to make of the answer what he would.

"Can I see Gareth?"

"Yes, when her father knows, and with his consent."

He shrugged his shoulders and sneered again. "You take me for a villain, of course. You said so once."

"I will gladly revise my opinion if you will give me occasion."

"I told you you were not so sharp as you thought. If you were, and if there is what I suppose there is behind those words of yours just now, you would see that I might be as anxious as yourself for Gareth—if only I could see the way."

"I should be glad to think it—for her sake."

"You can. It's true. And if you could see a way I'd forgive you all the rest."

"I have no more to say—to you," I said, rising.

"You are going to tell him?"

"Yes—now. There is no good in delay."

He got up, frowning, his face anxious but resolute. "No; this is my affair. You have done enough mischief. Send him to me. I'll tell him."

"I will not have violence in my house."

He came close to me and stared into my eyes. "Do you know what Colonel Katona can do in this?"

"I know he has sworn to have the life of the man who has wronged his child."

He waved this aside with a shake of the head and a toss of the hand. "Is that all you know?"

"Yes—but it is enough."

"I will tell him myself. Not alone if you say so. Karl can hear it too."

"You had better go to them. You will of course tell him everything. If you do not, I shall."

"You don't understand. This is beyond you now. I shall tell him one thing which you have been too prejudiced and blind to see—that Gareth is already my wife, legally—as you like to insist."

"I don't believe you—nor will he."

"Believe it or not as you please—it is true; if a priest of the Holy Church can make man and woman husband and wife."

He swung away with that, and I watched him cross the hall with

165

quick, firm steps, and enter the room where Colonel Katona and Karl were waiting.

I was glad to be spared the ordeal of that interview, and was still standing thoughtfully at the closed door on the other side of which that scene of the drama was being enacted, when a carriage drove up rapidly.

I knew it was General von Erlanger and the Duke, and I told the servant to show them into one of the larger rooms in the front of the house.

CHAPTER XXVII

"THIS IS GARETH"

I was in the act of going to the Duke and my fingers were all but on the handle of the door, when I recalled the idea which had flashed upon me an hour before when with Gareth, and instantly I resolved to act upon it.

Running back into the room where I had been with Count Gustav, I wrote two lines to his Excellency.

"I have made one mistake. Count Gustav's marriage is legal. Gareth is really his wife. Let the Duke know this."

I sent James Perry in with this note to the General and a message that I would be with him in one minute.

Then I ran up to Gareth. The poor child was sick from the suspense; but I noticed with intense satisfaction that she had been filling up some of the weary time of waiting by making herself look as pretty as possible.

"Is he here, Christabel? Oh, how my heart beats."

"Yes, dear, he is here. He is with your father now, telling him all; and you are to come with me to the Duke." I put it so intentionally, that she might believe Gustav had expressed the wish.

"What do we not owe you, Christabel?" she cried, kissing me tenderly. "But I'd rather see Kar—Gustav, first. I've been practising that name ever since you left me; but it sounds so strange. The other will come out first."

"Try and remember it with the Duke, Gareth. It doesn't matter with any one else so much."

"Oh, I can't go to him. I can't. He is such a stern and terrible old man, so—Gustav says. I got it nearly right that, time, didn't I?" and she laughed.

"It will soon come quite naturally, dear. Are you ready? He may not like it if we keep him waiting."

I looked at her critically, gave a touch or two to her fair hair, and kissed her. "You look very beautiful, Gareth."

"I feel very frightened," she said, and clung to me as we went down the stairs. I believe I was almost as nervous as she could have been; for I was indeed drawing a bow at a venture. But I dared not let her guess my feelings, lest she should run back upstairs.

So I took her hand and pushed on steadily, and when James opened the door of the room I led her right across to where the Duke sat, and, with my heart thumping against my ribs I said, just as I had thought to say:

"This is Gareth, Duke Ladislas."

His bird-like face was as black as a night-storm. His keen eyes watched us both, glancing swiftly from my face to Gareth's, and from her back to me as we hurried across the room. The heavy brows were pent, and when we stood in front of him there came an ominous pause—like the calm when the storm is to burst.

Gareth was so frightened by this reception that the clutch of her fingers tightened on mine. I felt her trembling and saw her colour go, as she flinched with a little gasping catch of the breath all eloquent of fear.

His Excellency had risen at our entrance, and I saw him stare with a start of astonishment at Gareth, and from her to the stern old Duke; and then he lowered his head and closed his eyes, and I noticed that he clenched his right hand. He feared as much as I did for the result of my experiment.

The silence was almost intolerable; those vulture eyes fixed with deadly intentness upon us both, and the hard unyielding face set in the stern, cold, impassive, expressionless scrutiny.

Bitterly I began to repent my rashness, when a great change came, wrought by Gareth.

With surely one of the happiest instincts that ever came to a child, half helpless as she was with fright, she slipped her fingers from mine and, throwing herself on her knees at the Duke's feet, she caught his hand and held it and looked up frankly in his face and cried:

"It was all my fault, sir. I pray God and you to forgive him."

Just that; no more. No tears, no wailings, no hysterics. Just the frank statement of what her pure, innocent, simple heart believed to

167

be the truth—the whole truth as it seemed to her; as no one looking down into her eyes could doubt.

The Duke could not. I did not look for emotion from him. He stared down at her; but gradually I saw the furrows on the forehead relax, and the eyes soften. Then the lids shut down over the glitter, his free hand was placed gently on the golden head, and bending forward he kissed her on the forehead.

"Gareth."

Then his Excellency did what I could have kissed him for doing; for I was past thinking what to do just then.

"I wish to speak to you," he whispered to me; and we both crept away out of the room as softly as though we had been two children stealing off in fear from some suddenly discovered terror.

The moment we reached the room where I had spoken to Count Gustav, his Excellency surprised me. "You knew it, of course; but how? You are wonderful, Christabel!"

"Knew what?"

"Do you mean you did not know? Then it is a miracle. I thought you knew and had planned it; and I marvelled that even you had courage enough for such a daring stroke."

"I drew a bow at a venture; and don't understand you."

"Do you tell me that you believed any mere pink and white young girl picked out at random would make an impression upon that crusted mass of self-will, obstinacy, and inflexibility of purpose? You—with your keen wit and sense of humour, Christabel!"

"You could see the impression for yourself, surely," I retorted.

"This is positively delicious! I really must enjoy it a little longer without enlightening you. You do really believe that the Duke was melted because that child is very pretty and has innocent eyes? You must give up reading us humans, Christabel; you really must, after this."

"It seems strange to such a cynic, I suppose, that innocence can plead for itself convincingly to such nature as the Duke's!"

"You intend that to be very severe—but it isn't. Innocence, as innocence, would have no more chance with Duke Ladislas, if it stood in the way of his plans, than a troutlet would have in the jaws of a hungry pike. The humour of it is that you should have thought otherwise, and actually have—have dangled the pretty troutlet right before the pike's nose."

"It has not been so unsuccessful."

"I am sorry for you, Christabel," he answered, assuming the air of a stern mentor; "but it is my unfortunate duty to administer a severe corrective to your—what shall I term it—your overweening self-confidence."

"I have given you considerable enjoyment at any rate."

His eyes were twinkling and he shook his forefinger at me with exaggerated gravity. "I am afraid that at this moment, very much afraid, you are rather puffed up with self-congratulation at the result of this master-stroke of yours."

"It is more to the point to think whether it will succeed."

"Oh yes, it will succeed; but why, do you think? Not because of that child's innocence or pretty pink and whiteness; and certainly not because the Duke was in any mood to be impressed. Now, there is a problem for you. When I gave him those three lines you sent into me, his fury was indescribable. Not against Gustav, mark you: he stands by him through any storm and stress—but against the wife. He was speechless with suppressed rage; and right in the midst of it in you came with your—'This is Gareth'—and you know the rest. There's the riddle; now, what's the answer?"

I thought closely, and then gave it up. There was obviously some influence at work which I did not understand. "You have your wish. You have pricked the bladder of my self-conceit; I've been floating with somebody else's life belt, I see that."

"Do you think you feel sufficiently humble?"

"Yes, quite humiliated," I admitted with a smile.

"Then, I'll tell you. The clue is to be sought for in the years of long ago. The Duke has been married twice; and his first wife was named Gareth, and the only child of the union was Gareth also; just such a girl as that sweet little thing you brought into him to-day—and so like both the idolized dead wife and dead child as to bring right up before him in living flesh the one dead romance of his life. Now you see what you did?"

"What will he do?"

"I should very much like to know. I am afraid you have got your way, and that he'll accept her as his daughter; and then—phew, I don't know what will come next. Only recently a very different sort of marriage had been planned for Gustav; one that would have strengthened the position as much as that child there will weaken it. I don't envy the Duke his decision. How does Gustav feel toward her?"

"I believe he still cares for her—but you know him."

"I wish I could think there was happiness for her. Those whom the gods love, die young—I'm not sure that if I were the gods, I wouldn't choose that solution."

"It is not for you to settle, fortunately, but for the Duke."

"True; but he can only give her Gustav—and that may be a long,

long way different from happiness." He paused and with a slow smile added: "This may affect you as well."

"I am thinking of Gareth just now."

"The same thing—from a different angle, Christabel, that's all. If this marriage is publicly recognized, Karl will be again the acknowledged heir; the axis of things will be shifted; and the motive for the Duke's promise to you last night will be gone. It will be hard if you should have done so great a right and yet pay the price. It is well that you are strong."

"I have the Duke's word."

"Can you keep water in an open funnel?"

I turned away with a sigh and looked out of the window. His Excellency came to my side and laid a hand very gently and kindly on my shoulder. A touch of genuine sympathy.

"Almost, I could hope, Christabel—but thank God, I am not the Duke. I was a very presumptuous old man—only a day or two back—but you have made me care for you in a very different way. I am presumptuous no longer; and all that I am and all that I have shall be staked and lost before I see injustice done to you."

"I know what a friend you are."

"Pray Heaven, this may not be beyond our friendship."

I could not answer him. I stood staring blankly out into the garden realizing all that was behind his words. I knew he might have spoken no more than the truth; and that in gaining Gareth's happiness, I had ventured my own future.

Not for a moment did I distrust Karl; but I knew the influences which might be brought to bear upon him. If Gustav was no longer to be preferred as the Duke's heir and Karl was not to be allowed to forego his rights as elder son, our marriage became impossible.

I had worked for this, I know; had planned that it should be; had forced it home upon Karl himself; and had even found pleasure in the thought of the sacrifice it involved.

But since then I had taken to my heart such different thoughts. The Duke had with his own hands swept away the barrier to our marriage; and Karl himself had shown me within the past hour how much it was to him.

It is one thing to stand outside the Palace of Delight and, in the knowledge that admission is impossible to you, be firm in a refusal to enter; but it is another and a very different thing, when the gates stand open and your foot is already on the very threshold and loving hands are beckoning to you with sweet invitation to enter, to find the portal closed in your face, and yourself shut again in the outer darkness.

It is little wonder, therefore, if my heart began to ache again in dread of the cold solitude which threatened to be the reward for my share in that day's doings.

It was all quite clear to me, as I stared out into the garden, seeing nothing that was actually there; nothing but the troubled forms which my thoughts assumed. And although I murmured and rebelled against it all, I knew in my heart that at the last neither Karl's desires nor mine would be allowed to decide what should be done.

My kind old friend, discerning the struggle that was taking place in my thoughts, left me at first to fight it out in my own way, but presently came, and in the same sympathetic way laid a hand on my arm.

"You must not take too black a view, Christabel," he said. "It may all be yet for the best. I thought only to prepare you."

"It is over," I said, with a smile. "I have taken my decision. It shall be as the Duke decides."

"I know how it must be with you," he replied, very gently.

The kindness of his manner seemed in some strange way to hurt me almost; at least it made me conscious of the pain of everything; and I lowered my head and wrung my hands in silence.

Then a door opened in the hall.

"Christabel, Christabel!" It was Gareth's voice, sweet and glad.

"Go to her, please, I—I cannot for the moment."

He went at once and did what was of course the best thing to do—he brought her to me.

"The Duke wishes to see Gustav alone," he said. A glance at his face told me my plan had succeeded.

Gareth caught my arm nervously. "I heard angry voices in one of the rooms, Christabel—my father's and Kar—Gustav's. What does it mean?"

"All will be well now that you have seen the Duke, dearest. Stay here a minute until I come for you."

I believed it now and felt very happy as I kissed her and she kissed me in response.

"I owe it you, Christabel," she whispered. "I will wait."

I went out with the General and closed the door upon her.

"You must do all that may have to be done now," I said, weakly. "I have finished, and can do no more. Count Gustav is there with Colonel Katona and Count Karl. Will you fetch him?" and I pointed to the room from which the sounds of voices loud in anger were to be heard.

But even as I spoke, the door was flung open violently, and Colonel Katona and Gustav came out.

"No, by God, no, you are too great a villain," cried the Colonel fiercely, and then seeing who was with me, he stopped abruptly.

In the pause I glanced through into the room and saw Karl staring after the other two.

Our eyes met, and he flung up his hands with a gesture of consternation and despair.

CHAPTER XXVIII

THE COLONEL'S SECRET

Instantly I thought of Gareth and raised my hand, hoping to still the Colonel's angry, strident tone lest it should reach her.

"He is a villain," he repeated. "I care not now who hears me say it. He lured her from me, planned to make me do murder, and now would have me join in dishonouring my child. You must hear this, Miss von Dreschler, for you know much—and shall know the rest."

"For Gareth's sake, Colonel, she is in that room and may hear," I protested.

"Let her come and let her decide this," said Gustav.

"No. This is for me. I will tell all. I have kept my secret long enough—for your sake, as you know—and will keep it no longer. You came here," he said, turning to me, "to clear your father's memory of the charge brought against him. I can prove it false, and will. He was charged with having murdered the young Count Stephen. It was a lie. This scoundrel here knows it was a lie. Ask him if he dare deny that."

There was no need to ask the question; Count Gustav's face gave the answer, clear and unmistakable.

"You will ruin everything, Colonel Katona," he said. "Not me only, but the Duke, your master, and the great cause—everything."

"To hell with any cause which would sacrifice my child's honour. I will tell the Duke to his face," was the hot reply, very fiercely spoken.

"I am here ready to listen, Colonel Katona."

We all started and turned to find the Duke himself had come out.

172

"What is this lie which threatens ruin to everything, sir?" he asked very sternly, after a pause.

Colonel Katona drew himself up.

"It is right that I should tell it to you. It was for you and your family that the lie was planned; that you might have the Throne when the time came; and it was continued that this man—your son—might succeed you. Your son, who has rewarded me for my fidelity to your house by stealing my child. It was for you and yours that I consented to dishonour my friend—this lady's father; and have kept the secret inviolate through years of remorse and sorrow."

"Enough of yourself," said the Duke, with a contemptuous wave of the hand. "Speak plainly."

"The scheme has failed, and through this villain's dastardly conduct. The man whom Colonel von Dreschler was accused of having murdered, and whose death would have cleared the way for you and yours to the Throne—Count Stephen—is living, a close prisoner in my house."

"Thank God for that!" I cried, fervently, understanding all now.

Then a gasp of pain, or rage, or fear, or of all three, escaped the Duke's pallid lips. He staggered so that his Excellency put out his hand to help him.

"Is this true?" fell in a whisper from the Duke, his eyes on his son's face, now as white and tense as his own.

There was no answer, and in the silence, I heard the door behind me opened softly, and Gareth came out.

"Ah!" The soft ejaculation, born partly of gladness at the sight of Gustav and her father, and partly of fear at the wrought looks of both, drew all eyes upon her. The silence seemed to deepen suddenly; as though a common instinct of mercy inspired all to attempt to keep what was passing from her knowledge.

A look of bewilderment came over her face as she gazed from one to the other; tender but questioning for the Duke; half fearful anxiety for her father; and infinite love and yearning for her husband. She glanced at him last; but her first word was for him, and it was toward him she moved, murmuring his name and stretching out her hands.

Her father drew his breath quickly, with a sound between a gasp and a sigh; and I thought he was going to step between them, but the Duke glanced at him and raised his hand.

"She is his," he said, his tone no more than a whisper, but distinct to all of us.

The Colonel drew back a pace and put his hand to his forehead.

Gareth passed him. She had no eyes for any but her husband in that moment.

I waited with fear-wrought anxiety to see how he would greet her, for his face had given no sign which we could read.

But she had no fear for him as she had no thought of us. Her faith in him was as staunch and patent as the love which lighted her face and sparkled in her clear shining eyes. Our presence gave her no embarrassment; I believe that we were all forgotten in the absorbing delight of that one supreme moment.

He played the man for once. As she placed her hands in his with just a simple—"I am so glad," he took them, and bending down kissed her on the lips before us all.

But this was more than her father could bear. With an angry "Gareth," he turned to part them.

Scared by his stern look and tone, she shrank back with a little piteous cry: "Father, he is my husband;" as if indeed she would defend him.

I saw the cloud on his face deepen and the words of a harsh reply were already on his lips, when the Duke, who had been watching intently, intervened.

"Colonel Katona, the rest is for us men to settle," he said, waving his hand to the room behind him.

His Excellency glanced at me and motioned toward Gareth, and I crossed to her.

"For a few minutes, Gareth," said the Duke.

She hesitated, and then, as her father was moving away in obedience to the Duke's command, she stepped past me and seized his hand. "Father, you forgive us?"

Just a little yearning plea, pathetic enough to have touched the hardest heart, I thought it. But he had no ears for it. His passion was too hot and fierce against the man whom she included in the appeal.

He turned and looked upon her quite unmoved—his face hard like a rock, and his voice rough and harsh as he answered: "No. You have to choose between us; and if you choose him, you are no longer my child;" and shaking her hand off, he went into the room.

Gareth gave one soft, piteous cry, like a stricken fawn, as I put my arm round her.

I hated him for the merciless cruelty of the rebuff; and I believe all shared that feeling, as we saw how it had cut deep into her tender heart. I know that Karl and his Excellency did, by the glances of pity they cast upon her as they passed me to follow the Duke.

Count Gustav hesitated, seemingly at a loss what to do. I thought he would have taken her from my arms to his; and much as I detested him, I think I would have forgiven him everything had he done so. But, after a second's hesitation, he shrugged his shoulders, passed on and closed the door behind him.

I led her away upstairs to her room, and by the time we reached it she was clinging to me feebly and helplessly. She sank down on her bed with a deep-drawn sigh, and lay there deathly pale and trembling violently.

I hoped that the tears would come to relieve her; but they did not. The shock had been too sudden. The suspense of the separation had worn her down; then the joy of the meeting with Gustav had wrought upon her nerves so that her father's stern and almost brutal repulse had been a blow struck just at the moment when she was at the weakest. The sorrow was too deep for tears, the suffering too acute and numbing.

I threw a rug over her and bent and kissed her, as I whispered: "I think it will all come right, Gareth, dear."

She took no notice; and feeling I could do no more then but just let her grief have its way, I sat down by the bedside, wondering whether I believed my own words; whether, in such a tangle, all could possibly come right; or whether in striving to right things in my own way, I had only succeeded in creating just an impossible bungle.

My thoughts were soon down in the room below. What was occurring there? Far bigger things were in the doing, or undoing, than the breaking of poor Gareth's heart. Fate had bound up that issue with others of much greater import.

If Count Stephen was alive, the whole of the Duke's plans and Count Gustav's scheming were shattered. Would Colonel Katona insist upon making his story public—or would some means be devised to prevail upon him to keep that secret still inviolate? On that question would hinge the future of the Patriots' cause; and so possibly the future of the whole Empire.

In such a balance what weight was the mere happiness of two girls like Gareth and myself likely to have? None; absolutely none. Nor could I bring myself to think it should have, considering the critical consequences there might be to thousands, aye even millions in the Dual Empire.

The Colonel was a hard man, however, how hard he had shown himself within the last few minutes; and I believed he would hold on to his purpose like a steel clamp. If he did, what would result? Either the leadership of the Patriot cause would pass from the Duke to Count Stephen, or the Duke's enemies would seize the occasion to promote a schism which would ruin the cause irreparably.

In that case the main obstacle to Count Gustav's open acknowledgment of Gareth as his wife would be removed; but her husband and father must remain open and bitter enemies; and her choice must be made between them. Poor Gareth!

175

And so I sat in long, weary suspense, tossed hither and thither by my distracted thoughts, while I waited, my nerves high-strung, to learn the result of the conference below stairs.

I was roused by a long, shuddering sigh from Gareth.

"I am here, dear," I said, bending over her.

"I am so cold, Christabel," she cried, shivering. I felt her hands; they were as cold as stones; but when I laid my fingers on her brow, it was hot with the burning heat of a fever. In much concern I called up Mrs. Perry, and together we applied such remedies as we could devise.

She was quite passive in our hands. Thanked us with sweet smiles, doing just what we told her like a submissive child.

"What has caused this, Miss Christabel?" asked Mrs. Perry. "She is really ill, and should see a doctor."

"She has had a shock," I replied; and the good soul shook her head dismally.

"She is just the sweetest girl that ever happened, but not weather proof against much shock," she said.

Then I heard sounds below; and my pulse quickened. The conference was ended,—how? "Stay here and watch while I am away," I said, and went downstairs.

His Excellency and Count Gustav were in the hall speaking together eagerly.

"Where is Gareth?" asked the Count.

"Upstairs, in her room."

"I will take her away with me. A wife must go with her husband," he answered; his tone curt and bitter.

"She is ill. A case for a doctor, I fear."

"She was well enough just now. Is this another trick? Tell her I am waiting for her. She has cost me enough. I may as well have as much of her as I can."

"You will have her life if you take her away now. But that may be your object." I could not help the taunt, his manner so enraged me.

"Thank you," he said, with a curl of the lip.

"It is no case for harsh words," put in his Excellency.

"And more certainly none for harsh deeds. Gareth cannot go until a doctor has seen her," I declared firmly.

"But for your meddling none of this would have happened," declared Gustav. "Let me see her."

"In your present mood, no. The shock of her father's cruel rebuff has quite unnerved her," I said to his Excellency. "Tell me what doctor to send for, please."

He wrote down the name of a Dr. Armheit and his address, and

I sent off James Perry at once. "What has been decided?" I asked next. "Where is the Duke? He should be told of Gareth."

"I will speak to you presently," said the General, very kindly.

Count Gustav laughed maliciously. "You have made a mess of things for yourself as well as for the rest of us, thank heaven. It serves you right. Karl has——"

"Stop, if you please, Count Gustav, this is for me to explain," broke in the General very angrily. "Be good enough to leave it to me."

"Why? What do I owe to you or to this meddler here that I should hold my tongue at your bidding? She has set herself against us, and must take the consequences. The Duke has about as much affection for you, as I have; and neither of us relishes the honour you would do us by becoming a member of our family."

"Silence, sir," exclaimed the General, hotly.

"Not at your bidding, or that of any other man."

"Nothing that this—this gentleman can say can affect me, General," I said, smoothly.

The words seemed to add fuel to Count Gustav's anger. "My wife shall not stay in your house and in your care," he said with great heat.

"The moment the doctor says she may leave the house, she can go—but not before."

"Oh, it's only another lie," he cried, passionately; and raising his voice he called loudly: "Gareth, Gareth. I am waiting for you. I, Gustav; Gareth, I say, Gareth."

"You may kill her," I murmured, wringing my hands.

As if gloating over my trouble, he sneered: "You act well; but we'll see;" and he called again loudly: "Gareth, Gareth, come to me."

I caught the sound of her footsteps above. The door of her room opened and she answered: "I am coming, Gustav;" and a moment later she came down the stairs and threw herself into his arms.

"She told me you were too ill to come to me, but I knew it was false. You feel well enough to come away with me?"

"Yes, of course, if you wish it. I must go with him, Christabel; he is my husband," she cried, wistfully. "He called me."

The General saw her condition as plainly as I.

"She is more fit to be in bed than to leave here," he said.

"Do you suppose I cannot take care of my own wife, sir?" cried Gustav, fiercely. "Get your hat, Gareth."

She left his arms and began to climb the stairs.

"Mrs. Perry will bring it, Gareth," I said, hastily.

But there was no need for it. She clung to the balustrade feebly and turned back to look at Gustav.

"I'm afraid—I'm—I'm——" No more; for the next instant he had to catch her in his arms to save her from falling. She smiled to him as if trying to rally her strength. "My head," she murmured; and then the hand which was pressed to it dropped, and she fainted.

"You had better carry her up to bed," said his Excellency, practically.

"She has only fainted and will be better in a minute," answered the Count. "She shall not stay here;" and he carried her into one of the rooms and laid her on a couch, standing between me and her to prevent my approach. Every action appeared to be inspired by hatred of me instead of care for her.

Happily the doctor soon came, and his first words after he had examined her were that she must be carried at once to bed.

"I wish to remove her from the house," said Count Gustav.

"It is impossible," was the brusque, imperative reply.

"It is necessary."

"It is for me to say what is necessary in such a case," declared the doctor; and being a strong as well as a masterful man, he picked Gareth up in his arms and told me to show the way to her bedroom.

And in this way she was given back into my care.

CHAPTER XXIX

A SINGULAR TRUCE

It was more than an hour before I could go down to General von Erlanger, and I carried a heavy heart and a bad report of Gareth's condition.

"She is very ill," I told him. "The doctor fears brain fever. At best but fragile, recent events have so preyed upon her that the climax to-day found her utterly broken in nerve and strength. I have left her muttering in half-delirious terror of her father's anger. Where is Count Gustav?"

"Gone away with the doctor, to return later. And now of yourself, Christabel?"

"In the presence of this I feel I do not care. I gathered the gist of all from what Count Gustav said. What was decided? Did the Duke know that Count Stephen was living?"

"No. The thing was planned by his supporters, as he told you last night, to make sure of his leadership being secure at a time when, owing to the Emperor's illness, it seemed that the hour was at hand for the Patriots' cause to be proclaimed. They meant to kill the Count, but some one saved him, and then Katona was persuaded to undertake his guardianship."

"What is to be done?"

"The Duke is a broken man. The knowledge of his favourite son's guilt; the break-up of his plans; the bitterness of the loss of virtually everything he cared for in life has completely unstrung him. He has sent Katona to take Count Stephen to him; he has given Gustav the option of voluntary exile or public exposure; and he has reinstated Karl in his position as elder son and his heir."

"It is only right. I am glad," I said.

"Glad?" he echoed, with a meaning glance.

"Yes, very glad."

"Your tone is very confident. You know what it carries with it—for you, I mean?"

"I do not care what it means to me. It is right."

"The Duke is very bitter against you, Christabel."

"He would scarcely be human if he were not. In a sense this is all my doing. I have brought it about, that is. But he cannot harm me, nor prevent my dear father's memory from being cleared. True, it seems he can influence Count Karl."

His Excellency smiled with deliberate provocation. "Possibly; yet Karl, although not a Patriot, is still a rebel."

"He has gone with his father," I answered, with a shrug.

"That is not fair. The Duke was too ill to go alone."

"He came with you, General."

He shook his head. "Christabel! If matters were not so sad here, I might almost be tempted to put that forbidden question."

"If you were so minded, I might not now forbid it, perhaps."

"I think I am glad to hear you say that. The girl in you can perhaps scarcely help resenting Karl's going away just now; but then any girl can be unjust at such a moment."

"Are you pleading for him?"

"Oh, no; there is no need. You will do that very well yourself when you are alone."

"You are very provoking."

"All I mean is that"—he paused and smiled again—"Karl is and will remain a rebel."

"I must go to Gareth now," I said.

I gave him my hand and he held it. "I am going with the news of

179

her to the Duke; and when there I shall see—the rebel. Shall I give him any message?"

"No—except that I am glad," I answered steadily.

"That, of course; and—that he had better come as soon as he can for the reasons;" and with a last meaning glance he was leaving, when I asked him to let the Colonel know of Gareth's serious condition.

I was full of anxiety for Gareth, and I had been so greatly wrought upon by the events of the day that, as I had assured the General, my own concerns seemed too small to care about; and yet I could not put them away from me. "Karl was a rebel; Karl was a rebel." Over and over again the words came back to me, and all that they meant, as I stood by the window at a turn of the staircase, looking out and wondering.

Yes, it had hurt me that at such a time he had left the house without waiting to see me; but—he was a rebel. He had gone at the stern old Duke's bidding; but—he was a rebel and would come again. The Duke hated me, and as Gustav had said would never sanction our union; but then—Karl was a rebel.

The sun might shine, or the rain might fall; political plans might succeed or they might fail; great causes flourish or be overthrown; Karl was a rebel—and we should find our way after all to happiness. Love must have its selfish moments; and to me then that was just such a moment, despite all the troubles in the house.

For Gareth we could do nothing but watch, and nurse, and wait. She was very restless; very troubled in mind as her wayward mutterings showed; very weak—like a piece of delicate mechanism suddenly over-strained and broken.

An hour later Count Gustav returned, and I went down to him. The doctor had convinced him of the seriousness of Gareth's condition, and I was glad to find him less self-centred and more concerned for her.

"While Gareth is here, Count Gustav, there must be a truce between us," I said. "And she cannot possibly be moved."

"I know that now," he agreed.

"Then there must be a truce. For her sake all signs of the strife between us must be suppressed. She may ask me about you; and you about me. She has grown to care for me in the last few days; and it will help her recovery if we can make her believe the trouble that divides us all is ended. It rests with us to give her this ease of mind."

"I am not quite the brute you seem to think," he answered.

"I have my own opinion of you and am not likely to alter it—but for her sake I am willing to pretend."

"You are very frank."

"The terms of our truce are agreed, then?"

"Just as you please," he said, with a shrug.

"There is another thing to be done, somehow. Her father must be brought to agree also."

"Shall I go on my knees to him?" he sneered.

"I care not how it is done so long as it is done. But her mind is distracted by the thought of the breach between you two—and of her need to choose between you."

"That was not my doing," he rapped out.

"I see no need for a competition as to who has done the most harm," I retorted, coldly. "The question now is how that harm can best be repaired. Gareth is very ill—but worse in mind than in body; and she will not recover unless her mind is eased."

"Not recover?" he cried, catching at the words. "There is no need to talk like that. Dr. Armheit does not take any such serious view as that."

"Could Dr. Armheit be told all the facts?"

"My God!" he cried under his breath; and turning away looked out of the window.

In the silence I heard a carriage drive up to the door. "Here is the doctor, I expect. You can tell him and get his opinion when he knows."

But it was not the doctor. It was Karl with Colonel Katona; and James Perry showed them in.

On the threshold the Colonel, catching sight of Gustav, stopped abruptly, with a very stern look, and would not have entered the room had I not gone to him and urged him.

"There is something to be done here which is above all quarrels, Colonel. You must come in, please."

"I have told him that Gareth is ill," said Karl.

"What do you mean, Miss von Dreschler?" asked the Colonel, with a very grim look at me.

I struck at once as hard as I could. "Gareth's life is in danger, and it rests largely with you whether she shall live or die."

He pressed his lips tightly together for a moment. "In plainer terms, please."

"Dr. Armheit, who knows only that she has had a shock and has something on her mind, says that she is very ill. We who know what the cause is, know how much graver her condition really is. He will tell you that her chances of recovery depend upon her ease of mind; and that ease of mind can only be secured in one way. It rests with you for one and Count Gustav for the other, to secure it and save her."

He began to see my meaning and he glanced with an angry

181

scowl at Gustav who, I am bound to say, returned the look with interest. Neither spoke, but waited for me to finish.

"I have just arranged a truce with Count Gustav to last until Gareth is strong enough to be told the facts. You two must do the same."

The Colonel drew himself up stiffly and shook his head, and Gustav quick to take fire, was about to burst in, when I continued: "Are you to think of Gareth or of yourselves? Is she to die that you may glower at one another in your selfish passion? Will it profit either of you to know that her life was sacrificed because you could not mask your tempers over her sick bed? Is this what you call love for her? You, her father; and you, her husband?"

I was beginning to win. I saw that from the slight change in the bearing of both. Hot indignation began to give place to mutual sullenness. "It is your quarrel which may kill her; your apparent reconciliation that may save her. Her mind is restless, fevered, and distraught with the horror of the cruel choice which you, her father, laid upon her. You can hear it in every murmur of her half-delirious fever as she lies tossing now. The terror of you, love born as it is, will kill her unless together you two can succeed in removing it."

With a groan the Colonel fell on to a chair and covered his face with his hands, while Gustav turned back again to the window.

I was winning fast now, and I went on confidently: "You can see this now, I hope. What I would have you do is to wait here until she is calmer, and then together go to her, and let her see for herself that the fear which haunts her is groundless. Let your hate and your quarrel stay outside her room; do your utmost while you are inside to make her feel and believe that you are reconciled. That will do more to win her back to health and strength than all the doctors and nurses in the empire. The trouble is in the mind, not the body. Happiness may save, where misery will kill her."

Neither answered, and in the pause some one knocked at the door. It was Mrs. Perry, come to tell me that Gareth was calmer and conscious, and was asking for me.

I told them the good news and added: "May I go and tell her you are both here waiting to see her—together?"

Neither would be the first to give way.

"I will take the risk," I said. "I will go and tell her, and then whichever of you refuses shall have the responsibility;" and without giving them time to answer I went upstairs to Gareth.

She was looking woefully wan and ill, her face almost as colourless as the linen on which she lay. She welcomed me with a smile and whispered my name as I bent and kissed her.

"I am feeling so weak, Christabel," she murmured. "Am I really ill? Or why am I here?"

"Not ill, dearest—but not quite well. That is all; and I have such news for you that it will soon make you quite well."

Her sensitive face clouded and her lips twitched nervously. "About Karl—I mean Gustav,—and—oh, I remember," and clasping her hands to her face turned away trembling.

"Remember what, dear?"

"My father—his look, oh——"

"You have been dreaming, Gareth. Tell me your dreams," I said, very firmly. "I know you have been dreaming because you spoke of your father's anger. And he is not angry with you."

She looked round and stared at me with wondering eyes.

"Not angry? Why, when I—oh, yes,—when Karl—oh, Christabel, I can't get his look out of my eyes. He said...."

I smiled reassuringly, and kissed her again. "Gareth, dear, what do you mean? Why your father and Gustav—Gustav, not Karl, dearest—are together downstairs. We have been talking about you; and they are both waiting to come and see you together."

I think I must have told the half-lie very naturally, for the change in her face was almost like a miracle.

"Is it all a dream, then?" she asked, her voice awed, her eyes bright with the dawning of hope.

"It depends what it is you dreamt, dearest. You have frightened yourself. Tell me all." I was making it hard for the two who were to come up presently; but the change in her rendered me somewhat reckless as to that.

"Has Duke Ladislas been here?"

"Oh, yes. He is Gustav's father."

"He petted me, and said I was like his own lost Gareth, and that now I was his daughter. Then I came to you to fetch Gustav to him; and after that——"

"You saw Gustav and he kissed you—and then in your delight you fainted, and I brought you up here."

"But my father——"

"You have not seen your father yet, Gareth. He is eager to see you." I told the flat lie as sturdily as I had told the other, and didn't stop to consider whether it was justified or not. I just told it.

"But he was there, and he—all but cursed me, Christabel; and oh, his eyes...."

"You have only dreamt that part, Gareth," I said, using a sort of indulgent tone. "You have been frightening yourself, dearest. You have always been afraid of what he might say to you, and—you have been imagining things."

She found it difficult to believe me, strong as her desire was to do so.

"But it was all so real, Christabel."

"It is more real that they are both waiting for me to say if I think you are strong enough to see them."

"Do you mean—oh, Christabel, how happy you have made me;" and with that, thank Heaven, she burst into tears.

She was still weeping when the doctor came; and noting the change in her, he gave a ready consent to her seeing Gustav and the Colonel for a short interview.

I took him down with me to fetch them. I told them what I had said to Gareth, and that they were to insist upon it that she had fainted when in Gustav's arms, and that everything after that was no more than her imagination.

They could not quarrel before the doctor; could indeed only look rather sheepish, as even strong and stern men can at times; so I carried my point and led them upstairs.

"Gustav and your father, dearest," I said, as I opened the door and stood aside for them to pass.

I saw her face brighten and her eyes light with a great gladness at the sight of them together and apparently friendly; and then I closed the door and left them to carry out their part of the agreement in their own way.

My face was glad too, and my heart light as I ran down to my "rebel."

CHAPTER XXX

THE END

Why do we women like to tease the men we love? Is the sense of coquetry innate and irresistible in some of us? Or is it merely a defensive instinct warning us of the danger of being won too easily?

I knew quite well how the interview with Karl would end; I knew he loved me and that I loved him; I was hungry for the feel of his arms about me and the touch of his lips on mine; and yet my face wore a quite aggrieved look as I met him with words of somewhat petulant reproach on my lips.

"I am glad you were able to go with the Duke," I said.

He gave a start at my tone and then laughed. "It was very fortunate. I am glad that—you are glad, Christabel."

"I am afraid you must have found it inconvenient to leave him so soon."

"Are you?"

"Had you not better hurry back to him?"

"Yes. I am going straight back from here."

"Don't let me keep you, pray."

"Very well."

What can you do with a man who refuses in this way to be teased, but just accepts what you say with preposterous good humour? I shrugged my shoulders. "Why don't you go then?"

"That is exactly it. Why? Of course you can't guess such an abstruse problem! It's altogether beyond you; but try. I should like to hear you making a number of ingeniously wrong guesses. Now, what reason can I possibly have for being here?"

"It is not worth the trouble."

"Well, then, try the obvious. That won't be much trouble."

"You wish to know the latest news of Gareth, you mean, to take to the Duke."

"That's not the obvious, Christabel; that's only an ingeniously wrong one. I'm afraid I've disappointed you a little."

"In coming away from the Duke so—soon?"

"Not a bit of it. In not letting you tease me just now. I ought to have taken you seriously and fired up, and all the rest of it. But I didn't. I didn't misunderstand you in the least. You see—but shall I tell you why?" and he came close to me.

"You did go away with the Duke," I persisted; rather feebly, I fear.

"And who would have been the first to blame me if I had not, when he was ill and could not go alone? You see you can't plague me because, for one thing, I know you too well; and for another—I've had a chat with the General. Didn't he tell you I was—a rebel?"

"I always understood you had no sympathy with patriots," I answered, looking up innocently, but prepared for defeat and surrender.

"It won't do, Christabel," he laughed. "You're looking too innocent. The General gave you away, I mean, and you know that I mean I am a rebel against my father's latest act of tyranny."

He paused; but somehow I couldn't meet his eyes. I tried, and at my failure he was very tactful. He seemed to guess that it would have hurt me, if he had laughed then. Instead of laughing he took my hand.

185

"I am not going to give you up, Christabel, just because the Duke is unreasonably angry. Not all the dukes and princes in the empire shall make me do that. We may perhaps, have to wait a little longer yet; but even that's for you to decide. You see, I'm so sure of you, dear. There's where it is."

"I would not come between you two," I whispered.

"Nor shall he come between us two. I was only a shiftless sort of ne'er-do-well till you came here and helped me to be strong again. I was going down the hill full speed with no brakes on; and, as you know, I didn't care. But I care now and have a will again—as you'll find out if you try to cross me in this; and having found my right mind again I made it up. You mean to side with the—rebel, don't you?"

He proved that he had a will then; for without giving me time to reply, he just put his arm about me and made me kiss him on the lips. And after that, what was the use of protesting, even if I had the wish? But I hadn't. At the touch of his lips, the Duke and his opposition and his dislike of me, and everything else in the world was blotted out, save only—my love for Karl and his for me.

*****

I wish that this story of the chapter of my life could end with that pledge-kiss of ours; and that I could say all ended as happily for others as for Karl and myself. But I cannot.

I had done my utmost to gather happiness for Gareth from the seeds of trouble which her loving but thoughtless hands had sown so innocently.

The deception I had contrived and had caused her father and husband to continue was successful in its first object. They did their part well in the short strange interview by her bedside; and when the doctor called them away, she was entirely happy, holding a hand of each of them in hers in perfect belief in their reconciliation.

The doctor told me that the risk of brain fever which he had seen was at an end, and that she would soon recover her strength, unless that occurred which was in all our thoughts.

And it did occur.

A crisis came in the night. I was dozing by her bedside, for she had fallen asleep, when her cries of pain roused me. I called Mrs. Perry, the doctor was summoned at once; and everything that his skill and our care could do for her was done. But there was no doubt of her imminent danger now.

In the grey of the dawn the life, which was yet never full life, came only to be snatched away instantly by the remorseless Reaper, who lingered by the bedside as if to garner with one sweep of the sickle the mother as well as the child.

Fearing the end I sent news at once to the Duke, to Count Gustav, and to Colonel Katona. Both the latter came hurrying to the house; but by the time they arrived, the doctor was able to announce a respite. There was danger, grave danger, but just a faint hope that all might yet be well.

Long, anxious, wearing hours followed while we watched the flame of life flicker up and down as she lay, white as wax and death's very counterfeit for stillness.

More than once I thought she had passed; and held the mirror to her mouth to catch just the faintest dew of breath.

Both Gustav and her father came up to see her, creeping into the room to gaze and sigh, and turn away despairing.

She knew none of us; but just lay as though she had done with all the matters of earth: hovering on the edge of the thinnest line that can part death from life.

The two men stayed in the house: nursing I know not what angry thoughts each of the other; but both afraid to leave lest the moment of consciousness should come to her and find them absent.

I scarcely spoke to either of them, except to carry a brief message of her condition. If Gustav had brought this all about by his selfishness, it had been the Colonel who had made matters so desperately worse by his ill-timed harsh looks and words on the preceding day. And toward both I felt too hardly on her account to do other than leave them to the bitterness of their belated, unavailing remorse.

That both suffered acutely I could tell by their looks when I carried my brief news. But pity for them I could not feel. It was all absorbed by the gentle girl whom between them they had brought to the threshold of the grim portal.

All through the hours of that long autumn day, the coma continued, until the doctor confessed his fear that she would pass away without even a minute's lapse into consciousness.

"If she should be conscious may I bring them to her?" I asked him when he was going away at nightfall.

"There is risk either way; but if she asks for them, bring them— for a minute only, however."

"There is no hope?

"If she lives through the night—yes; but..." and he shook his head very gravely.

In the evening the last solemn pathetic offices of the Church were solemnized; and through it all she remained unconscious—

mercifully, as it seemed to me, since it would have roused her to the knowledge that she was dying.

I went back to my chair by the bed with a heart full of foreboding. I recalled the General's words—so sadly prophetic—"Whom the gods love, die young." The saying had galled me as he quoted it; but it did so no longer.

She looked so frail and fragile in her sickness; a tender floweret so utterly unable to bear up against the rough cross winds of anger and strife which, held in restraint only by her weakness, would assuredly burst forth to blight her life, that one could only feel with sad resignation that the dark verdict was the best for her happiness.

And yet so loving and passing sweet she was that with resignation to the will of Heaven was an irresistible, almost passionate, regret that she should go.

Hours passed with that solemn slowness one knows in a sick room. The time was broken by my errands to the two watchers below stairs, to whom I carried news of her condition. More than once during the night Karl came also, as he had come frequently during the day, sent by the Duke in his anxiety for tidings of Gareth.

It was some time past midnight when I noticed a change. She took the nourishment I gave her, and when I laid her back on the pillow, she sighed and made an effort to open her eyes.

I took her hand and held it and, after some time, I felt a slight pressure of her fingers upon mine.

"Gareth, dearest," I whispered.

At first there was no response; but when I called her again, the pressure of the fingers was distinct; and a little later she opened her eyes and looked at me.

That was all then, and she was so still afterwards, that I thought she was once more unconscious. She was not, however; and presently her eyes opened again and her lips moved.

I bent down over her, and caught the faintly whispered words:

"Am I dying?"

"No, dearest, no. You will soon be strong again."

She looked at me, and tried, I think, to smile.

"Poor Karl." Just a soft, sighing whisper, and she was silent.

"He is here, dearest. Would you like to see him?"

She made no reply, but I told Mrs. Perry to bring both Gustav and the Colonel to the door of the room. Then I went back and gave her some stimulant, as the doctor had told me.

It lent her a measure of strength.

"Karl is here, Gareth, and your father—shall I bring them?"

"Yes—both."

I went to the door and opened it, and they crept across the

188

room to the bedside. Gustav knelt down on one side and took her hand and pressed his lips to it. The Colonel stood on the other side; and I lifted her other hand from beneath the bed clothes and laid it where her father could hold it.

She thanked me with a look, and whispered: "Kiss me, Christabel."

I bent and kissed her; and the tears were standing thick in my eyes as I drew away.

"Father!"

Just the word and the look of entreaty; and he stooped down and kissed her too.

Her eyes lingered on him a moment, and then she turned her face slowly round to Gustav, whose head was still bowed over the hand he held:

"Husband!"

He did not catch the faint whisper; and I touched him on the shoulder. He started up to find her eyes on him, and then understood; and he too kissed her. She kept her eyes on him; and he kissed her again.

"My darling wife," he murmured.

She looked at him intently.

"I am so sorry, Karl."

It was her last word. The flickering remnant of her strength was spent in a smile of love to him; and as it died slowly from her face, she closed her eyes, and her spirit passed into eternal peace.

As soon as I realized that she was gone, I whispered to Mrs. Perry and hurried out of the room, to find Karl there. He had come for news. He read it in my face and by the tears in my eyes, as he put his arm about me and led me away.

THE END

www.ingramcontent.com/pod-product-compliance
Lightning Source LLC
Chambersburg PA
CBHW020437180626
46812CB00003B/1275